# POWER
# AND
# JUSTICE

## PETER O'MAHONEY

Family is the world's greatest masterpiece.

Power and Justice A Legal Thriller
Tex Hunter 1

Peter O'Mahoney

Copyright © 2019
Published by Roam Free Publishing.
peteromahoney.com

Cover design by Belu.
https://belu.design

# POWER AND JUSTICE

## TEX HUNTER
## LEGAL THRILLER
## BOOK 1

### PETER O'MAHONEY

# CHAPTER 1

SHE DIDN'T fight much.

The girl tried to struggle, but not as much as the woman had expected. Carrying the girl into the basement was easy. The cocktail of Valium, cocaine, and alcohol had worked.

It was a quiet street, practically lifeless at 3 a.m. The woman made sure of that before she planned her setup. Giant oak trees lined the upmarket street, and during the day she'd expect to see children dressed in Ralph Lauren polo shirts selling lemonade in front of freshly painted fences. She would never drink that lemonade. She hated the idea of those grubby little fingers squeezing their dirty germs into her juice.

The girl tied to the chair had been working as an escort, making herself available through various web pages, hardly even trying to hide her adult profession. Not that she judged the girl for her choices. Life offered many different paths, and the girl tried to do the best she could. At least she was working for the money.

The girl struggled in the chair. Her right arm jolted upwards, tugging at the rope, but the rope was tight enough to prevent any large movements. It was a reaction from her nervous system, trying desperately to metabolize the overload of drugs. Even without the massive intake, the girl couldn't call out anyway. The cloth tied around her mouth made sure of that.

As the woman wiped down the edge of the wooden dining chair, cleaning off any fingerprints, she spotted the scratches in the crease of the girl's elbow. It made her sigh. She'd seen it so many times before, more times than she cared to count, and she empathized with the pain so much. But even as she fought her depression, even as she fought back the black dog that tried to attack her, she could never think about turning to the artificial highs that illicit drugs provided.

The girl groaned and moved again. She was getting louder.

Under the low roof of the damp, enclosed basement, the woman moved a box to the right, emptying the space around the girl. There were tools and half-empty paint cans to her left, boxes of memories to her right, and old gardening tools near the door. Despite all the mess, despite all the distractions, the girl was the focus in the cramped space, directly under the only fluorescent globe hanging from the roof.

The girl started to swing her head left and right. Maybe she was trying to see where she was, or maybe she was trying to shake the blindfold off her eyes. The girl tried to yell, but the cloth around her mouth muffled the scream.

The woman couldn't let her make a noise, not with the man sleeping upstairs in the house. He couldn't know she was there yet. Not when payback was within her grasp.

The woman had no choice but to swing her left hand across the girl's face.

She connected hard. The girl's head fell to the side, her voice and movements silent again. She had nothing against the girl, but she was a necessary pawn in the plan. Part of the retribution.

The woman checked for a pulse. It was slight.

The woman knew she could've hired someone to do the work, someone with the skills to haul a drugged-up escort into a basement. Those people would've made sure the girl survived. They would've been cleaner, quieter, perhaps even more effective. But none of that mattered now. The woman's work was done.

And revenge was a sweet, sweet feeling.

# CHAPTER 2

IN LIFE, there are places that are etched into memory, places that are scratched so deeply into the recesses of one's mind, that no amount of drugs, therapy, or alcohol will ever erase what happened there.

For Tex Hunter, the Cook County Jail was imprinted into his mind, branded onto his brain like a mark on a bull. It had been more than thirty years since the criminal defense attorney first stepped inside the walls of the building, thirty years since his life changed forever. He was only ten years old when his father was arrested for the murders of eight teenage girls. The building still smelled the same, the furniture hadn't changed, and the same beige coat of paint, now faded and cracked, lined the walls. Some of the same guards still hustled through, although the years had taken a toll on their vibrancy.

Tex Hunter was only a boy when he was first escorted through the narrow halls, an impressionable child who didn't understand what was happening, and didn't understand why people in authority were harassing him. He was questioned for five hours straight, stuck at a metal table in a windowless room, not even allowed a toilet break. The cops pressed him so hard, so ferociously, screaming in his face, squeezing every piece of information out of his young brain. He shouted, they yelled, but he told them nothing. By the time they allowed him to see his father, his head was throbbing.

"Your scumbag is in meeting room five. Another dirty killer." The Correctional Officer standing behind the reception desk nodded down the hall. "I thought you were the biggest scumbag I'd ever met, but this guy's another level."

Hunter stepped forward, his tall figure towering over the guard.

"Hey, settle down, big guy." The guard retreated, throwing his hands up in the air. "It was just a joke. Let's not get violent."

Hunter didn't respond to the guard. He turned and walked to the meeting room, briefcase in hand, his mind focused on the job. He brushed his hand through his thick black hair, unbuttoned the jacket of his Italian-made fitted suit, and opened the door.

As he stepped into the meeting room, Robert Sulzberger didn't move. Sulzberger stood in the back corner of the room, arms folded across his orange jumpsuit, hair a mess, eyes staring at the floor. He'd spent ten years fighting for the ideal of freedom in the United States Army, traveling across continents, fighting dust and smoke, bombs and people. And now, in his own country, in his home city, that freedom had been taken away from him.

Although the space in the meeting room was tight, only big enough for two chairs and a small desk, it was the most space Sulzberger had seen in the last fifteen hours. The walls were an off-white, as were the chairs, the floor was covered in stains, and the round metal desk in the middle of the room looked like it was placed there twenty-five years ago and hadn't been cleaned since.

"Robert Sulzberger." Hunter moved forward, holding out his right hand. "My name is Tex Hunter. I'm the defense attorney you called to take on your case. As I'm here in my capacity as an attorney, anything you say will be covered by the attorney-client privilege."

"Mr. Hunter." Sulzberger shook Hunter's hand with a tight grip but didn't raise his eyes from the ground. The smell of Sulzberger's body odor was pungent. He smelled like he hadn't had a shower in the hours since he'd entered the building, but that was common for most males on their first visit to prison, even ones the height and width of Robert Sulzberger. "Thank you for coming at such short notice. I've heard about you as a lawyer. Read about you in the paper. Seen you on the news. Your history..." He shrugged. "Well, your family history is one of the reasons I called you."

Hunter had heard that a lot from his new clients. His family's past had been the subject of many journalism files, repeated television documentaries, and even a college course studying the media coverage of his father's trial. His name alone presented him with substantial amounts of work. When faced with a criminal conviction, the newly charged naturally turned to the man they felt was already on their side.

"Then we should get started." Hunter placed his briefcase on the table littered with deep scratches, and sat down on the metal chair, much too small for his long legs. "An unidentified woman was found unresponsive in your basement. I need to—"

"Do they know who she is yet?" Sulzberger interrupted.

"They're working on it, but right now, she's a Jane Doe."

"Then I guess your next question is going to be whether I did it or not." Sulzberger came to sit opposite Hunter. He rolled his fingers over each wrist, the marks of the handcuffs still on his skin, and the force of his arrest still fresh in his mind. He struggled to find a comfortable position on the metal chair. "I didn't do it. I'll be clear about that. They showed me the photos of the girl, and I've never seen her before in my life. Never. I was as shocked as anyone when the detectives walked into my office and started questioning me about a dead girl. Of course I answered their questions, every single one, because I had nothing to hide. Do you think I would've gone to my office if I killed her? Not a chance. Any sane person would've been on the next flight to South America. You've got to find the person that did this, you've got to find this killer. Someone has set me up, and that means there's a cold-blooded murderer out there on the streets, and they'll do it again."

"The woman found in your basement was drugged, beaten within an inch of her life, tied to a chair and then left to die. All the while you were home alone, lying in bed, claiming you didn't hear a thing. If you didn't do it, how did she get there?"

"Someone set me up. Don't you get it? They set me up. Someone is out to get me. I have my haters out there." Sulzberger ran his hand through his brown hair, tinged by gray on the sides. For a man in his mid-forties, he still had a great head of hair.

Genetics, or a hair replacement company, had blessed him.

In the public's eye, Sulzberger had the picture-perfect life. He had a beautiful wife, a young daughter, investments in shareholdings, a white picket fence around his yard, a house with all the trimmings. From the outside, his bright white teeth, fitted suits, and cheeky old-world charm was admired.

When he returned from duty, he starred in a reality television show, winning the survival contest, and winning the hearts of the general public. With that success, he became a local celebrity, and he used that status to become elected as a Chicago City alderman for the 44th Ward. He entered politics on the back of his mission, on the back of his popularity, going to the City Council with the intention of increasing funding to support veterans. Within six months of his election, he'd been forced into a corner—approve the rezoning of an area for the development of a new multi-billion-dollar ice hockey stadium, or see his political donors, and the Mayor, withdraw their endorsement for his reelection. But the approval of the stadium meant the demolition of a building that housed the community assistance offices for veterans. It was their hub, their home for more than five decades. The veterans' organizations were offered new offices, but the new building was in the suburb of Buffalo Grove; a very nice, family suburb, but an hour away by train from Downtown Chicago, and not easy to get to.

Sulzberger chose to support the Mayor.

"If you think someone set you up, then who was it?"

"I can't say." Sulzberger shook his head and

looked at his hands. He looked over his left shoulder, and then the right one. He stared at the door for a long moment before turning back to Hunter. "I can't say because I don't know her name. All I know is she's called 'X'. She set me up. It had to be her."

"X?"

"It's a code name. She wanted to protect her identity. She insisted on it. She called me S, and I called her X; they were our names for each other. The secret code names only added to our excitement. It made everything seem mysterious. We would determine a different meeting point every week, and go from there."

"You were having an affair."

"Not just an affair, but…" He looked back to the door. "It's complicated. My wife and I separated around five months ago. We were still living in the same house, but we were sleeping in separate rooms, and we agreed we would start to see other people. I think she was seeing someone else already." He looked away. "We kept staying in the same house because it was better for my public image, and we weren't ready to tell our five-year-old daughter, Lucy, about it yet. My career would've taken a massive hit if I started to go through a divorce, and I was already on the ropes. And I didn't want to move away from Lucy. I wasn't ready to move away from my family." He looked at his hands. "But the grass is always greener, right?"

"If the grass is greener, you can bet the water bill is higher." Hunter removed his legal pad and began to write notes. "X was your lover?"

"X and I were lovers, but we also…" Sulzberger rubbed his fingers along the edge of the table. "We stole things together. Usually we only stole small things, like a chocolate bar or a bottle of water. That's how it all started. Just small things. It was a harmless rush. It's what I did as a kid, and it…" Sulzberger shrugged. "The rush of stealing took me back to the days when I was a teenager. Before all the stuff happened. Before all the death I saw in Afghanistan."

"You stole chocolate bars with X, and then she kills a woman and leaves her in your basement? That's quite a stretch. I've defended a lot of clients in court, but this isn't a usual, nor foolproof, defense."

"It started out as chocolate bars." He ran a hand over his chin, the stubble growing thick. "But then it wasn't thrilling enough. We had to do something more dangerous to get the same rush. We started doing more and more. Sweaters, shoes, electronic goods. The last thing we stole together was a laptop. She caused a distraction at the store, and when the staff member wasn't looking, I stole it." He held his hands up again. "But we never hurt anyone, and I always gave the goods to charity."

Hunter stared at the man opposite him. The fire in his client's eyes, the pain in his face, was evident. "Did she give you the black eye?"

"No."

"That was from in here?"

"Things aren't easy in here. Everywhere I turn, people hate me, and I've been told there's a target on my head." He struggled to hold back his distress, blinking back a tear. "But the black eye was from Cindy Mendel, the politician. Two days ago, I was in a meeting with her and my assistant, Teresa Hardcastle. We were talking about the stadium vote. Teresa is very passionate about helping veterans. She never forgave me for my decision, and when I started talking about it, she snapped and yelled that I was a traitor to the army. I yelled back, but Cindy intervened. I said something I shouldn't have said, and then Cindy slapped me so hard that I almost passed out."

Hunter wrote a note on his pad. "At this point, we'll apply for bail. It's likely you'll make bail, given your ties to the community; however, I suspect you'll have to give up your passport. The 'D' Bond is likely to be at least $100,000, and you'll have to wear an ankle monitor. Our best chance of proving your innocence will be finding another suspect." Hunter wrote more notes. His messy handwriting was almost as good as a coded message. "You're a controversial person, Robert, and the list of people that could've set you up is going to be quite long."

"I'm sure every person associated with the veteran's community group would also hate me. Veterans are born fighters, and they fought the development of the stadium all the way. There were marches, protests, letters, rocks through my windows. It's not hard to find people that despise me. Walk down the street and do a poll—I'm sure you could find a suspect there. I don't even know where you should start looking for the person that set me up."

Hunter spent the next fifty-five minutes discussing the situation, and it became clear that Sulzberger was a man adrift in a sea of regret.

"I'll take the case," Hunter closed his legal pad once he'd heard enough, "and this is what will happen next. We'll begin to investigate and sort through the evidence the prosecution has gathered. It's a first degree murder charge under the Illinois Criminal

Code, 720 ILCS 5/9-1, and while Illinois doesn't have the death penalty, the minimum sentence is twenty years. The prosecution isn't going to approach this case lightly."

"I need to get out of here. If I stay in prison, then I'm dead. They'll kill me. I've already heard people talk about it. I can't die behind bars. I can't let my Lucy grow up without a father. I still have so much to give the world. I still have so many people to help." His head fell into his hands. "I'm innocent. Isn't that what the system is for? Defending the innocent? I didn't do this. I didn't kill that girl."

"I'll get you out of here on bail, but this case is going to get dangerous." Hunter stood. "Because if you didn't do this, then the real murderer is still out there, and they may kill again."

# CHAPTER 3

BRIEFCASE IN hand, Tex Hunter walked through the halls of the Cook County Jail, following a path he'd walked countless times before. But no matter how many times he walked through the prison, he still hated it. It stunk of fear. Anguish. Pain. There was a frenzied nature to the air inside the halls, an overriding scent of panic, an anxiety that violence wasn't far away.

"Still defending killers?" Prosecutor Michelle Law stood at the end of the hallway, waiting for Hunter.

"As long as you keep trying to put innocent people away, I'll keep defending them." Hunter walked past her into the foyer.

The low ceiling on the first-floor foyer added to the sense of claustrophobia, enhancing the sense that this was a place where hope was lost, not found. A long reception desk sat behind the wall of security checkpoints, with a forgotten row of vinyl seats to the left and two dying indoor plants to the right. Beyond that, there were elevators to the various floors and numerous signs detailing the strict rules that governed the building. Hunter understood why the chairs looked outdated but still unused; this wasn't a place where anyone wanted to linger.

"I've always thought your title was misleading, Tex. It's missing the word 'and.'" Law followed Hunter as they approached the exit. "It shouldn't be Criminal Attorney Tex Hunter; it should be Criminal and Attorney, Tex Hunter."

"Witty. How long have you waited to say that?"

"I've been sitting on that joke for months." Law held herself with a straight, rigid, posture, a result of punishing herself at the gym for hours every day. Her dark hair was pulled back tightly, her glasses were bright red and her blue suit was creaseless. "I've heard you've been doing a lot of pro-bono work for disadvantaged youths lately. That's great that you defend street kids, but I guess it'd give you a chance to clear your conscience."

Hunter stopped and turned to Law. His smile showed off his dimples. "A clear conscience is usually a sign of a bad memory."

She let out a laugh. The guards near the exit turned around. Laughter wasn't something they were used to hearing. "I suppose you live by the defense lawyer mantra—just because your client did it, doesn't mean they're guilty."

"What even is guilt?" Detective Daryl Browne interrupted as he passed the security checkpoint in the foyer. He came to stand next to the lawyers, rubbing his plump stomach in the same way a pregnant woman did, almost looking proud of the years of alcohol abuse that it took to develop it. "Or innocence?"

"You wouldn't know." Hunter turned to the cop. "You've never been interested in either."

Standing next to the lawyers, Browne was a contrast—the lawyers, fit and tall, were neatly dressed, and the detective, round and short, had his shirt untucked at the front. There was enough artificial glow from the fluorescent lights to spot the abundance of ear hairs on Browne—not something Hunter wanted to notice but something he couldn't stop looking at.

"It won't be long before the handcuffs are on you, Hunter." Browne touched the badge on his belt. "You're just like your father. It's in your blood, in your DNA, and I'll take great pleasure in the day I see you behind bars. If there's one thing I've learned on the streets, it's that being a criminal runs in the family."

"My father is innocent, Browne. You know it, and I know it, so why must we always have this dance? Haven't you got better things to do?" Hunter leaned closer to the detective to talk near his ear. "Like extorting money from small business owners."

The comment piqued the prosecutor's interest, and Browne stepped back, the panicked expression on his face signaling that Hunter had rattled him.

"The only thing I know for sure is that your parents are as guilty as your new client in that room." Browne's voice lowered as he changed the subject. He pointed down the halls, but avoided eye contact. "A dead girl was found in his basement, I hear. It's funny—Robert Sulzberger presented himself as a moral politician, but it was only a marketing tool to win votes. He's as bad as the rest of them. It just goes to prove the old saying, 'power corrupts.'" Browne rubbed his stomach again, stepping back from Hunter. "They all crack, Hunter. Just like your father—everyone thought he was a normal person, living an ordinary life, but in reality, he'd buried those girls six-feet under."

Hunter made up the space between them again, and Browne's hand went to his holster on reflex.

"Settle down. This isn't a schoolyard." Law threw her hands out, stepping between them. "And I don't feel like being a witness in a case about the lawyer who knocked out a cop in the foyer of a prison."

Browne grunted, stepped back from Hunter, and bumped into a passing guard. "I'll get you, Hunter. One day you'll make a mistake and I'll be there with my cuffs waiting for you." Browne turned and walked to the elevators, scratching his behind as he went.

"You always had a way with words, Michelle. One of your many talents." Hunter watched the detective enter an elevator, then turned back to his University of Chicago Law School alumni. "You're more than a pretty face, and it's a very pretty face."

"Thank you, Tex, but flirting will get you nowhere with me. I'm immune to it." She shrugged. "The media has reported that you're taking on the Sulzberger case. I'm assigned to it, so I hope you take it."

"You might even enjoy it enough to break out into a smile."

"I don't smile much these days. The world's a horrible place, you know?" She ran her hand over her hair, patting it down. "Cases like this are the only thing that keep me going. He's been charged under 720 ILCS 5/9-1. That's first degree murder, Tex."

"You know the Sulzberger case well? He's only been in here a day."

"He's big news. The media's all over it, and a name like that in prison, well, I've heard that he won't last long. He'll be dead within a year if he stays behind bars. A lot of status goes to the prisoners that kill big name detainees. And I've always been a reality television fan. Robert Sulzberger was the oldest guy ever to win Island Survivor. You don't get bigger reality television stars than that." She smiled. "I don't want him to die, but if he killed the girl, then he has to do the time. And if he does the time, he dies. His life is in your hands."

"Thanks for the pep talk, Michelle. I'm sure we'll talk soon."

Hunter turned and proceeded through the exit. Once outside the walls of the prison, he paused, blinking as he looked up to the cloudless sky.

He understood what taking Sulzberger's case meant. A high-profile client meant months of stress, scrutiny, and burnt out adrenaline reserves. It meant his face was going back on news bulletins, with competitive reporters hustling outside his office, and people yelling at him in the streets again. More significantly, perhaps more painfully, it also meant his father's legacy, the long shadow cast by the murders of eight innocent girls, would be thrown back into the spotlight.

But he hoped, as he always did, that the wild ride was going to be worth it.

# CHAPTER 4

THE WOMAN walked around her dimly lit living room, studying the photos on the wall. She clinked her wine glass against a picture, stumbling a little as she finished the last drop of the bottle. Life was exciting. Thanks to a rediscovered passion for guns, she was experiencing the highs of a thrill again. That rush of adrenaline. That urgency of pulsating veins.

"It's amazing how heavy you are in real life," she said to her latest purchase. "And, boy, you feel good. So cold, and so powerful. If you were a man, I'd marry you."

The 9mm Glock 17 sitting on the table didn't respond.

Her home was spacious, roomy, but it was her prison. It was a family house with bedrooms to be filled, joy to be experienced, but at night, it was only drenched in the emptiness of solitude. She never switched on the lights after dark, preferring to wander her home in obscurity, lit only by the streetlight flooding in through the large front window. Her neighbors probably thought she was never home, but she didn't care for their gossip anymore. She'd given up caring about what other people thought a long time ago.

She needed the girl to wake up from her cocktail of drugs in the basement, screaming for help, desperate to be saved. She needed to see what Robert would do—would he report the situation to the police? Would he call for help? Or would he brush it under the carpet and pay the girl off to keep quiet?

The girl wouldn't have remembered her, and even if she had, her presence could've been explained. It was the perfect set-up. Fill the homeless girl with too many drugs, carry her light frame into the basement with outdoor access, and leave her there, confused and worried.

When she'd heard Robert had been charged with murder, she expected him to roll over and take a deal. How could he fight against such a charge? What sort of defense lawyer would even take that case on?

The son of a killer would.

She hadn't factored him into the equation. She thought every decent lawyer in town would run for the hills, but some people thrived in the glory of infamy, having their name spoken about no matter how badly, and Tex Hunter was more than used to that level of pressure.

Every day Robert rejected the deal, the Chicago PD came closer to the truth. She couldn't take the fall for murder. She couldn't go to prison. She wouldn't do that. Not now. Not with everything she'd been through.

If they started to suspect her, she could run, but she wouldn't know where to go; in all her travels, in all her life, she'd never found a place she could call home.

As she ran her hand over the cold metal piece sitting on her dining room table, her heart rate accelerated, her pupils dilated, and her shoulders tightened. It felt so real, so cold and powerful.

It was her answer. Her vengeance.

Robert wouldn't escape her wrath. She wouldn't let him get away with what he had done to her family.

She smiled. Not because of the impending danger, not because of the threats, not because of her life of torment; she smiled because, next month, in only five weeks, everything would be different.

One way or another, her life would have changed.

She would have her revenge.

# CHAPTER 5

"THANK YOU, Tex. You're a lifesaver."

The handshake between Tex Hunter and Robert Sulzberger was solid, manly; the type of grip that would make any farmer proud. They stood in the foyer of the George N. Leighton Criminal Courthouse, floods of people hustling past them, life frantic under the bright lighting. It was here that crime seemed most real, the atmosphere quivering with suffering and agony. The foyer was almost always full of a churning mass of people, a place where wives and girlfriends cried and wept, where officers yelled instructions, and where lawyers huddled together and whispered in subverted tones. It was the entrance to where justice was served, where punishment was dealt, and where freedom was taken away from so many.

"Don't thank me yet." Hunter grabbed Sulzberger's elbow, leading them away from the courthouse's hectic crowd, down a steep set of stairs marked 'Security Only', and to a thick metal door with more alarms than needed.

Hunter rapped on the door twice, and it unlocked from the other side, opening into the cold Chicago air. The massive Samoan guard, squeezed into a suit one size too small, nodded, and then allowed them to exit. Hunter shook the guards hand, two hundred dollar bills hidden in his palm. The guard slipped his hand into his pocket, and walked off in the other direction. The waiting throng of media were out the front of the building, desperate to snap a picture of Sulzberger as a disgraced mess.

"We've got a long way to go, and this ride is only getting started," Hunter lead his client away from the building. "The 'D' Bond was enough to get you out, but it's only going to get harder. You're lucky that Judge Lemont sided with us today. Your connections to the community, your family ties, and the lack of direct evidence are the only reasons why you're breathing fresh air right now."

"Honestly, I mean it when I say thank you." Sulzberger stopped on the sidewalk. The engine of a black Chevy Suburban was rumbling across the street, waiting for them to escape the media attention. "I don't know what would've happened if I didn't make bail. I don't think I would've lasted long in there. One guard said there was no way I was going to make bail, and if I didn't, he would leave me with the other prisoners. There was already a target on my head. These people want me dead. I don't know if they would've even let me live long enough to see my trial. I would've died in there."

The smell of urine on the street was strong. There were stains on the edges of the sidewalk, puddles of wetness still leaking out from the night before. After being released from the nearby Cook County Jail, many convicted cons took great pride in relieving themselves near the building that put them away. It was a right of passage for some, a middle-finger to the system, a way to take the power back from the institution that locked them away.

"It was my job to get you bail, but we need to keep moving right now." Hunter rested his hand on Sulzberger's shoulder as a man on a bike, carrying a backpack too large to be comfortable, zipped past them. "The reason we snuck out the side exit was so the media didn't see you. If they get a photo of this, of you, right now, your story will be front-page news. Without a photo of you, without something visual, this story will be resigned to page four or five in the Tribune, just a little write-up."

Hunter stepped towards the edge of the busy street, towards the Chevy waiting on the other side. He checked over his shoulder. No media yet.

Behind him, standing on the sidewalk, Sulzberger didn't move, his eyes focused on the ground. "A girl died."

"Robert." Hunter's tone was firm. "I understand this is tough for you, but we need to move. Now. It won't take long for the media to realize that we've gone through the side exit. They won't like that. They're desperate for a photo, desperate for a sound grab, and they'll come rushing over here, searching for us. We can't afford to have you on the front page. The jury for this trial, the people that are going to judge you, are going to be selected from the general public. We don't need them reading this story. Not now. If you're on the front page of the paper, if you're the headline news, then everyone in Chicago will develop an opinion about you. That won't work in our favor."

"Do you understand what I just said? Someone died. A girl. That's someone's daughter. Someone's friend. She died in my house. Someone I didn't even know. Who would do that? Who would try to set me up like that?"

"Robert." Hunter lowered his tone and slowed his voice. Behind them, pedestrians pushed past each other, not stopping to notice the two men that were about to be the center of a media storm. "This isn't the time for a meltdown. You can do that later when you're alone. Right now, we need to move off the street and into that car."

Hunter looked over his shoulder. There was a woman moving quickly at the end of the street.

"I have to see my daughter. I can't go to the apartment you organized. I can't stay holed up in there. I have to go home."

"You can't go home. Kim doesn't want you there. And the more people that see you out in public, the bigger the story. The bigger the story, the less chance we have to influence the jury." Hunter looked again. More people. "Settle down, get back to the apartment, and shut the door. That's our focus now. No media. No talking. No phone calls. We need to keep this story off the front page." A white van pulled up fifty yards away. "We've got to go."

"I can't stay in that apartment," Sulzberger whispered. "I have to go home. That's where I need to be. With my family. I have to see my Lucy."

Three people jumped out of the van. One had a news camera on his shoulder.

"You can't go home. Every media crew in the city has someone there waiting for your return, and your wife won't let you in the front door. She's told us she doesn't want you there. The more you're in the media, the more people will think you're guilty. We don't want to fight the people of Chicago as well as the jury."

"I can't stay in an apartment."

The people ran closer, eager for the breaking story.

"Would you prefer to die behind bars?"

Sulzberger looked away. The cameraman steadied. A woman ran towards them with a microphone.

"We have to go." Hunter grabbed Sulzberger's arm and pulled him across the street, with no care for the on-coming traffic.

"Mr. Sulzberger?! Robert? Can we ask you a few questions?" The reporter yelled as she came closer. "Mr. Sulzberger! Can we have one moment of your time? Robert!"

"No comment," Hunter said as he protected his client, his back to the reporters. "We have no comment."

"Mr. Sulzberger? We need a comment about the murder case. Please! Robert!"

Hunter hustled his client into the back seat and closed the door as a desperate pack of reporters pressed up to the Chevy.

"I said nothing to them," Sulzberger stated as the driver raced them away.

"It doesn't matter. Your worried face is going to be on every news bulletin tomorrow." Hunter grunted. "And they're all going to paint you as guilty."

# CHAPTER 6

BEAUTY IS a gift given randomly at birth, and Esther Wright had been blessed with the full package.

Her eyes were a rare shade of cobalt, her sandy-blonde hair rested just beneath her shoulders, and her figure boasted a healthy feminine curve. Add to that lightly tanned skin, perfect teeth, and a smile that would bring any guy to his knees. Tex Hunter would've thought she was flawless, except for her severe lack of table manners.

"Remind me never to have a coffee meeting with you again." Hunter watched as Esther grabbed a chunk of blueberry muffin, eating it like a teenage boy who hadn't seen food in days.

"Why not?" She questioned as she slurped her coffee.

Her lips almost vibrated as she sucked back the drink, turning the heads of the people next to her. Even in the busy Downtown Chicago café, filled with many suits refueling before their next deal and workers looking to escape their offices for a brief moment of respite, everyone heard her slurping.

Even some of the customers with headphones turned their heads.

Trying too hard to be alternative, the café instead

just matched the style of every other alternative café in Chicago—dim lighting, Swedish furniture, dance music humming in the background. Their showpiece was the edgy art on the walls; pencil drawings of half-naked women holding animals, the art attempting to make a statement about the primal acts of human nature. Or perhaps they were attempting to make a statement about the lack of half-naked veterinarians. Only the artist would know.

"Have you ever been told you're the loudest coffee slurper in the world? You sound like a vacuum cleaner that's been charged up by a NASCAR mechanic."

"I've been told something similar many, many times. The last time was yesterday in fact. A guy next to me on the train platform asked if I could 'consume my coffee a little quieter.'"

"Any man who messes with you is either plain stupid or stupidly brave." Hunter slapped the wooden table in laughter. "What happened to the poor guy?"

"I told him I could shove the coffee up his tight butt if that would make him happier."

"That's my Esther." She might look like a model, but this woman would be more at home on an oil rig in the Gulf of Mexico than in a photo shoot on the beaches of Malibu.

"Want to hear a joke?" She slurped a drop of coffee off her finger.

"Is it racist, sexist, or really, really terrible?"

"Don't know." She grinned. "I'll tell you the joke, and you can make your own decisions."

"Go on then. Tell your joke."

"My uncle died the other day because we didn't know his blood type. It was hard, but he helped us through it. He was a good guy. As we struggled to find out his blood type, he was encouraging us, even though he was dying. He kept shouting 'Be positive, be positive!'"

Hunter laughed and shook his head. He was sure Esther was a construction worker in a past life.

"If you don't like that one, then you'll like this one. It's a lawyer joke." She tried hard not to giggle. "My dad took an airline company to court for misplacing his luggage. He lost his case."

Hunter shook his head again before his dimples gave his smile away. "That's an old joke and the years haven't made it any better. You should stick to new jokes."

"I've given up many things lately, including asking rhetorical questions. I mean, what's the point?"

"Ha!" He clapped his hands. "That's good. You've got a winner there. How's the plan for your stand-up comedy routine going?"

"Not yet." The smile disappeared from her face, replaced by a look of anxiety. "I'm not ready to stand up in front of people yet."

"If you want to be a comedian, then you'll have to stand up in front of a room. That's how it works, but I wouldn't worry about it if I were you. They'll love you. People always love you. No matter where you go, people adore you. Even if your jokes are really disgraceful, people would still love you."

"But what if they don't? What if I get up there and freeze again? I couldn't even tell a joke last time, remember?"

Hunter wasn't used to seeing a nervous attitude from his legal assistant. She was the one that always made her presence felt, her name remembered, but the fear of public speaking was holding her back, keeping her dreams locked up inside a little box.

"Courage is the acceptance of fear, not the absence of it." Hunter tapped his index finger on the table. "My only advice would be—don't eat or drink on stage."

"Maybe one day I'll get back up there." Esther broke out in a nervous smile. "Maybe."

She placed her coffee cup down, gulped hard, and returned to her muffin sitting on its side, slightly destroyed by her attack.

"So, what have you got for me?" He changed the conversation back to the case.

She stopped munching on her blueberry muffin, licked each finger twice, and then reached into her handbag to pull out a file. "I've got—"

Hunter raised his hand. She understood, finishing her mouthful before she continued.

She loudly gulped down the food after minimal chewing and started again. "I've got some preliminary information about Robert Sulzberger. Son of a construction worker and stay-at-home mother, both long deceased. Grew up in poor housing in Naperville, Illinois. Dropped out of school, left his small town at sixteen, moved to Chicago, got into drugs and stealing. Got caught stealing a sweater during a snowstorm, and was arrested but not charged. Turned to the army as a way out. Said in one of his political speeches: 'The army provided me the structure and family that I needed.'"

"He's been very vocal about how the army was his 'real' family."

"Got out of the army after ten years, and went on the reality show Island Survivor. He won it, and the public loved him. The lovable giant with integrity. With that level of popularity, someone convinced him to go into politics, and it was all downhill from there." She leaned forward. "As a politician, he's been the complete opposite to what we saw on Island Survivor. He's lost his spine. He flipped between different ideas all the time, and never stood up for his constituents. I have no idea how he got voted onto the council."

"He was charismatic, good-looking—and thanks to good investment decisions—wealthy. After his success on reality television, he wanted to do good for his fellow returning veterans, and he entered politics believing he could make a difference to someone, somewhere. He believed politics was the way to change society, make the world a better place, but he quickly found out he was wrong."

"But where was the substance?" Esther appealed. "The policies? He ran for office on the back of nothing. He used his fame to win votes. Politics is about the best person for the job, not the most popular."

"It's a lot more complicated than that, Esther." Hunter swirled his espresso, the tiny cup almost swallowed by his huge hands. "He united a group of people who felt their voice wasn't being heard. Veterans felt they finally had someone in office who they could trust; he was one of their own. His whole campaign was built around what he could do for his fellow vets. There are a lot of vets in his council ward, and he said all the right things for them."

"But when push came to shove…"

"He changed his mind. He agreed with what his donors and mayor wanted. They wanted to demolish the current community center to make way for the new stadium, so they could try and corner the younger voters. He was told that if he didn't change his vote, he would lose his donors, and then the Mayor wouldn't endorse him in the next election."

"It shouldn't be like that, and it shouldn't be about keeping your job." She shook her head. "Politics should be about doing what's right for your people."

"Henry Kissinger once said that ninety percent of politicians give the other ten percent a bad reputation." He smiled. "Sulzberger's a politician. That's his job. He's got to look at the whole picture. He could do more good for the people of Chicago by voting for the party politics than he could by standing up for his vote. He would've achieved nothing if he stuck to his vote. They still would've found a way for the stadium to go ahead. The development was too important to the Mayor's next election."

"Well, from the outside, he appeared to be the perfect politician. Good teeth, nice wife and child, nice house, nice suits. From the outside, it looked like he had the ideal life..."

"I feel like that's not the end of your sentence."

"But you never know what happens behind closed doors."

"Meaning?"

"I found a record that his wife, Kim Sulzberger, bought a registered gun only a month ago."

"Interesting." Hunter paused. "What sort of gun?"

"A Glock. She walked into the Midwest Sporting Goods store on Plainfield Rd, filled in the registration papers, and bought a handgun. It's all on file. I fluttered my eyelids, and the owner slipped me the information."

"You do have nice eyelids," Hunter said. "Do you think it was for protection? Worried about the public's reaction to her husband's choices?"

"Who knows? Could be revenge. Obviously, things weren't right in their perfect life, and the wife would've known about Robert's new woman. Nothing would've gotten past Kim Sulzberger. She's on community boards, on the neighborhood watch, an active member of many blog websites. It took me hours to go through all her Facebook comments in the last year alone, and they were all quite attacking. This is a woman who loves drama and being a part of it all. Maybe that's how she gets her kicks."

The child of a Chicago beat cop; Esther had seen enough of that side of the law growing up. After she watched her dominant father arrest her boyfriend for a minor drug infringement, she knew she had to stick up for the disadvantaged.

Her father tried to push her into becoming an officer, but she hadn't been able to bear the thought of picking on the 'little guy'. When Hunter employed her, her father hated the fact she was working for a defense lawyer, and pleaded with her to change her mind. He was more concerned about his colleagues' reactions than her career. He even told her to go out to a bar, meet the right guy, get married, and stay at home to raise his grandchildren.

That statement made the decision for her, and five years later, Hunter couldn't be happier with that choice.

"What happens next to our new buddy?" she asked.

"I'm filing a number of motions this afternoon, and we'll apply to suppress his name on the files. I don't think we'll get the suppression order, but it's worth a shot. Then we can start to build this defense. I've already got Ray on the case."

"Ray Jones?"

"Only the best for this case, Esther. He didn't think twice about working on it—he's already researching all of Robert's connections. As for me, I'm going to talk to the arresting officer, and see if we can get any extra information."

"Chances of winning?"

"At this point, slim to none. We don't have much to go on yet, and we don't have any information about the only real lead. Robert's a good man who's done a lot for his country and people, but I don't think that's going to keep him out of prison for long. He's the type of man we need in politics." Hunter finished his espresso and threw a few bills on the table, leaving a sizable tip. He stood and began to make his way to the door of the busy café. "And it's my job to make sure he stays out of prison."

"Wait," Esther complained as she stood to leave. "I haven't finished my muffin."

Hunter turned around to say something, but Esther had already shoved the remaining half into her mouth.

"I'm... ready... ugh," she mumbled with food dropping out as she dusted down the front of her jacket with her hands. "I'm good. Let's go."

Hunter sighed, shaking his head. "Just finish chewing before you get back into the office."

# CHAPTER 7

THE WORLD buzzed around Hunter as he stood next to the Union Park outdoor basketball court, a takeaway coffee cup in each of his hands.

Looking out of place in the area dominated by loose T-shirts, long shorts and brand-name socks, Hunter stood tall in his fitted suit. Not only did his fashion choices look out of place, but he also felt like dishing out life advice to every young person that whizzed past him. Union Park was situated between a nice suburb on the north side, and a not-so-nice suburb on the south side, creating a space that felt comfortable enough for a family picnic under the evergreen trees during the day, but not a place to walk through at night without a police escort.

The basketball courts were separated from the adjoining tennis courts by a tall, chain-link fence, creating an enclosure that seemed like a prison yard. And the pickup basketball games were played in the same manner.

Chicago PD Detective Jemma Knowles looked at home on the other side of the white line, bouncing the basketball in her left hand, holding out her right hand as a defense, and mouthing off to the young men on the court. Despite being at least twenty years older than them, she moved between them with agile ease, springing up to lay the ball into the hoop.

There were two places the forty-one-year-old, six-foot-tall, African-American woman felt comfortable—flying around a basketball court, taking down macho young men, and wearing her badge as a Chicago PD detective, taking down macho older men. With one tattoo sleeve, usually covered during working hours, Knowles could be mistaken for a rough street player, but whoever thought that would do so at their own peril.

Knowles aggressively high-fived one of her teammates, staring at the opposition while muttering something inaudible, and then turned to greet Hunter.

"What are you doing here?" She flapped her white T-shirt to try and catch some cooler air.

"You wouldn't answer my calls."

"Because I know what you're calling about, and I shouldn't be talking to you about it. If you need to talk, do it through the official channels."

"All I need is a few minutes, Jemma. That's all I'm asking for."

"We're five points up; it's the first to twenty. It'll be five more minutes, and I'll have finished with this lot."

She bounced back onto the court, muscling one of the nineteen-year-olds out of her way. With a burst of speed, she found space on the crowded court. The ball bounced into her hands, and she sprung back into the air. Another layup, and then another one, followed by a block, a grunt, a pass and then another two-point layup for the win.

Hunter grimaced as he watched her land. One wrong step here, one wrong position, and no amount of beauty products would cover the damage the hard concrete could inflict.

Not that Detective Jemma Knowles would mind. Beauty products weren't her thing.

"Still like a soy latte?" He presented his peace offering as she stepped off the court, another win under her belt.

"You do know a way to a woman's heart." She felt comfortable next to his figure. As a tall woman, there weren't many times she felt feminine, but next to the defense lawyer, she felt rather girlish. Knowles took a long sip of her coffee, adjusted her cap, and passed the coffee back to Hunter before stretching out her arms. Her black hair was pulled back tightly, almost like she wanted nothing to do with it. It had betrayed her many times; men saw her feminine locks and immediately thought she was an easy target, that she was soft. That would be their mistake. Hunter knew that from the days when she was his girlfriend.

When Hunter dumped her a week before her twenty-first birthday, and only two days before Valentine's Day, she slapped him so hard that his ears were ringing for a week. Despite the decades that had passed, he still remembered the slap. Vividly.

"I'm a busy woman, so hurry up and get those words out of your mouth." Knowles puffed, flapping her shirt again.

"What can you tell me about Robert Sulzberger?" Hunter asked.

"Tex, it's my day away from the job. It's not what I want to hear when I come here to play some pickup. I come out here to escape the job, not to be hounded about it. If you need to ask me something like that, send a request to my desk. We may be old friends, but there's got to be a line between work and life."

"This is important, Jemma. I wouldn't be here otherwise."

She drew a long breath, sighed, and stared at the man she respected.

"There was a 911 call from a woman, the cleaner for the house, screaming that there was a dead person in the basement. The cleaner came once a week but only cleaned the basement once a month. She had no idea how long the woman had been there. Detective Rodman got there, searched the house, and found the woman in the basement. She's a Jane Doe. They have no record of her. No fingerprints, no DNA, no match on the missing person's file. She was obviously drugged, beaten, tied up, and then left to die. I got the call to go to Robert's office and take him in for questioning. I asked him a few questions, then took him in, and they arrested him an hour later. I'm sure you know all this—it's in the report."

"I need to know what's not in the report."

"Possession is nine-tens of the law, right? Robert had the girl in his house. He admitted he was the only one home for over a day. He denied ever knowing the girl, but it's hard to argue against the evidence. We took him in for questioning as soon as the body was found, he talked very freely, and Rodman made the arrest within an hour after that."

"But?"

"But as guilty as he looked, I wasn't convinced he knew anything about it. I was the first to talk to him when we arrived at his office. We were just around the corner when uniform got the call, and we went straight in. I was a little nervous because I was a big fan of Robert when he was on reality television, and we didn't really know the extent of the crime yet. We found Robert at his desk, working on a file—not unusual, and in no way prepared for what was about to happen. When we were there, explaining what happened, he was in shock—no doubt about that. When I started questioning him, he looked utterly confused. He had no idea what was happening. He said we must have the wrong person or the wrong house. I've seen a lot of people tell lies in this job, but it was real shock on his face. He said he hadn't been in the basement for at least a week. It's a place he rarely went into, but his wife was out of town, and nobody else had keys to the house. Of course, we had no choice but to bring him in for further questioning. But, again…" She sighed. "Some things at the scene didn't add up."

"Like why would he tie the woman to the chair and leave for work, knowing his cleaner was coming that morning." Hunter responded. "He didn't keep the basement locked or shut down. This guy's not dumb, and he basically framed himself. Unless he wanted to get caught, it was a terrible move."

"We went to talk to the wife, Kim Sulzberger. She'd been out of town on a hike and had left their daughter at her mother's house for a few days of babysitting. Kim runs a small soap making business but told us she was taking a digital detox. She had no alibi, and no other evidence to prove where she was. She said she needed a mental health break, and didn't touch her phone for two days. She had no photos, or any other evidence, from the trip. The only person who verified that information was Robert, and all he knew was what she told him. Sounds like a fairly big coincidence to me." She looked back to the basketball court, eager to play again.

"Your impression of the wife?"

"There was something off about her. I know Robert said he was going through a midlife crisis, at least that's the way all the gossip magazines reported it, but Kim was probably going through one as well. She looked lost, like something was missing. Probably from all the drugs she'd been taking."

"I'd imagine she's on the normal rich housewife set?"

"All prescribed by doctors, but man, it was almost a pharmacy in her cabinet. Valium, Xanax, codeine; if it could be prescribed, she was taking it. It doesn't prove she had anything to do with the murder, but she seemed off. If Robert had been murdering women in the basement, then she could've joined in and not remembered it." Knowles ran her hand over her hair, keeping it flat. "These people—they try to live their perfect lives, keeping up with their friends, checking on each other's progress, but they don't know what's happening in their own home. They try to keep up with their next-door neighbor, but one day they find out there isn't much love to be found in a new washing machine or a bigger kitchen, so they pump themselves full of prescribed drugs, trying to squash those feelings."

"Instead, they should be pounding the pavement with people half their age?"

"Hey, I'm not saying I've got it all worked out, not even close, but I don't need to take half a bottle of pills to get me through the day. I've always said that a little bit of danger, excitement, and adrenaline goes a long way. And what's life without a little bit of danger?" She paused. "What are your thoughts?"

PETER O'MAHONEY

"I'm a man of action. I'm not paid to think." He smiled.

"Just as well." Knowles laughed. "You wouldn't earn much money if that was your only income."

Hunter smiled before watching a young teen land a shot from halfway down the court, followed by a round of high-fives. "It's possible Sulzberger was set up. He's got enough enemies out there who want him out of the picture."

"Pretty big set up though. If it was a set up, a lot of effort was made to make it look perfect. There's no sign of a forced entry, no sign of a struggle outside, and nothing out of the ordinary in that basement. The only thing that wasn't perfect in that whole picture-perfect life was the bloodied girl tied to a chair."

"The picture-perfect life, eh?" Hunter sipped his coffee as the ball bounced near them. Knowles picked up the ball and threw it back onto the court, followed by a number of statements about how bad her opposition were playing. "What about the assistant, Teresa Hardcastle?"

"I've spoken to her over the phone, and I've taken her statement, but I haven't met her in person yet. She's a hard woman to track down. If you find her, you need to let the PD know."

Hunter nodded. "The file's been handed over to the prosecution. And Michelle Law's name is on top. She took over the case yesterday. Apparently, she requested to take over this one."

"Michelle Law?" Knowles smiled. "It's just like old times—like one great big high school reunion."

"I looked at our yearbook last month when I was moving some old boxes, and Michelle was on the front and back cover. An overachieving A-type if there ever was one."

"Watch out for her; she's always had a thing for you. She was the good girl cheerleader that always liked the bad boy type," Knowles said. "But it's funny you mention her name because she's starting to fall apart at the edges as well. I picked her up a few weeks back—rotten drunk on a street bench in Burnham Park. No charges were laid, but she was a mess after we woke her up—swearing and throwing things."

"Michelle Law in lockup? Now I've heard it all." Hunter stared at the woman that had been in and out of his life for the best part of two and a half decades. "You look good, Jemma. You look like you're still in your twenties."

"Don't do that." She shook her head. "Not now."

"How's your husband?"

"I kicked him out. He turned into a slob. He drank too much beer, didn't do anything around the house, and had become disillusioned with life in general. Like you said, a common theme for our age. I'm still married to him, and deep down, he's a nice guy, but I couldn't do it anymore. We're living apart for a while to see if there's anything left to save in the marriage. It would seem a waste to throw all those years away." She looked up at him with wide eyes. "What about you? Any women on the scene?"

"You know me, Jemma; no woman deserves the pain I would put them through. I've got too many issues to sort out first."

"You're a good-looking man, Tex. Tall, successful, charming—what's not to like?"

"I'm the son of a serial killer. Any woman will run for the hills when they hear that."

"Well, maybe you shouldn't bring it up on the first

date. That shouldn't be the title of your online dating profile."

"Then I'm lying to them. I can't hide it for long."

"Your parents' actions don't define you. Your father killed those girls, not you. You do amazing things in this world. You make a difference in people's lives. You're better than being your father's son." She brushed a strand of loose hair behind her ears. "You can't keep waiting, Tex. There has to be a day when you let someone into that cold heart of yours."

"No one deserves this."

"I hope one day you realize that someone does. And when you do, give me a call." She touched his arm, and started to smile. "Just look after yourself until you're ready. I don't want to hear that they've found your body at the bottom of the Chicago River. These politicians have a lot of powerful enemies, and they'll kill to get what they want. I've seen it before. You're stepping into a dangerous world by defending Robert Sulzberger. Lots of people want him dead. I don't even know why you're doing it. The further you go in this case, the more dangerous it's going to become."

Hunter sipped his coffee again, and began to walk off the basketball court, before he turned back to her. "You said it yourself, Jemma—what's life without a little bit of danger?"

# CHAPTER 8

THE WALKWAY was abuzz with children's laughter, a light spray from the Buckingham Fountain filled the breeze, and an atmosphere of joy hung around the park. Tex Hunter couldn't help but smile as a child ran past with a red balloon, giggling as it bounced on a string. The pure joy was infectious.

Grant Park, full of green space, flowers, trees and freedom, was a place a child could escape the restrictions of the city that lay close by. The large park was a distinct contrast to the skyscrapers only a block away; here, life felt open and spontaneous. Sitting on the edge of the Chicago Harbor, freedom abounded. There was a sense of adventure, a sense that one could achieve anything if they were brave enough to sail out into Lake Michigan and take on the world.

The frail woman waiting for Tex Hunter on the park bench was jittery. The sun poked out from behind the cloud on the gray afternoon, bringing a sense of warmth with it, but even that warmth couldn't comfort Kim Sulzberger.

A former army nurse, she was used to not wearing makeup, used to not spending hours in front of the mirror, or caring about her appearance at all. When she first returned to civilian life, she enjoyed getting dressed up, enjoyed feeling like a princess again, but now, in the midst of the chaos, her cosmetics cabinet had grown cobwebs around it. Her hairbrush had about the same amount of use.

When she'd woken up that morning, in anticipation for a meeting with her husband's criminal lawyer, she'd tried to brush her hair. It was a frazzled mess. She'd pulled hard on the knots, and no amount of anti-frizz spray made it any less painful.

"Mrs. Sulzberger?" Hunter approached the woman waiting on the bench. Her arms and legs were crossed, her eyes hidden behind a pair of large sunglasses.

"Hello." She looked up and attempted to smile, but her mouth cracked in the corners. It had been months since she'd tried that expression.

"Thank you for finding the time to meet, Mrs. Sulzberger. I've got to say—I was happy when you suggested we meet here. Any excuse to get out into the sunshine and absorb some vitamin D is a good one." He sat down next to her on the wooden park bench, and she shuffled slightly to her right, away from him.

"Call me Kim," she stated in a tone that was neither friendly nor attacking. "I'm not here to make small talk with you, Mr. Hunter; I'm here to talk about Robert. What your parents did to those girls was awful, and I don't want to talk with you any longer than I have to. I need to know what Robert's been saying. Everything. I need transcripts of what he's said."

Hunter squinted. "I must tell you that anything discussed with a client is covered by attorney-client privilege, so I can't discuss anything he hasn't said to you directly."

"But I'm Robert's wife."

"Estranged wife."

"Still married by law."

"And I'm still bound by law not to discuss my conversations with him."

She sat upright. "I'm talking to you because I need to know how the case is going. I love Robert, even though it's hard for us to talk at the moment. He's in a lot of trouble, and it hurts me to see him so sad. I'm angry about what he did to the girl, in our house, but he's still the father of my daughter." She stared at Hunter. "I need to know where the case is heading. I know things about Robert, things that may change this case."

"Such as?"

"I know why he's in this mess."

"Go on."

"Not long ago, I started seeing a change in him."

"What sort of change?"

She hesitated, biting her fingernails before answering. "With all the trouble we've been through, we decided to take a break from our marriage. I suggested it. I said we would still live together, but we were free to see other people, as long as we didn't bring them home. He was reluctant, but I told him it was for the best. After a while, he accepted it. I know he started looking outside the home for support, and I know he found it. I saw the change in him. He was dressing better, smelling better, going to the gym. He was a new man."

"What about you? Did you start seeing another man?"

She looked away, rubbed the tip of her nose, and

crossed one leg over the other. "Not a man."

"A woman?"

"It's… It was complicated. We weren't—I mean; I didn't have a real relationship with anyone." She brushed a strand of hair behind her ear. "Even though I wanted the break, even though I was meeting someone, I was heartbroken by what Robert did. The happier he looked, the more it hurt. I felt like I was the one being left behind, and he was off living an exciting life, even though I pushed for it."

"What did you do about those feelings?"

"Nothing." She shook her head. "But I should've done something. I should've made him pay for it."

"What do you mean by 'made him pay for it'?" Hunter leaned forward.

She turned to look at him directly again, her stare almost cutting through him. "I didn't have anything to do with what he did to the prostitute. I didn't even know he was seeing prostitutes. What could he get from her that I couldn't provide? Sure, she was younger, but that was it. I was right there. In his house. Why did he have to see hookers to get that?"

Hunter didn't answer.

"I'm asking a question of you. Why did he do that?"

"How did you know she was a prostitute?"

"I assumed she was a prostitute. How else could you explain it?"

"Had you ever met the woman found in your basement?"

"Me? No. Of course not. No." She brushed the tip of her nose. "I've never seen her before, but I think Robert was seeing prostitutes. Hookers. Escorts— whatever the right term is for them. I thought she was another one of his paid helpers."

Again, Hunter didn't respond.

"I read online there was no evidence to say they slept together before she died. Wait…" Her hand covered her mouth. "So that means that Robert hired her? He tortured her like some sort of kinky fantasy? Is that what this was? A kinky sex session gone wrong?"

Hunter shook his head.

"I'm asking you—is that what happened? Was this some sort of dungeon fantasy? Oh my. This is worse than I thought. In my own house. In my basement."

A woman with a stroller walked close to them, close enough to overhear their conversation, but that didn't stop Hunter.

"Did you want Robert out of your life?"

"About one week before all this happened, I asked him to leave the house, move out to an apartment."

"And what did he say?"

"He refused to leave. He said this was his home and he wasn't going anywhere."

"So you devised a plan to have him sent to prison?"

"Pardon?" She jolted in shock. "What are you saying? That I did this?"

"It's very convenient you were on a two-night hike by yourself when this happened. You drop your daughter off at your mother's house, and then no one else sees you. No alibi and no phone reception. Nobody can verify your whereabouts, and you don't strike me as the hiking type."

"My therapist recommended hiking. He said I needed to get out into nature. Away from my phone. Disconnect. He said social media was making everything worse for me." Her voice was frantic. "I didn't expect Robert to lose it like this when I was gone. I didn't expect this."

"If he lost it."

"Are you saying he didn't do it? I'm confused."

"I'm saying it's very coincidental that you were away for your first two-night hike in ten years, with no one there for an alibi, and then this happens to the man that you want out of your house."

She stood, her muscles tensed, shocked by the accusation. "I didn't have anything to do with this, Mr. Hunter."

"If he was here, what would you say to him right now?"

"That he's my husband and I never wanted to share him." She hesitated for a moment, before turning and marching away from him, towards the city, leaving a nervous feeling in her wake.

Hunter sat forward on the park bench, elbows resting on his knees, stunned by the final statement of Kim Sulzberger.

# CHAPTER 9

SHE HADN'T fired a gun in a long time.

She hadn't felt that desire to shoot a weapon for more than a decade.

Now, with everything that had happened, she needed to. She needed to feel that cold metal against her skin. She needed to feel alive again. City life had drummed her into numbness, a mess of avoiding pain, marching towards emotional emptiness.

With the 9mm Glock 17 in her right hand, she remembered the feeling. She remembered what it felt like to be alive. When the metal pressed into her hand, squeezed tight, with no chance to make a mistake, the pleasure began. It was when fate took over, driving her actions, tingling her senses, forcing her to make decisions. Life-changing decisions. Decisions that would impact more than just her.

He used to be good to her.

He used to look after her, staring at her with a heart-warming gaze. He used to smile when she walked into view. She felt like they were on the same team, but she hadn't felt those days in a long time. She tried to quash the memories of those days, tried to force them out of her head.

He abandoned her. She tried to ignore that fact,

but there was no denying it. Wine had helped her deal with her emotions. Lots of wine.

But nothing would take those days away for long. That love, that passion was etched so deeply into her mind that no amount of alcohol would ever rid her of it. She longed for those days, the days when he'd placed his hand on her shoulder, whispering into her ear.

She had never felt so loved. She had never felt that cared for.

But one day, suddenly, it was all gone.

"Ma'am?" The voice came from over her shoulder. She smelled the man first. He stunk of smoke, beer, and gunshot powder. "Do you need any help?"

"No," she mumbled without turning around. "I'm taking my time to get ready."

"Are you sure, ma'am? I can help you—show you how to hold a gun."

She turned. "I know how to hold a gun."

The man took a step back, intimidated under her stare. He'd seen lots of angry people at his gun range, and he knew when to step back and give them space.

She moved her attention back to the target. She'd been at the range for fifteen minutes, psyching herself up to pull the trigger, edging herself closer to action.

Her revenge was so close.

It wasn't easy to go back when she had been trying to be such a good girl. It wasn't an easy thing to break free.

She set her sights. Focused on the board. Held the piece steady. Her finger gripped the trigger. Squeezing closer to action.

The shot fired.

Dead-on target. Exactly what she needed.

# <u>CHAPTER 10</u>

THE FIRST taste of whiskey hit him hard.

It was a taste that Hunter was all too familiar with, one that had got him through many hard times. He had just passed his fifteenth birthday when he first tasted the burn of whiskey. At that time, both his parents were in prison, and he was in the care of an emotionless aunt. His older brother, at twenty-five, had gotten his hands on a bottle of whiskey and decided that was the answer to all their problems.

Hunter went to his brother, confused about what the papers were saying about their parents. The hatred towards his family was overwhelming, and going to the mall became a battle against verbal abuse. Instead of providing a consoling hand, a hug, or a nice word, Patrick Hunter put the bottle in his younger brother's hand.

"It's only going to get worse," he said. "Nothing I do will change that. This bottle is the only thing that will help ease your pain."

And since then, that had been Hunter's truth.

The narrow dive bar was lit by dull orange lights. Neon signs, advertising beers that hadn't been sold since the '80s, hung behind a collection of cheap spirits. The floor was sticky, the smell of hops was overwhelming, and the nuts at the bar were stale, but this was the place Hunter felt most comfortable. He'd been a regular for more than a decade, and the bar stool had almost become as comfortable as his couch.

"Tough day?" Ray Jones, Hunter's investigator, patted Hunter on the shoulder as he sat next to him at the bar.

"They're all tough days," Hunter replied.

In a moment of male bonding, they nodded to each other.

With ripped biceps and scarred knuckles, Ray Jones had been Hunter's go-to man for half a decade. Slightly unstable, and with ignorance to match, the role of investigator suited him perfectly—from quietly breaking into homes to finding a small piece of information hidden on the internet, Jones flourished in his job. Standing as tall as Hunter, the man with West African heritage dominated most situations through pure intimidation. Tattoos covered his arms, his hair was cropped short, and his shoulders were wide enough to have to turn sideways when he walked through narrow doorways.

Hunter was sitting on his regular barstool, half-watching a replay of the Cubs game on the television in the corner. His phone was open on the bar next to him, displaying the latest news headline: 'Serial killer's son defends reality star.'

"You would think that after all these years they would've moved on. Does it make you angry? The way they still say that? It's not like you killed those girls." Jones indicated to the bartender for a pint of Goose Island Pale Ale. "You're a person, not a headline."

"My name brings in clients, lots of them—there's

no doubt about that. People remember me and aren't ashamed of hiring my services because they think that if my father was a serial killer, then I must sympathize with criminals. It's good for business. The Hunter name always has been."

"Throwing rubbish on the street keeps street cleaners in a job, but it doesn't make it right."

"I can't change my past, Ray." Hunter looked at the article. It was exactly what he didn't need. Sulzberger had become a walking headline, and unfortunately, there was no stopping the media now.

"But does the name bring in the right type of clients?" Jones threw a few notes on the bar when the server placed a beer in front of him.

"The right type of clients are the ones that pay."

"You don't believe that," Jones stated.

"Some days I believe money's the most important thing, especially the days when you send me your invoice."

"Ha!" Jones laughed. "Well, the way I see your current case; he couldn't have done it. He couldn't have killed the girl."

"Why not?"

"Because he's a war hero. He protected the people of this country. He risked his life to save innocent people, and then he stepped up to help the people that needed it. When I used to watch him on Island Survivor, he was a man of true honor and integrity— that's how he won the whole thing. That's why the people loved him—even in the face of losing the game, he stood by his morals. He went into politics to make a difference. He kept trying; he didn't give up like he could have. That's not the actions of a killer."

"He rezoned an area so a new stadium could be

approved, displacing a community for returning veterans who had been in the same place for fifty years. That's not supporting your own people, or standing by your morals."

"But that's politics." Jones shrugged. "If you want to make a difference, you have to stay in the game. He might've had the deciding vote, but if he voted the bill down, then the Mayor and his donors would've abandoned him at the next election. The best thing he could do is stay in there and make a difference to future votes. Be a voice of reason in the room. We need more people who want to make a difference."

"The people who want to make a difference, the people who can change the world for the better, the people who are devoted to helping others, don't belong in the political game. Those people, the ones that hold our misdirected hope, are laughed out of the game by the players."

"Well said."

"And that's not the idea of politics. You can't be at the whims of someone else's beliefs. You have to stand up for what you believe in."

"It's strange." Jones chuckled, shaking his head. "I never pictured you to be so idealistic, Tex. I always thought you were a man of reason. You know that's not the way the game is played. You know that isn't how the big picture works. Certain decisions equal private funding. Funding equals better advertising. Better advertising equals a better chance at reelection. He voted for the stadium to get reelected."

Hunter stared into his drink, drawn into the conversation by his long-term pal. "His life wasn't all roses though."

"How so?"

"It's no secret he was falling apart at the edges. He was struggling to keep it all together." Hunter tipped the glass sideways, comforted by the familiar clink of ice cubes tapping on the glass.

Laphroaig's ten-year-old scotch whiskey had always been one of his favorites. The punchy peaty taste, delicate smoky overtones, and smooth finish had always taken him away from normality. It was his quick escape from the mundane moments of life.

"Do you want to know what I think about the murder?" Jones leaned both arms on the bar.

"Go on."

"Suspect number one has to be the wife. It makes perfect sense. She didn't want to lose her lifestyle, but she didn't want to get divorced. I've seen it many times—people cheat before they accept their marriage is over. They want out, but they don't know how to do it."

"Killing an unknown woman is an extreme solution to marriage issues."

"Maybe Kim Sulzberger found the woman in the house and went into a rage." Jones shrugged. "She could've lost control, and accidentally went too far. I've heard some bad stories about what jilted wives do."

"I need you to start with her." Hunter placed a file on the bar. "I need to know her every movement and every purchase in the month before the murder. If she set him up, then I'd say that she'd been planning it for a while."

"I'll see what I can find."

"But she's not the only suspect right now." Hunter slid another file across the bar. "Teresa Hardcastle is a hard person to track down. I need you to track her down so I can talk to her."

"If she's in Chicago, I'll find her." Jones turned to the door as five college students walked in. "If I'm looking at the wife and assistant, where are you going to start investigating?"

"I'm going to start with the people that hated Robert Sulzberger the most."

# CHAPTER 11

THE MEETING room in Cindy Mendel's office was cramped. The beige walls looked like they'd been pushed in on each other, the narrow space could've passed for a hallway, and the small window at the back of the room did little to brighten the mood. The décor was neat, tidy, and completely soulless. A small watercolor painting by a local artist hung on the left wall, their name proudly attached underneath, and heat poured through a vent that looked like it hadn't been cleaned since the turn of the century. Tex Hunter squirmed on the firm office chair, unable to find a comfortable position. It was the McDonald's seating plan—comfortable to enjoy for a few moments, not comfortable enough to linger on. He stood and walked around the white Formica table, noticing his office chair had been lowered and the politician's had been raised. With a smile on his face, he switched them around.

After fifteen minutes, Cindy Mendel entered the room through the wooden door, holding out her hand for an introduction, a chill in the air around her.

"Mr. Hunter." Her suit was creased, and her breath stank of wine, but for a woman in her late fifties, she moved with ease. Her hair had recently been dyed dark black, covering any gray strands, and her skin was wrinkled, but not in the places where she smiled. "I'm so sorry to hear about all this drama. I wish we could meet under better circumstances. Obviously, I was close to Robert so I'm happy to help you any way I can."

"A pleasure to meet you, Cindy." Hunter shook her hand.

"Robert's done a lot of good for this country. His service has been appreciated, but unfortunately, it's a story we hear all too often. That's why veterans need our support. That's why they need us more than ever. That's why funding needs to increase."

"Of course."

"I understand you've been trying to track me down." She sat down on the chair, and her eyes squinted with confusion as she noticed it was lower than usual. "Robert and I were colleagues, and we were close once, but I'm not sure how much help I can be. What he did to that girl was terrible, absolutely shocking, but I wasn't surprised. Many men and women return from the horrors of war, try to assimilate into normal society, but then just... snap." Cindy leaned forward and she stared at the table in front of her. "Robert and I used to be friends. To think that I had that cold-blooded murderer at the dinner table in my house…"

"He hasn't been found guilty yet."

"It's only a matter of time." She frowned and tried to flatten out her skirt. "And this is why veterans need support. They need to be supported after they return from war; otherwise, things like this can happen. They lose their cool; I mean, PTSD is real, it's not a made-up condition, and this is exactly why places like the

Returning Veterans Center are so important to our community. Places like that provide support for the men and women who've served our country, and protected our freedom."

"Is that what you think happened?"

"In my line of work, I've seen it many, many times before. Men and women return from combat, and the images of war are too much for their brains to take in. It's all too frightening, too intense, and they snap— they lose control. Some people become very violent, others just breakdown and aren't able to function."

"Is that what happened to your husband?"

The look on her face instantly changed. Gone was the pleasant, but forced, smile, replaced by a steely gaze. She stared at Hunter for a few long moments before replying. "It's well documented what happened to Liam. It's very well known that's why I went into politics, and some days, I struggle to keep it all together. Some days, I feel like my world is falling apart as well, but I don't want anyone else to suffer through the pain I had to suffer through. He hung himself and that was his choice. He saw it as his only choice to escape the pain. It hurts your soul when your significant other does that, the mark it leaves on you is permanent, but fortunately, Liam only hurt himself when he snapped, unlike Robert."

"I'm sorry to hear that."

"He decided to check out. Leave us all behind. He abandoned the people that loved him because he couldn't handle the thoughts in his head. That's what war does to people. I served for a short period in my early twenties before I was medically discharged. That was a long time ago now. It's been many decades since I lived that life."

"In interviews, you've stated before you were running from a past life when you went into the army. What were you running from?"

"My parents were addicts, and I grew up in an explosive environment. I became pregnant at fifteen after I was kicked out of home. I had no choice. I had to give up the child. I was forced to put her up for adoption because I couldn't care for her. I was never the same after that. Don't judge me for that mistake; I was only young. I've paid for that mistake many times over."

"I'm not judging. My family history is littered with many faults."

"Of course it is." Cindy laughed, and the tension eased. Most family issues looked minor next to the Hunter family tree. "I found the daughter I was forced to give away. I know who she is, and I'm a part of her life, but she doesn't know who I am. I've protected her over the years, but I don't want her to know about me. Not yet." The sadness grew in her eyes. "But we're getting off topic. You didn't come here to listen to my life story. How can I help you, Mr. Hunter?"

"Why did you slap Robert two days before he was arrested?"

"Straight to the point. I like that in a man. You see, people who are straight to the point tend to have a line of questioning in mind about their cause. I can see that you've got a focus in mind and that's what you're working towards. When Robert first started in politics, I had an ally. He was on my side when we stepped up to look after the veterans. But, unfortunately, in the end, he put his political needs before the people that elected him."

"Answered like a true politician," Hunter stated, looking over Cindy's shoulder to the filing cabinet in the corner of the room. Sitting on top of the cabinet were two books—The Courage to be Disliked and How to Handle Hatred. "But I'll ask again—why did you slap Robert?"

"My relationship with Robert was very tense after he voted down the motion to support veterans and approve the stadium development. There were times when I would consider him a friend, a buddy to our cause, but after that vote, I didn't feel we had a connection. My political career rested on his decision to rezone his area, and now, it looks like I'll be out at the next election."

Hunter waited, a grin on his face.

"Okay. I get it. You want the answer to your question, but I'm not quite sure how to answer it."

"How about we get you to answer that question under oath."

"Well…" She looked to the door, which had been left slightly ajar. "I imagine you'll ask me that question under oath anyway, but first, I would also be interested to know whether Robert is going to plead guilty or not?"

She raised her eyebrows, waiting for a response; however, Hunter didn't give her one. He'd dealt with enough politicians to know they took every opportunity to avoid answering tough questions. Redirect the conversation here, throw in a distraction there, ask a question in return. Her answer was as textbook as it was frustrating.

"Okay." Cindy conceded defeat, looked down at the table, and rolled her fingers over each other. "Is he going to press charges for the slap?"

"You still haven't answered my question."

"You get used to certain things in politics. You build up many skills, including how to avoid answering questions you don't want to give a direct answer to. I'm sure, as a lawyer, you've built up many different skills that come in handy in everyday life. What would be your best skill, Mr. Hunter?"

Again, Hunter didn't respond verbally. He just raised his eyebrows.

She nodded. "I imagine Robert has already given you his version of events and you're looking to verify them. He did get a black eye in the office that day, and yes, I was there with his assistant, Teresa Hardcastle. She was very angry that day."

"But why did you slap him?"

"Is that not what I just answered?"

"You said he got a black eye in the office and Teresa Hardcastle was angry."

"Isn't that what you asked?"

"I asked why you slapped him."

"I can see you have quite a formidable intellect, Mr. Hunter, but the reality is that I'm not going to answer that question today. You'll have to get me under oath to answer that."

"You could've said that from the start."

"But then we wouldn't be having as much fun, would we?" Her expression was emotionless. "You can understand my confusion here. These questions seem to be all about me, and not about the case with Robert. What angle are you going for here?"

"Robert's vote effectively ended your career as a politician. You had all your eggs in that basket, supporting veterans, and now, nobody is going to vote for you at the next election. Nobody is going to vote for someone who can't get anything done in office. Rumor has it that you might even resign."

"I'm not going to resign. Why would I? I will always do what's best for the people. Just because Robert murdered a prostitute doesn't mean I should stop trying to do my job."

"A prostitute?"

She squinted. "Isn't that who she was?"

"Nobody knows who she was. She's still unidentified. A Jane Doe."

"I must've heard it on the news. You know what news reports are like. They take a piece of information and twist it until they get the story they want."

Hunter leaned forward. "Where were you on October 5th?"

"October 5th? I have no idea. What day was it?"

"A Tuesday."

"Tuesday is usually my stay at home night. A night just for me. I work all the time, always at different places helping someone, but I keep Tuesday night free. I usually sit down with a good book and a nice glass of red wine. I say glass, but I mean bottle. Is that a crime?"

"Can anyone verify you were at home?"

"As I said, it's my time. I was alone." Her teeth ground together. "I'm not on trial here."

"You might be."

Cindy stood, the chair almost falling over behind her. She walked to the door, opened it, and waited for Hunter to leave.

"Thank you for taking the time to meet." Hunter stood and paused just beyond the threshold. "I'm sure we'll talk again."

# CHAPTER 12

A BED, a television, a microwave. Only the essentials. In the tight entrance of the apartment, a generic photo of the City of Chicago hung in an attempt to relieve the blandness. It didn't work.

Robert Sulzberger sat hunched forward on the two-seater black leather couch, elbows resting on his knees, staring at the shoebox full of memories. He hated the small apartment. Its darkness, its lack of direct sunlight, hindered by the neighboring apartment blocks, only added to his misery. It was a two-bedroom rental which included a small galley kitchen, the main living area, and a bathroom, which was only just big enough to fit the toilet, sink, and shower.

The rope, placed on top of the box, broke his heart. It was the first thing Robert Sulzberger saw when he picked up the box. Digging deeper through the items, he found a photo of himself, smiling, carefree and happy.

Staring at a photo of his much younger self, the crinkled picture from a time before digital-everything, Sulzberger's mind drifted back to the first time he stole. At sixteen, he walked into a convenience store, its bright lights in contrast to his dark outlook, and he stared at the shop assistant, knowing he didn't have the money to pay for a chocolate. He stared at the assistant as he slipped a candy bar up his shirt sleeve. A rush of blood, an excitement, a feeling of escape from his dark sadness, filled his body. When he stole a second time, another candy bar, the adrenaline rush was even bigger. Then he did it again, and again, and again.

It was his most vivid memory of adolescence, the one he thought about the most, the one where he was happiest. The bigger the challenge to steal an item, the bigger the buzz was afterward. The moments after he walked out of a store carrying a microwave, when he laughed so much he couldn't breathe, his childhood friend next to him, was one of the happiest moments of his life. The two boys developed a bond through thieving, driving each other to do bigger and better each week.

It was why he went back to it.

When he returned from the reality television series about surviving on a remote Pacific island, he had all the support in the world around him, everyone adored and admired him. He couldn't walk down the street without someone asking to take a selfie. People yelled their admiration as they passed in cars, and he was often greeted with applause after he entered a restaurant.

He saw politics as the best way to make a difference. Unfortunately, he didn't understand the political game. After he was backed into a corner over the decision to rezone an area to make way for a new stadium, he lost his support network—the support of his brothers and sisters in arms.

Months of protests outside his office followed,

which triggered his first post-traumatic stress episode in over five years. The flashbacks to the world of Afghanistan, the violence, blood, and horror that he saw, spun him out of control. In one of the worse incidents, his assistant found him crying in the corner of his office late one evening, the desk overturned and all his files on the floor.

After numerous PTSD episodes in the next month, he took to stealing again. It was his way to feel relief from the painful images, his way of going back to a simpler time, a time when he felt the happiness of adolescence.

It was a rush. An escape. A rebellion. When the stakes were so high, when there was no margin for error, when perfection was demanded, the harmony would begin. When he pushed past the fear, when he tempted destiny, the adrenaline kicked in, singing through his body, tingling his senses, bringing a smile to his face that he couldn't wipe off. Beyond what was considered reasonable, he found his escape.

He never expected sensible people to understand. The risk was too much, so they eased back. They stayed in their normal lives; doing sensible things: dusting, vacuuming, working nine-to-five. But past the limit of sensible, past the edge of sane, was excitement, exhilaration, and maybe, expiry. And that was the place he needed to go. That was the place that took him away from the pain.

In the Lincoln Park short-term rental apartment his lawyer organized, he moved the box in his hands. Kim, his wife, left the box on the porch for him to collect. She refused to open the front door when he arrived, and she'd already had the locks changed. Through the living room window, he could see his five-year-old daughter crying, before she was dragged away by his mother-in-law. Her tears broke his heart.

It was bad enough the neighbors were watching the drama unfold, but with the news crews outside, and cameras targeted on him, the situation was being broadcast to the world. He had no doubt it would be on the front pages by the next morning.

Heartbreak in front of the neighbors was one thing; heartbreak in front of a whole city was on another level.

He talked to Lucy on the phone after he left. She asked when he was coming home, and he promised her it would be soon. He promised he would read her a bedtime story soon, but he didn't know if he could keep that promise. Kim wanted Lucy kept away from the drama that was unfolding. His wife told him it was for the best, the only way to protect Lucy. He was reluctant, but he agreed.

The box she left was filled with his war medals, a bunch of old photos, and the item designed to hurt him the most—her wedding ring.

After a decade of marriage, he was surprised at how quickly love had grown into hate. They met when she was an army nurse caring for people, and he was a sergeant, hunting them down. Their love blossomed under the intensity of warfare, their passion an escape from the horrors they'd witnessed.

While he entered into politics to make a difference, all it did was drag him further away from his wife. They had barely talked in the past year, living next to each other as icy housemates rather than anything more.

He'd spent countless hours searching for X, scrolling through pages and pages of social media profiles online. The only thing he really knew was she lived in Chicago. He knew her face, he knew her body, and he knew her smell, but finding her online was proving difficult.

Every day, he looked for her. Every day, he searched through the profile photos of women in Chicago until he couldn't focus anymore. Every day, he tried to remember what she looked like. What color were her eyes? What shape was her face? Did she have any distinguishing features? He remembered little.

He rested his head in his hands. The rollercoaster of life had taken many turns for him, many ups and downs, and he didn't like the track he was riding now. His father, hard and cold, would be turning in his grave.

His phone buzzed again, and it made his heart jump.

He didn't want to read another message of hatred—he'd had enough of those—but he couldn't resist checking the phone, hoping at least one person in the world was sending him a message of support.

He turned the phone over and unlocked the home screen.

*I spoke to your lawyer today. You deserve to die in prison, scumbag.*

It was Cindy Mendel, his old ally. His old friend. They'd stood side by side as they fought for the benefit of veterans, but when he lodged his vote for the stadium, he sacrificed everything he stood for.

When she slapped him, he was glad there were no cameras to see it. As much as she hated him, he could never hate her, not after what she had done for his fellow vets.

He'd been surprised by the force of the slap. It was a solid left in the right eye socket. Blood had dripped from a cut above his eye onto his office floor, and neither Cindy or his assistant, Teresa, helped him. He understood why Cindy was angry—she lost her husband to suicide after he could no longer take the images that kept coming back into his head. That loss drove Cindy to ensure that others never had to experience the pain she suffered. She was as single-minded in her approach as she was strong.

Teresa had been through similar heartbreak—her sister, also a veteran, had suffered PTSD episodes after she returned from war, but survived her numerous suicide attempts.

They weren't the only friends he'd lost over the past months. Many others had ignored his phone calls; while others sent messages of outright hatred. People he thought he could count on.

He wouldn't last long in prison. Not with what he'd done. How he'd turned on his own people. They would target him, and ensure his life behind bars was short. He knew the veterans wouldn't allow him to see his sentence through.

They would take great joy in taking him out.

He removed the photos from the bottom of the box and stared at the last item his wife left in there. One photo of Kim, Lucy and himself, carefree, smiling and hugging, but with a red scribble drawn over the top of his face.

He held the rope she left in the box, the texture stabbing into his hands.

She was giving him a way out.

He looked up at the roof. The arch would be able to take his weight.

"Not today," he whispered to himself. "Not yet."

He knew X was the reason he was in this predicament.

He knew all of it stemmed from their relationship, but he couldn't see a way to get to her. He had no doubt she was the reason he was in trouble, but he knew nothing about the woman.

He opened his laptop and started searching profiles of women in Chicago. X was the only chance he had left.

His only hope.

He had to find X.

# CHAPTER 13

*One month earlier...*

THE WALLS of the ground floor electrical store were splattered with a confusion of colors, a smattering of oversized words and a collection of boisterous posters showcasing the store's amazement at their own mid-year sale.

A baseball cap pulled down and sunglasses covering his eyes, Robert Sulzberger wandered through the aisles of the well-lit shop, waiting for his opportune moment, pretending to gaze over all the electrical options for the useless waste of his hard-earned cash.

He glanced to his left and noticed his friend, slim and brunette, engrossed in a conversation with the teenage male shop assistant, who was wearing a work uniform two sizes too big. X smirked as she listened to the teen explain the intricacies of a particular videogame, edging closer to the boy's personal space with each breath.

Sulzberger and X had been friends for five months, but still, he didn't know her name. She insisted no information was to be exchanged between them. He only knew her as X.

"We have to protect our privacy, our identity," she'd said. "What we're doing is too risky, too illegal. It would risk it all if you knew my name."

Sulzberger didn't care. X was giving him what he needed—an escape from the life he'd built. Their moments in the car after a steal were the highlights of his mundane days. He would think about them all week; the way she couldn't keep her hands off him, the risk of being caught in the car, the adrenaline still coursing through his veins after a theft.

But he'd had his fill now. He was done with that life. Mundane and average was enticing to the tired and worn-out people of the world.

Choosing his moment to perfection, Sulzberger bent low, lifting a new laptop off the bench in one fluent motion, tugging just hard enough to pull the security cord from the wall. He tucked the silver computer under the arm furthest from the sight of the shop assistant.

The assistant didn't even look his way. No one did.

As he approached the automatic doors, he felt no sense of exhilaration, no charge in his heartbeat, and when he realized he would walk out of the shop without a hassle, when he realized his escape was clean, he coughed brashly and switched the laptop into his most visible arm, gathering the immediate attention of the teenager.

"Hey!" the boy yelled. "Where are you going with that?"

Sulzberger's reflexes sprung into action—his muscles clenching, hands tightly gripping the possession, his legs exploding him forward out the door.

The teenager reacted, leaping into motion after the

fleeing thief.

X lunged her left foot into the boy's path. With a tangle of lanky arms and legs, he tumbled, grasping at X's jumper on his way down to the floor. Sensing the chance to slow him even more, she feigned a fall, landing on top of his awkward frame, pressing her body firmly into his.

The teenager was stunned with a flurry of hormonal activity, forgetting about the chase for the computer, his face flush with an embarrassing redness.

With deliberate slowness, X raised her body off the teenager's, the hair from her messy wig over his face, maintaining eye contact as she rose. He was slow to rise, having completely forgotten about his chase, and offered a stuttering apology for the mishap.

It took a few moments before the teenager realized Sulzberger had well and truly escaped out the door, and when it dawned on him, he snapped his face toward the exit to see the doors wide open. After apologizing for the fall, X left while the teen began his phone report to his boss.

Outside, in the smoky Chicago air, she searched for her man and found him waiting at their predetermined meeting point next to a bus station two blocks away, leaning against his car.

"What the hell was that all about?"

"What a rush, eh?" Sulzberger grinned as he pulled off his mustache and removed his sunglasses, forcing them into his backpack covering the stolen laptop. He stepped forward to embrace her, but she reacted, stepping back.

"What a rush? Are you serious? We almost got done! That kid saw you walk straight out of the shop with the computer!" She didn't close the gap between them.

"Such a rush." Robert's pupils were dilated, his hands were shaking, and a wide grin was spread across his face. "And we didn't get caught."

"It's not about getting caught! It's about getting the goods with minimal fuss."

"And having fun."

"A criminal record is not fun. Trust me—I've seen enough criminals to know it destroys your life."

"But it's a good way to finish, don't you think?"

"Finish?" X looked at the backpack sitting on the ground next to his car, the top of the silver product poking out of the bag. "What are you talking about? We can't finish now."

"I'm sorry, but that's it for me." He leaned forward. "I told you last time that I would only do it once more. It's been amazing, but this is it. I told you this couldn't be a long-term activity."

"I didn't think you were serious."

"I'm serious—I'm out. It's been an amazing ride, but we've stolen enough. This isn't healthy. I need to confront my emotions, not cover them up with distractions."

X stared at him with confusion.

She had never loved a man this much. She had never felt this close to anyone.

Even though he didn't know her name, she knew everything about him. A quick Google search revealed everything she needed to know. The countless nights of internet surfing that followed revealed everything she didn't need to know.

"What are you going to do instead? Start visiting prostitutes?"

"Pardon?" He looked at her strangely. "Why would you even say that?"

"That's how most middle-aged men get their kicks, right? Craft beer and prostitutes. Your marriage has broken down, so you chase hookers and then drown your thoughts afterward," she whispered, blinking back the tears.

"How would you know about my marriage?"

"You wouldn't be sleeping with someone in the back of your car if your marriage was good." She pointed towards the back seat, then folded her arms across her chest. "You can't stop. Not now. We're such a good team. What about us?"

"Us? There is no 'us'. You won't even tell me your real name! I know nothing about you. How could you possibly think there's something between us if you won't tell me anything?"

She drew a breath. "My name is—"

"Wait." He held up his hand. "I don't need to know. Not now. This is over. I—we—have to stop this. We're pushing the boundaries too far. Kim wanted this, she wanted us to see other people, but she's starting to get really jealous, and I don't want to make her angry. She's not a nice person when she's angry, and I'd hate to think what she'd do to me, or you."

"No," she whispered. "Not now. Please."

"It's been amazing, but it has to end here."

"But think about the rush. Think about the thrill of it being dark, not knowing if the cops are coming, or if the security cameras have seen us... Think about the kick! You said it yourself—that's why you do this. It's the most exciting part of your dull life! Where else could you find something to match this?"

"Maybe dull is good sometimes." He shrugged, standing tall. "Thank you, X. I mean it, thank you. It's been incredible."

A lustful affair with her would've been simpler. It would've been easier to explain. How would he even start to tell his wife what he had done over the past five months? But if he wanted a second chance with Kim, a second chance as a family, he would have to be honest, and he planned to be when the time was right.

"Have a good life, X. It's been fun."

After Sulzberger took his car keys out of his pocket, he flattened down his shirt, made sure it was tucked in, entered his car, and then began his journey home, away from the world of thrills and adrenaline, back to his middle-class, middle-aged world. At that moment, he was sure he would never see X again.

"She doesn't even love you," X whispered as he drove away. "But I do. And I'm going to make sure she can't have you."

# CHAPTER 14

*Present day.*

TEX HUNTER'S shoulders tightened, the grip on his briefcase strengthened, and the muscles in his face stiffened. The walk through the narrow corridors of 69 West Washington St, Downtown Chicago, never failed to increase his heart rate. The 37-story building housed the Executive suites of the Cook County State's Attorney Office, and Hunter had walked the halls more times than he cared to count. The more he thought about the sweat building in his armpits, the more it did, but he thrived under the pressure of the first meeting with the prosecution. One wrong slip of the tongue, one wrong statement, and either side could jump on the hint and destroy a case. Some people leaped out of planes, others climbed mountains, but Tex Hunter got his thrills from having somebody's life, hopes, and dreams resting in his briefcase.

Michelle Law knew him better than any other prosecutor, knew his style and strengths, and more importantly, she knew his weaknesses. Her willingness to exploit them had caused him many headaches in the past, but Hunter was a man familiar with headaches.

He stood in front of the secretary's desk and waited for her to greet him; however, she seemed more interested in her computer screen than his presence.

"My name is Mr. Hunter, and I have a two o'clock with Ms. Law."

"A pleasure to see you," the secretary stated, but the pleasure did not translate to her face. She barely raised her eyes from her mid-afternoon attack on the keyboard. "Miss Law is expecting you, and she's free now. Please go on through. Second door on the right."

He nodded, smiled, and then walked past the rows of administration staff working in office cubicles. He understood the workers were there for the money, but he could never work in a place like that—the mundane chicken-coop existence would drive his rebellious streak into submission. When he came to the wooden door that stated the prosecutor's name, title, and the many degrees earned through years of studying textbooks, he took a breath and knocked.

"It's open."

He turned the doorknob and stepped inside the public office. Dark wood paneling lined the walls, old textbooks sat on the shelves, unused and forgotten about in the age of the internet, and the leather couch at the side of the room, although luxurious, was more than two decades old. The only personal item in the room was an unsolved Rubik's Cube on the middle bookshelf.

"Tex. It's good to see you again." The prosecutor stood and noticed his eyes looking at the brightly colored puzzle. "One of the staff left it here last week.

She said it was a present for my birthday, but I don't have time for such frivolous activities. Actually, I'm surprised anyone has the time for that sort of thing."

"You never know about these sort of things; you may enjoy the challenge of the Rubik's Cube." Hunter shook her hand firmly, but with care.

Her dark mahogany desk was flawlessly organized, with loose paper lined up with the edges of the table, pens in a perfectly straight line, files stacked from largest to smallest. The entire room felt barren and sterile. There wasn't a mark on the carpet, there wasn't a scratch on her desk, and there was barely a speck of dust on the shelves. There was a drenching sense of perfection, a sense that incompetence would not be tolerated and any mistake would be punished. It was here where her OCD was most pronounced, her way of maintaining control in a workplace full of chaos.

With straight black hair, a body toned from too many hours in the gym, and a lackluster look in her eyes from years of secret alcohol abuse, her physique made the statement that she was still fit, but the yellow in the whites of her eyes told a story of addiction.

"It was good to see you last week; I should've mentioned you look stunning." Hunter turned on the charm as he sat in the leather chair old enough to be in an antique show. "You look like you haven't aged a day since high school."

"Flattery will get you nowhere." She tried to smile. "And trust me, I've aged many days since then. Botox keeps the wrinkles at bay on the outside, but on the inside, I've had more hard days than a one-legged duck trying to swim upstream."

"Strange image—a one-legged duck."

"A one-legged duck swims in circles. That's my point. Life is a merry-go-round of days now. Another day, another case. Another case, another file. Another file, another mistake to find. You must be feeling the routine now too. It's middle age—that's what my therapist keeps saying to me each week. Attacks the best of us."

Raising his eyebrows, Hunter looked around the office. "At least you've got all this to show for it. Look at that view of Chicago behind you. That's got to be worth something."

"Worth what? The years of pain that I've given? Worth the breakdown of my marriage? Was it worth watching my husband leave?" She shook her head and sat down with a posture so rigid she could've had a metal pole down the back of her white shirt. "Sometimes, I wonder what life would've been like if I'd gone on to become a painter, or a writer, or a naturist. What would I be like now? Would I still be so bitter and twisted? Does middle age still hit those people with real freedom? I don't like this Western freedom anymore, not this capitalist-consumer 'freedom'." She used her fingers as quotation marks to indicate her disgust for her apparent independence. "I need real freedom. The sort of freedom that comes with doing what you want, when you want."

"You can always step out of the rat race. There's nothing to say you've got to keep living this life. You may want to consider that while you're still young."

"Young?" She scoffed. "Tex, stop kidding yourself. You and I aren't young anymore. Those days we had in high school were two decades ago. I barely even remember the girl that was so full of life, popular, and used to flirt with all the boys. I saw one of our teachers last month; she was being sentenced for theft from a Walmart, and she didn't even recognize me. I don't blame her though. When I look in the mirror, I barely recognize myself some days."

"I remember that girl."

Waving him away, she leaned across her desk and removed a file. "All this leads me to think about my birth mother. She had me at fifteen years old. Can you believe that? Fifteen. That's so young. I've been around now for more than four decades, and I still haven't found someone to reproduce with. My therapist said it might be my biological clock that's causing all this mental pain, along with the pain of not knowing my birth mother, but I don't agree. I think I've just had enough of it all."

"Did you ever look for her—your biological mother?"

"I searched for the adoption records in City Hall, but my file was missing. Apparently, missing files happened a lot back then. I've looked for her, over and over, and I would love to know who she is. Before my time is up, I hope to have found her, or at least her family."

"I'm sorry to hear that."

"My dream has always been that someone will walk into my office with a file that states who she was. What a dream to have." Law stated. "I just wish it was that easy."

"Be careful what you wish for." Hunter smiled. "Family isn't always perfect. Trust me, I know."

"Enough about family and my birth mother. I've already thought about her too much. Talking about it only makes me miserable, and I'm going to have to pop another Valium if we keep going." She looked at her cupboard, the one where she kept her spare stash of prescribed pills. "Enough of this small talk."

"You have a very strange idea of small talk. Most people like to talk about the weather or sports."

"The older I get, the worse I get at social interactions, but I guess that's what happens when you live by yourself, and your whole life revolves around work." She coughed deeply. "What are we discussing today?"

"The Sulzberger case."

"Ah, yes…" Law placed the file down and scrolled through what was on the computer screen, happy to be distracted by her work. "Of course. The remarkable case of another innocent man. If you win this case, you should write a book about it. The only thing is—the librarians would put it in the fiction section as nobody would believe the case was real."

"It's not that clean cut."

"I'm afraid it is." She smiled as she leaned back in her black leather chair, hands resting comfortably across her lap. "We've got an unidentified woman, who was found deceased and tied to a chair in the basement of a three-bedroom house. His prints are all over the room. So is his blood. He has no alibi, no excuses, and no other explanation. How could you possibly win?"

"He was set up."

"Is that what he's saying? That's going to be very, very hard to prove based on the weight of this evidence. Have you even read what the papers are saying? They've already convicted him. Some people are still on his side, trying to explain why he did it, but even some of his strongest supporters are conceding he did it. There's no other possible explanation for what happened. We had no choice but to lay these charges."

"There's no blood at the scene of the crime other than a spot near his power tools. There's no evidence the attack took place there, and the lack of evidence speaks louder than the evidence you have. You must know how that's going to look in a courtroom. There'll be doubt in the jurors' minds from the start. It's going to be easy to exploit that."

"Maybe. But it also doesn't raise enough doubt that he didn't do it elsewhere. All it says is he killed her somewhere else and carried her into the basement. If that's what you're building your defense around, then this is going to be a very easy case for us. There's missing pieces, but it's not enough to get him off."

"If we can locate a particular person, then we can break this whole case apart." Hunter looked over the desk for any clues about the case—a file or a note accidentally left out.

"Who?" Law leaned forward, her hand covering the notepad to her left. She turned the notepad over, covering up any potential hints.

"The right person."

"Of course." She tried to smile again. "You're not going to disclose that yet."

"There's nothing to disclose yet, but we're getting closer. We'll find her before this case hits the courts."

"Is that your play? Drag it out as long as you can—see if you can get a good deal from us? Well, I'm afraid that isn't going to work. We're in this one for the long haul. He's a high-profile public figure, a popular reality television celebrity and now a politician, and we can't let you walk over us. There's more than a case at stake; there's our public reputation to protect. We've requested the case be pushed through for the sake of public interest. The State's Attorney is very keen to have this one wrapped up quickly, and I'm sure the courts will feel the same and find an opening for us."

Hunter didn't respond, staring at her, letting her continue the conversation.

"I see Robert made bail. You did a very good job there—give up his passport, post the bond, and convince the judge he actually cares about his community. I apologize for not being there, but I was impressed when I heard about it. Are you going to bring him in to a case conference? I would love to see him."

"See him?" Hunter questioned. "Don't you mean meet him?"

Her mouth hung open for a moment. "I've seen his face on television a hundred times. I was a big fan of Island Survivor, and that was my favorite series— I've watched it four or five times online. I loved the characters, and Robert's mental toughness was so clear. Did you know that no other contestant in the show's history has won as many challenges as he did?"

"I've never watched the show," Hunter replied. "Robert's lying low for a while. The media aren't playing nicely at this point, so we've got him holed up in a secret location. We're giving him some space to work through what's happening. It must be hard for an innocent man to deal with these sorts of accusations."

"Innocent?" She laughed. "I can tell you now he's

not innocent. He rejected his vets so he could get more funding for his next election campaign. That's why he voted for the stadium development. It was about money—it's always about money. Always. When the evidence is presented in court for the public to see, they'll all see how guilty he is. And who knows what else he's done? He's stolen from the people of Chicago, and he's probably stolen from others. He's a thief as well as a murderer."

"We'll be working hard to keep a lot of your evidence quiet, Michelle. You should expect that from us."

"Of course. You and I both know how this works—we challenge, we challenge, we keep challenging until one of us makes a mistake. But, lucky for you, I've made a few mistakes lately. Maybe this is your lucky break, your chance to beat me in court."

There was a pause between them.

Hunter looked at her, not having to search hard for the cracks in her armor. They were in the open for everyone to see. He was surprised she was still working, still taking on the big cases, still risking the reputation of the office.

"At least you're still passionate about defending evil people. I guess it's in your blood." She pushed him for an angry response. "Nature or nurture, that's the big question. Do you defend evil people because of your killer genetics, or do you defend scum because of the upbringing you had? Tough question to answer."

He didn't bite back with anger. "This job helps you realize there are very few truly evil people in the world. There are evil people out there, but most criminals have good in them. The thieves, the violent offenders, the fraudsters—they're all still good people who've done bad things. A lot of people, they've hit a breaking point, and they make wrong decisions. There's still good in them. There's good in everyone. It's my job to make sure their goodness shines through in court."

"So you're going to push for leniency in the sentence because Sulzberger was a good man before his breakdown? You expect concessions because of his combat history? That's not going to work. Not in this case. The State's Attorney needs blood, the public needs blood, and I'm going to deliver it to them."

"What's the best deal on the table?"

"First-degree murder, a sentence of twenty-five years, but we can recommend minimum security. That's all I've got."

"First-degree murder?" Hunter's voice rose. "He'll be dead within a year on that sentence. He's a marked man behind bars. You're signing his death certificate if you put him away for that long."

"His death? What about the death of Jane Doe? When does that factor into your equation? I can't help what happens behind bars, and if he's a target, then it's because of what he did, and who he betrayed. If he's going to die behind bars, then that's his own doing. Not mine."

"It can't be first degree. You don't have enough evidence."

"It's easy to prove he knew his actions would result in the high probability of great bodily harm or death. That's murder in the first degree. No argument about that."

"720 ILCS 5/9-2. Second-degree murder. Five

years. How does that sound?"

"You're going to go for self-defense? Or are you going to say his actions were the result of intense passion caused by serious provocation from our unknown victim? That would almost be impossible to prove! The girl was tied to a chair; she wasn't responsible for this!"

"But will you consider it? Take it to your boss?"

"Not a chance."

He looked at her puzzled. "The courts are full. Your job is busy. Give us a good deal, and we'll consider it. But twenty-five years—we might as well take this to court and run the risk of a judge's sentence. There's no incentive for Robert to take the deal."

"Everyone feels the pressure of life!" Her fist hit the table. "Robert Sulzberger shouldn't be given leniency because he had a breakdown! What about the rest of us? Where's my break from life? Where's my chance to escape? No. He's not getting any help from this office. If he breaks down, he can deal with the consequences."

Hunter sat back, shocked my Law's statements. "How bitter has this job made you?"

"This job…" She looked away from her old friend. Pulling her shoulders back, Law swirled her chair to look out the window at her view of Downtown Chicago. She used to love this view, the way the sun hit the artistically designed buildings, reflecting the soft glow upon the busy streets. Now, it only represented her lost chances in life. "It takes everything away from you. Family, friends, your hobbies—after you've worked eighty hours a week, fifty weeks a year, there isn't much time for anything else. But I've been lucky. I've already hit my breaking point numerous times and dealt with it. Or perhaps, this is one big breaking point, and I'm still going through it. I don't know yet."

"I always wondered how long you could do good for. I remember after you left school, just when you were at the top of the popularity ladder, you changed overnight. You shaved your head and were suddenly getting in fights in bars. And then you became a prosecutor. You went from good to bad to good again in only a matter of years, so I always wondered when that bad would seep back out."

"Perhaps it already has." She stood. "I was lucky no one ever pressed charges. I was lucky my adopted father was a lawyer and threatened litigation against any person who dared to take me to the police." She looked down at the table, her fingers tapping her notepad. "Is that what happened to your client? After years of being a good boy, he finally had enough and let the inner animal free?"

"He's a good man." Hunter stood. "The question is: how long are you going to keep your animal down, Michelle? How long are you going to do 'good' for the world?"

"As long as I can." Law looked at him. Straight at him. "That's the trouble with our jobs. You realize everyone says they're good, but we all have a little bit of bad in us. Some more than others."

# CHAPTER 15

THE MAN that sat in Tex Hunter's office was a shadow of his former self. His shoulders had slumped, his shirt was un-ironed, and his face was unshaven. The whole city knew how much Robert Sulzberger had fallen apart. He was the lead story on every news bulletin, the lead talking point for every morning show, and the lead conversation at every water cooler. If he sneezed, the city knew about it.

"At least you made bail." Hunter stepped into the office, holding two cups of coffee, looking at Sulzberger slumped in an armchair in front of his desk. "How has the council taken the news?"

"I've been forced to take a leave of absence." Sulzberger drew a long breath. "I needed the break anyway."

"By the sounds of it, you needed the break a year ago."

With an office on the twentieth floor of a Downtown Chicago building, off busy West Jackson Boulevard, Hunter felt a part of the action, a part of the ever-bustling fight to work in the city. He loved his office. It was his place to think. His place to move through a case. His place to succeed. The space filled him with pride, a testament to the ability to overcome the worst odds to make something of his life.

But his office also left him within striking distance of the media news teams. If something on the case broke, they would have news crews in his building's foyer before he could ride the elevator down.

There was enough room between his desk and the door to dance the waltz, if he ever felt the need, or drink in solitude on the leather couch to the left, which he often felt the need. Law books lined the right wall, and a signed Michael Jordan jersey hung on the left. He'd never liked having stuff to fill a room. He would much rather sit in an empty room than one full of clutter. As such, his large dark Oakwood table looked like it'd barely been used. His assistant insisted he fill some of the space on his desk or his clients would doubt whether he did any work at all. As a compromise, he left a pile of files next to his computer monitor, but the gathering dust was a giveaway that they were nothing more than an ornament.

Hunter stopped at the large window to take in the view of Downtown Chicago, squinting in the natural light for a few moments, and then sat down behind his hefty desk, comfortable in his black leather chair. He opened a file and scanned his eyes over the notes.

"We've had a long think about how to approach the not guilty verdict. We've got a play that we can go with, but first, I needed to ask you about a plea deal."

"No deal."

"Will you even consider it?"

"No deal. Never. I'm innocent. I didn't kill the woman. I had nothing to do with it. I won't even entertain the idea of a deal. I don't know how many times I have to say this—I didn't do it."

"If the prosecution presents a deal, I'm obligated to bring it to you. That's how the system works. If they—"

"I'm not interested in what they've offered. What I'm interested in is how you're going to play this? What's your angle for getting me off?"

"X is our best chance of getting you off."

Sulzberger threw his head back. He didn't want to accept it. He didn't want to accept any of it. "Why her?"

"X is our best chance to create an element of doubt in the courtroom. That's what will get you off the charges—doubt. The prosecution doesn't have a witness of you committing the crime, doesn't have a witness that places you at the scene at the time of death, and doesn't have direct evidence that you committed the act. That leaves the window open to create doubt in the minds of the jurors, but we have to exploit it. We have to be able to take the tiny opportunity and rip it open."

"But why her?"

"If we can prove she exists, then we can frame the argument that it would be reasonable this woman broke into your house and left the deceased woman in your basement. We could suggest she had a key to your house, which makes our argument even stronger." Hunter looked at his notepad for a moment. "But we have to prove she exists."

"I've thought over and over and over again about what I know, and I've searched through thousands of social media profiles online. I've found nothing. Not a thing. Not even a lead. I guess she's a professional. She was always well dressed, always had new, expensive wigs, and her makeup was perfect.

Yesterday, I walked through a lot of the shops we stole from, with my disguise on, hoping to see her, but I saw nothing."

"That doesn't help."

"I'm just telling you what I know. And that's all I can think of."

"The jury isn't going to buy that. If we present this option as it is now, then it looks like you're making the story up, and trying to divert the attention away from you. It'll do more damage than good. We need evidence that she exists." Hunter held his pen over his notepad. Although Esther had told him he needed to start using the computer to take notes, he couldn't resist using the old-fashioned pen and paper. He found there was much more freedom of thought, much more creativity, in the use of a pen. "Take me through the last time you saw the mystery woman."

"The last time I saw her; we'd just stolen a laptop from the Best Buy electrical store in the Joffco Square Mall. We were outside the bus station on Roosevelt and Jefferson, standing next to my car. I told her it was over, and I didn't want to see her anymore. She was upset, but she didn't seem vengeful. I didn't think she could do something like this."

"Did you keep the laptop? Perhaps we could search for a fingerprint match?"

"No, I got rid of it. I left it at the charity shop like I always did."

"I need you to list all the moments you interacted with her." Hunter placed a piece of paper in front of Robert. "We can start to look at the surveillance footage for the times and places you said she was there, and hope we come across a clue."

"I doubt you'll be able to find anything."

Sulzberger began writing the dates and places he could remember. "She was very good at what she did. She always had wigs, hats, glasses, even fake noses. The whole works. I barely recognized her when she walked up to me sometimes, and she always seemed to know where the cameras were."

"Which means she had access to the information. Perhaps a cop?"

"She was too prim and proper to be a cop. She could've worked in the department, but there was no way she was a detective or a beat cop."

"Is there anything that might be able to lead us to her? Tattoos? Moles? Scars? Anything at all?"

"I've thought about it so many times. What she said, what she wore, where we were—but there was no pattern to it. Even with all this time to think, I've come up with nothing other than what I've already told you. I knew nothing about her. The best I can do is go to all the places we stole from together and wait for her to return."

"As your lawyer, it's my job to advise you on the best way to proceed. Right now, with the information that's on the table, the best way to proceed would be to take a deal."

Sulzberger grimaced. "Go on—if you must, tell me. How long is the deal?"

"First-degree murder with a minimum sentence of twenty-five years in a minimum security prison."

"Twenty-five years in prison? No way." He jumped forward, stood up, and started wandering around the room, his hand rubbing the back of his neck. "Not a chance. I wouldn't last a year. You know that. I've already got a target on my back. The only way I'd survive twenty-five years is to do it in solitary confinement, and at forty-five years old, that doesn't sound appealing. Can you imagine that? Spending all day locked up by myself in a tiny concrete room? And even if I did survive, I'd be over seventy by the time I got out! You've got to be kidding."

"If we take this to court as it is now, we're done. We can't win the case as it sits. That's the cold, hard truth. There's nothing to say that you didn't do it, and the jury isn't going to believe that a random, unknown assailant placed a drugged-up woman in your basement."

"Then it's over. I'm dead." He fell back into his chair, defeat etched on his face. "They'll stab me before I get to my next birthday. Lucy will grow up without a father."

"Due to the lack of direct evidence, the door is slightly ajar for negotiating a better sentence. But we have to take that door and put our foot straight through it. The best way to do that is present another possible suspect, evidence that the mystery woman exists. That'll be enough to create the doubt in their minds. If we want a better deal, then we need to convince the prosecution that we've got a better case. They'll only start to negotiate if they start to think they can lose the trial."

"Does it still mean prison time?"

"We can look at second-degree murder, and the minimum sentence for that still involves four years, but it depends on how well we present the case. With this sort of crime, any deal we strike will involve prison time, with part of it suspended, but that's our best option. We can't deny the deceased was in your house. She was on your property, in your basement, while you were the only one home. The best we can push for is a suspended sentence."

"Insanity?"

"Are you suggesting you attacked her while having a PTSD episode?"

"I don't know." Sulzberger's shoulders slumped further. "Would that help?"

"Possibly."

"No, no. Forget I said that. I would never use that to get something." He stared at the floor. "What can we reduce the sentence down to?"

"Before we can start to think about that, we need to convince the prosecution that they could lose. To even get to the negotiating table, we have to make them believe that we have an amazing case. We have to make them think we're taking this to court and fighting it on the basis of a new suspect. They have to start to doubt their ability to win the case in court."

"What would you tell them?"

"That we have a second suspect. It's possible that, even if you were guilty, you didn't work alone. There was someone else involved. We'd have to find surveillance footage that indicates someone was entering your home, perhaps the view from a neighbor's house."

"But what happens if we can't find X?"

"Then we find another suspect."

"Who?"

"One option is your assistant, Teresa Hardcastle." Hunter's tone was blunt. "But the best option is your wife."

"Kim? No way. Not her. No." Sulzberger shook his head. "She's prone to violent outbursts, but not her. I'm not going to try to pin this on my wife. She was out on a hike. It couldn't have been her."

"Entertain the thought that it could be her for one moment." Hunter paused, narrowing his eyes on his client. "And then tell me why she would've tried to set you up."

"I don't know." Sulzberger looked away. "Our lives fell apart. I think she would've known about my nights out with X. She would've sensed it, and I guess, in the end, she hated me. But I don't think she would've killed for it. I mean, why not just kill me and make it look like an accident? Poison me, perhaps. It makes no sense that she would've done that to the girl in the basement."

"Unless she wasn't trying to set you up. Unless she knew the girl and this had nothing to do with you."

"What?" Sulzberger whispered. "She accidentally killed the girl?"

"If we look at the big picture, then Kim fits the profile of a suspect. She needed revenge, she needed you out of her life, she had access to the basement, and you made her angry. She smashed your car with a baseball bat a week before the attack. She has no alibi. At this point, without the evidence that the other woman exists, she's our best chance." Hunter's pen hovered. "Maybe she knew the girl in the basement. She has ties to a lot of community groups—ones that deal with young women who sell their bodies for money. Has she shown sexual interest in women before?"

"Yes…" Sulzberger's mouth dropped open. "But she said she was on a hike?"

"And conveniently, there's no evidence of her whereabouts." Hunter flicked open another file. "She's our chance. This is our opportunity to strengthen the case. If you didn't do it, then your wife is the number one suspect."

"It can't be." Sulzberger shook his head, mouth still hanging open. "Please, not her. Not Kim."

# CHAPTER 16

"FORE!"

Patrick Hunter watched the golf ball fly from the tee, slicing through the air like a slow-motion bullet shot from a sniper rifle. Despite his failings at the game, despite his anger towards his clubs, he kept returning for the unique feeling of power, technique, and precision all rolled into one single swing. That one perfect shot a round, that one perfect shot a week, wiped out the memories of the hundreds of mistimed, misjudged, and misdirected strikes.

"We're on a driving range. There's nobody out there." Tex Hunter shook his head.

"You're right." Patrick grinned. "But I always yell that when I hit it so sweetly, even on the driving range. It's just a natural reaction when you can hit a ball this well, but you wouldn't know that feeling, would you?"

"You know, when I play golf, I always carry an extra pair of trousers in my buggy."

"Why?" Patrick looked confused.

"Just in case I get a hole-in-one." Hunter stepped up to the tee, took a practice swing, and then hit the ball just as sweetly. The men followed its trajectory, watching as it took one bounce, then another, and then slowly out rolled Patrick's shot.

"A lucky swing." Patrick groaned.

"Luck has nothing to do with it. That shot was a combination of chance, fate, and good fortune."

"All those words are synonyms for luck. And that's probably why you're a very good lawyer."

Patrick Hunter was a thoughtful speaker—his softly-spoken voice, slow sentence pace, and hypnotic green eyes captured attention everywhere he went. Although he looked meek against Hunter's broad stature, his intelligence more than made up for his physical shortcomings. Patrick's younger brother was blessed with more height, more width, and more speed, but while Tex Hunter spent his high school years playing football and smashing things, Patrick spent his time at school studying, his nose always in a book, his spare time in the library, and he hadn't stopped ever since. And that was why he was a very respected criminal psychiatrist.

"Had any good clients lately, Patrick?" Hunter stepped up to the practice tee again, watching other balls fly off the tees around him in the half-filled driving range, darting towards the distance markers. Just after 8 p.m. on the fall evening, the natural light was being replaced by the massive floodlights that highlighted the 300-yard fairway in front of them.

The men had taken up position in their usual spot—bottom level, furthest tee from the stairs—in the Diversity Driving Range, north of Downtown. Giant oaks lined the edges of the fairway, shut off by a large chain-link fence, and the city skyline dominated behind them. The heaters had been switched on, the radio turned down, and the distractions were at a minimum.

Patrick Hunter waited for the man next to them to pack up his clubs. The man was dressed in the standard middle-class set—shorts, sneakers, polo shirt, with expensive clubs to match, and a receding hairline and pot belly. The man has a mid-life crisis beckoning, perhaps a sports car, but most likely a mistress, Patrick reasoned to himself.

The brothers had always felt they could talk freely there, as most other customers were too obsessed with watching their balls bounce in the distance to notice the men or listen to anything they had to say. It almost felt like they were transported back to the time before their lives were torn apart, back to a time when they were part of a normal family and hadn't lived through a life of abuse.

"I've got one client talking about committing more murders when he steps out of prison. I've reported him and added the notes, but the parole board is going to review his file in a week."

"Do you think he'll get out?"

"I hope not. One of the people he talked about killing was me." Patrick laughed with a mixture of humor, nerves, and unease.

While his younger brother went into criminal law to defend people like his father, Patrick Hunter went into criminal psychiatry to understand why his father acted the way he did. Unlike his younger brother, he'd accepted long ago his father was guilty of being a serial killer. Acceptance was his key to moving past the pain that his family provided.

Ten years older, Patrick had felt responsible for his youngest sibling. As a young adult, going through a trial televised across the country was hard, but the infamy boosted his popularity with the girls on Friday nights. To look at the trial through the eyes of a ten-year-old boy would've been devastating. But the experience only hardened the resolve of his younger sibling, and now, Patrick looked to Tex for support.

"Any further leads with Maxwell?"

"We finally got something." Patrick bit his lip, nodding. "He checked into a police station last week, in Englewood of all places. I don't know if he was arrested or if he went in of his own accord; they wouldn't tell me. All they would tell me was he's off the missing persons' list, and doesn't want to be contacted. He's eighteen so he can do what he chooses." His head dropped. "It was good to hear he's still alive, but I wish I knew more. It's been over a year since I've seen my son. Do you know what that does to you? It breaks you. It hits you where it hurts." He tapped his chest. "He's my family. He's everything to me."

"You did all you could. At least you know he's alive. That's a start. He may take some time before he comes back to you."

"I hope he does come back and I hope he forgives his mother." Patrick shook his head again and looked back out to the driving range. Although Patrick talked about emotions and thoughts all day long, they were not his. Talking about his own feelings, the way life was proceeding, had always been difficult. His brother was the only person he felt comfortable talking about feelings with, but he redirected the conversation to avoid going any deeper. "How's the case with the politician coming along?"

"He went from weekend warrior to weekday slave."

"What's that supposed to mean?"

"Why do you always have to question my great lines? Why can't you accept them for what they are?" Hunter swung the club again, the smash of his driver echoing through the air.

"Because there's always something more to words. There's always a meaning behind them." Patrick practiced his swing. "And what sort of brother would I be if I didn't question everything you did?"

"Spoken like a true psycho. Sorry, I mean psychiatrist," Hunter smiled, swinging his club hard again, aggressively, and then watching his ball sail well left, landing near the fence. "I meant that he went from a life of adrenaline in the army to a life of thrills on reality television and ended up in a mundane suburban existence. His job on the City Council, with all the time he had to spend chained to a desk, was in contrast to life as a sergeant and celebrity. That's bound to turn anyone crazy. Deep down, he seems like a nice guy though."

"Just because you're nice doesn't mean you're a good person. Some of the nicest people I've ever met have been killers."

"Remind me not to attend any more of your dinner parties."

"Not in my personal life. At work." Patrick groaned. "All I'm saying is don't be tricked by a nice smile and nice words. They don't mean anything. Action means something. Rude people can make a bigger difference in the world than nice people."

"I really don't want to meet any more of your friends."

"Always the joker." Patrick shook his head again. "Ethically rude people change the world."

"Here we go. Patrick the Philosopher." Hunter

shook his head. "Ethically rude people?"

"The ones that are willing to be disliked to get what's best. The people that are willing to risk everything for something they think is right, and they don't care if you like them or not. Take your current client—voted against his ethics so he didn't lose his backers. He's not ethically rude; he's being nice, agreeable and likable. But his party room colleague, Cindy Mendel, went against all the odds, everyone, including her own council, to do what she thought was ethically right."

"I didn't realize being likable was so bad."

"Someone who chooses to be likable, instead of what's ethically correct, is actually being selfish and thinking about themselves. They're choosing particular choices because of the way they will feel about it."

"Being nice isn't all bad."

"Of course not. The world needs nice people, but it also needs ethically rude people. They're the people that get stuff done. It's like that saying by James Freeman Clarke— 'A politician looks to the next election, while a statesman looks to the next generation.' You have to be willing to be disliked to do something for the greater good." Patrick swung his club again. "So, do you think the nice guy finally snapped and did it?"

"I didn't say that. I said he was bound to turn crazy trying to please everyone." Hunter leaned on his golf club for a moment, checking the bays next to them were empty. "But between us, the answer is no. I don't think he did it, but I think he'll spend some time behind bars. At this point, it looks like we can still get second-degree murder. We'll push for a good deal, and hopefully, we'll get a reduced sentence, early parole, and an agreeable prison. The only thing is— I'm not sure how long he'll last in any prison. He'll be a big target, and I'd say he'd have a year to live, at the most. They'll kill him as soon as they have the chance."

"So you have to keep him out if you want to keep him alive."

"And the only way to do that is to find another suspect."

"But if not Robert, then who else?"

"The wife is my number one draft choice, but there's also a mystery woman floating outside of this case. I'm not sure what she has to do with it, but I'm sure she's somehow involved."

"Mystery woman?"

"Apparently, this mystery woman was going through a midlife crisis at the same time as Robert, and joined him on the quest to steal small items from stores, and then they slept with each other in the car after each steal. But they never exchanged any information about themselves—not where they worked, not where they lived, not even their real names. There's no evidence she even exists. She's a complete mystery."

"Interesting. Very interesting." Patrick pursed his lips. "Robert's quest for anonymity would most likely be caused by his need to escape his high-profile life. He could've felt the pressure, and the need to be a nobody—just a face in the crowd—could've led to his need to wear a disguise. It happens to more high-profile people than you think. They have a desire to stop being their public profile and become a nobody."

"I don't care about the reasons why he did it; I just

need to find the mystery woman."

"What about surveillance footage that places them together?"

"Tried that. They always wore disguises when stealing—a wig, a fake nose, or a hat. We can see her on some footage but we can't ID her."

"Classic move. Her quest for anonymity would most likely be the same. I suggest she would've been under a lot of pressure, perhaps she was going through a divorce or she had a job where the eyes are always on her. She would feel the need to escape that. Stealing, well, as you've suggested, it's an escape for some people. Most likely, they don't need what they're taking, but they need the thrill." He turned to his sibling. "But I would suggest being careful."

"Why?"

"Because people like this don't retreat. If they've gone this far, they'll be willing to go further. If you fly too close to their sun, they'll burn you. They'll kill someone else, or even possibly, themselves. Suicide is the best option you could hope for your mystery woman."

Hunter looked down the fairway and paused, the thoughts of suicide filling his thoughts. "It's Mom's birthday soon."

"Aw, come on, Tex." Patrick looked down at the ground. He continued softly, "Any mention of suicide and you have to bring her back up. We have to talk about something else. The past is the past."

"Have you heard from Natalie?"

"Come on, Tex. Let it go. Our conversations can't keep coming back to our sister either. She's gone. She moved to Mexico. Nobody has heard from her in thirty years. She's probably dead for all we know."

"Don't say that."

Patrick paused, looking up at the only family he still talked to. "I'm sorry. You know I didn't mean it like that." He sighed. "Can't we talk about something else?"

"Like Dad's innocence? Shall we talk about that?"

"Tex. I can't keep doing this." Patrick looked away. "I can't fight it anymore. In case you haven't noticed, no one else still thinks Dad is innocent."

"I'm sure we've missed something. He said—"

"Don't tell me." Patrick held his hand up as a stop sign. "I don't need to know what he said last time you talked to him. I'm not interested. I'm not interested in how he's feeling or how he's going in prison. I don't need to know. I want nothing to do with it anymore. I'm out."

"He's your father." Hunter's voice deepened. "You haven't been in to see him in years. He's your family, Patrick."

"But where does this crusade end?"

"When we find the truth. When we find justice."

"Can't we just talk about something normal? You know, if you wanted, we could just crack a few beers and watch the '85 Bears season again?"

"Again?" Hunter swung his club aggressively.

"I know you love that season, and you've told me you could never watch those highlights too many times. The way the defense works, the way they shut teams down. You've said it yourself—it should've been back-to-back, but it's only one perfect year, one perfect Super Bowl."

"Dad's case is our Super Bowl."

"How about the baseball then? Can't we talk about that? How about them Cubs, eh?"

"We don't have that luxury."

"We do." Patrick was soft in his approach. "We're brothers, and we've never even been to a baseball game together. Our father's crimes stole our childhood relationship, but it doesn't have to steal the rest of our lives too."

Hunter didn't respond, staring at Patrick, who was desperate to avoid eye contact.

"Way to spoil a moment." Patrick packed up his golf clubs.

He shook his head at his younger brother, knowing most of their interactions ended that way. The only place he couldn't avoid talking about his painful past was with the brother he loved.

Patrick took one last look at his brother before slinging his golf bag over his shoulder. "I'll be at Mom's grave for her birthday. 5 p.m. I'll bring flowers. I'll see you then. I love you, brother."

# CHAPTER 17

"NOT NOW." Hunter groaned as he walked into the busy Starbucks in the upmarket district of the Gold Coast. Hunter stepped through the door, past a young couple with their arms locked together, and proceeded to the back corner of the room, standing over a man staring into his coffee. "I thought I told you to stay in the apartment."

The aroma of freshly roasted coffee filled the café. The art displayed on the walls was edgy, the seats were a shiny vinyl, and the lighting was bright enough to make the place feel welcoming. Suits hustled through the takeaway line, students sat on laptops accessing the free Wi-Fi, and older customers sat near the entrance, desperate to feel part of the community.

"No one will recognize me here." The man with the baseball cap and sunglasses shook his head. He ran his hand over the light brown mustache. It was an obvious fake, and not just because the color didn't match his hair. "This disguise is too good. Nobody knows who I am."

"Are you serious? Your disguise draws attention to you. You look like you've just stepped off the set of Get Smart. I'm surprised you're not dressed as a tree."

"I'd answer the shoe-phone, but you're right; that would probably draw more attention."

"At least you've still got your sense of humor." Hunter sat down on the brown chair that was too small for him. His patience was being tested, but every client tested him in some way or another. Although it frustrated him, he knew this was part of a client's rollercoaster, and they had to deal with the thought of losing what they truly valued but absolutely underestimated—freedom. "What did you call me here for?"

"I've been thinking about the murder."

The men paused as a young woman sat next to them. She stared at her phone, the screen visible and displaying a news site. She sipped on her coffee that was much too hot. She took off the lid, blew the steam away, but never took her eyes off the screen.

"We can't talk about it here." Hunter leaned forward, moving his chair closer to Sulzberger's. "You shouldn't be here. We can't keep having your face in the media. The best thing to do is lock yourself in that apartment, and watch as many movies or read as many books as you can. Every time someone takes a photo of your face, you're inviting more media coverage. More media coverage means more people are going to have an opinion, and right now, they'll form the opinion that you're guilty."

"But what if this is it? What if this is my last taste of freedom? The last taste of life outside prison walls? What if this is my last chance to have a coffee in a café? If I'm convicted, I'll never get out. You know that. I'll be killed within a year. If I'm convicted of her murder, then it's a death sentence for me."

The woman raised her eyes from the glow of her

screen, turning to look at them, recognizing Sulzberger instantly after catching the last sentence. Hunter stared at her, making her uncomfortable, and she placed the lid back on her coffee, gathered her work bag, and moved away.

"This is what I do, Tex. I'm a man of the people. These people are still my constituents. They're still my fans." He held his hands wide. "This is my life. This is everything I've worked so hard for."

"You'll get your chance to be free, but it's not now. You've been suspended from the City Council, you don't have a job, and some people have expressed their hate for you online. Right now, you don't have any constituents, and you certainly don't have many fans left."

"But I've been thinking." Sulzberger leaned forward, wrapping his hands around the warm coffee mug. "Maybe I can work this to my favor. There's no such thing as bad publicity, right?"

"Not in this case."

"I'm going to tell you something, and I need you to listen to it. It may come in handy for you one day if you ever decide to run for politics—"

"I'm not going to do that."

"Don't write it off yet." Sulzberger lowered his voice, and shifted his chair closer to the table. "You see, people vote for who they admire, and people admire who they aspire to be. Remember this— aspiration equals admiration and admiration equals votes."

"Aspiration equals admiration?" Hunter raised his eyebrows.

"Absolutely. If you can understand who your

voters aspire to be, who they want to be when they're successful, then you can be that person. Think about every person you've ever voted for—if you didn't aspire to be someone like that, whatever values they held, then you wouldn't vote for them. If you can appear to be what the majority of voters want to be, if you can appear to represent their values, then you have a much stronger chance of getting voted in. Of course, policies are important, but mostly, they're not the reason the masses vote. Don't get me wrong, big policies matter—major changes sway votes—but the everyday policies, the bulk of our decisions, are so close to the center of politics that it doesn't matter. Policies only sway votes when it's a big change one way or the other. Think a big change to healthcare policy, or a big tax break, or a big immigration policy that changes votes, but for the most part, for the majority of decisions, the masses are mobilized through admiration."

"And what do your voters aspire to be?" Against his better judgment, Hunter humored him.

"My voters—they aspire to be strong, intelligent, and successful, so all I have to do is present that image to the public. I'm the strong army type, I'm a celebrity, I've got successful investments, and I'm well studied and well traveled. I dress well, and present the image of someone full of morals." Sulzberger raised his finger in the air. "And although I need people to aspire to be me, I also need them to feel superior to me. If I stand up and make complicated, uncomfortable, but entirely true statements, my appeal is going to be very low. But..." His finger waved again. "If I stand up as a successful person and make less intelligent statements, statements built around emotion, then I'm not challenging anyone. In fact, people look at a successful, less intelligent person, and think, 'Yeah, I could do that, I could be that person.' I'm accessible to my audience. My voters want to be me, but more importantly, they think they can be me."

"If there were no voters, democracy would be perfect." Hunter responded. "And put your finger down. You've clearly spent too much time by yourself over the last few weeks."

"In our modern society," Sulzberger continued, desperate for someone to listen to him, "success and celebrity dictate our social class. The more successful you are, the higher your social class. The more popular your celebrity status, the higher your social status. I didn't buy a meal for a year, one whole year, after the Island Survivor win because people loved having me around. They loved having me in their restaurant or bar." He went to put his finger in the air again before Hunter shook his head. "In our society, great success is achievable. Our society gives everyone a chance. Our society makes changing social classes admirable, and yet somehow, achievable."

"The great American Dream." Hunter ran his hand over his dark hair. "This murder trial isn't going to make you more accessible. Being charged with murder won't bring you up the social ladder."

"Not quite, but how I handle it will influence the voters. If I appear strong, honorable, and intelligent through this whole thing, then the voters will still side with me. I'm still a celebrity—people still remember that series, and they'll think I'm just an average guy that could also be them, just the wrong person at the wrong place at the wrong time. They'll vote for me again."

"Provided you get off."

"Of course." Sulzberger sat back, arms wide across the table. "We have to sort that bit out first, but I'm confident you will. I didn't do it, so I should be able to get off. That's what the justice system is for, right? But while you're sorting that side out, I'm going to appear resilient and noble. The publicity we get from this is going to help me win more votes for the next election. I may even run for the Senate. The public are desperate to hear my story."

For the mass media, more drama meant more readers. More readers meant more advertising sales. And more advertising sales equaled bigger profits. From a distance, the drama could become a welcome distraction for a consumer; an escape from the everyday, a holiday from the mundane. Celebrity drama was an escape from the daily grind for so many people.

The most-read online article for the Chicago Sun-Times over the past week had been: 'Eleven Ways Robert Sulzberger was Rocked by His Troubled Young Childhood.' There was nothing of substance in the article, but the article headline encouraged people to click through to the story. His young childhood wasn't troubled, and he wasn't rocked. And the article only listed ten reasons.

"I'm saying if people believe in your image, they'll tell themselves their own story. If people believe you're different, an everyday guy, a breath of fresh air, then people will find ways to confirm that. You just have to be ambiguous enough for them to find their own answers."

Hunter drew a long, thoughtful breath. "Why do

you do it, Robert? Why put yourself out there?"

"I've thought about that a lot over the past week."

"And the answer?"

"To make a difference. But politics is also about power. Influence. Respect. People respect me for what I represent, and I've fought for that my whole life. I enjoy that respect. My father never respected me—he was a different man to me, never said much, never cared for much other than his Jack Daniels— and he didn't respect the fact I had a voice. He used to tell me not to talk so much."

"And here you are, forty-five years later, still fighting for that respect." Hunter looked over his shoulder, watching a woman talking on her phone, staring at the disguised Sulzberger. "We should go. The media is not our friend at the moment. They won't help you get reelected right now."

"I need them to see me." Sulzberger removed his hat and sunglasses, pulled off his cheap mustache, and placed all three on the small table. "I need them to know that I'm not afraid."

"Robert, no." Hunter looked around the coffee shop again. People began looking in their direction. A car screeched to a halt outside the window. "Not now. Not yet. The time isn't right."

"Let them come."

A man exited the car with his camera ready. Outside the coffee shop, the cameraman met the woman that had been sitting next to them earlier, and she pointed to Sulzberger.

"You'll have your time, Robert, but it's not yet. We can't have your face on the front page again tomorrow. We don't need this to be trial by media."

"It's the beginning of my reelection campaign."

"Not here. Not now."

The man lifted his camera lens to his eye, ready to take snaps through the window.

"If you want me to represent you, we have to move now," Hunter said.

Click. The first whirl of the camera snapped.

Hunter stood, his back to the camera, blocking the shot of Sulzberger. "We have to move before they get the right shot for the front page."

Sulzberger didn't move.

"I promise you'll get your chance for publicity, but that time is not now." Hunter leaned down closer. "You need to move."

Sulzberger nodded, accepting Hunter's hard stare, and began to move away from the crowd gathering outside.

But before Sulzberger had taken two steps, he stopped, turned, looked directly at the camera, and smiled.

# CHAPTER 18

SHE SWUNG left.

Then right.

Then left again.

She followed the movements on the YouTube clip on the laptop in front of her, learning how to defend herself against the possibilities.

Guns hadn't always scared her, but the power of taking someone's life with one simple pull of the trigger frightened her now. When she was young, life was hard, and guns meant control, they meant power to the defenseless, but her life had changed since those days.

For the last month, she'd been following the instructions of a former UFC fighting champion, learning how to throw a hook, an uppercut, and a straight kick, among many other moves.

She skipped around her dining room table, past all the empty boxes, past all the useless goods she'd obtained over the years. She danced around the new couch, around the new dining room table, punching at the shadows.

She even made noises as she threw her fists.

Life was slowly creeping past her. Slowly edging her forward to death.

Time was escaping her grasp every day. Every day that she lay her head down in bed, she felt another day, another moment, slip through her fingers. With every day that came and went, she felt more tired, more rundown, and closer to her end.

Life, for all its great opportunities, was eating her away.

She'd had enough of being tired.

Enough of coming last.

It had to be her time to shine now.

She wasn't concerned about regaining her youth. Those days were past her. What she needed was to realize her greatness. She needed to fulfill her potential.

She was told she could have it all. She was told there were endless possibilities in her life. Possibilities that generations of women didn't have before. She should take those possibilities and use them.

But possibilities bring pressure.

Pressure to live up to them. Pressure to use them. Pressure to choose the right path. And if you didn't choose the right path, then you had wasted the opportunities that others fought so hard for.

The pressure was killing her from the inside out.

And she wouldn't have it anymore.

She couldn't.

Something had to change.

And that change began now. She would no longer be confined. She would no longer be held back. She would remove all the obstacles.

He was the biggest obstacle. He was holding her back.

She knew where to find him.

She knew where he was going to be.

She had tracked his movements for so long now. He thought he could keep secrets, but she knew more than he ever would. He thought he could hide things from her, but he would never know the amount of time she had spent tracking him.

His lawyer was fighting to prove him innocent.

His lawyer was more than competent, and he would find a way out of this; she knew that. Their path may even lead to her. That was why she had to put a stop to this.

She wouldn't let him get away with what he did. She needed her revenge. She placed her hand on the gun on the kitchen table.

The time for thinking had stopped.

Now, it was time for action.

# CHAPTER 19

"ANOTHER DAY, another dollar." Prosecutor Michelle Law said as she walked through the security checkpoint into the courthouse. "Although I hope they pay me more than just a dollar."

The guard, with his hand on his gun, only nodded his response, as the people behind her grumbled about the amount of time the checkpoint was taking, desperate to arrive at their next destination.

There was a feeling of history in the George N. Leighton Criminal Court Building, beyond the architecture that had stood for many decades, beyond the marble floors that had seen the likes of Al Capone, and beyond the paintings that had been hanging for more than a generation. For the past ninety years, movie stars, singers, celebrities, and politicians had shared the building with gang members, mobsters, rapists, and serial killers. The history of 2600 South California Ave was as lengthy was it was captivating.

Michelle Law felt the weight of that history in every case she took on.

If she were so inclined, she could claim she was in the depths of a midlife crisis. The question of 'why?' had constantly been in her head over the past year.

Why go to work and ride the elevator full of stinking people? Why does it make a difference? Why get dressed in the morning? Why even get out of bed? Why keep going?

That was the way her generation had been raised—always have a reason, always know the why behind your actions.

Her adopted father didn't like living that way. He was a 'no-questions, get-it-done' sort of guy.

"Buckle up, shut up, and let's get going," he used to repeat to her every time they drove anywhere.

Raised by her adoptive parents after her young mother placed her for adoption, Law felt like she was being raised by a generation removed from everything relative to her. In high school, everyone else's parents seemed liberal, progressive, and wanted their children to be free.

Not her adopted parents. They needed her home at 5:30 p.m. to eat at 6 p.m. One hour of television followed, then chores, and then bed. That was the only life she knew.

Despite the strict upbringing by her guardians, a voice in her head told her she was the daughter of a teen mum, a rebel, someone who hadn't followed the rules. She'd looked for her mother, time and time again, trying to find the answers of her genetic line. It was her truth. Who she really was.

To look her mother in the eyes, to be held in the arms of the woman who gave birth to her, would melt the coldness in her heart.

One moment, that was all she needed.

One hug. One kiss.

She tried to forget about it, tried to move on from the reality, but her birth mother's identity was a nagging truth in the back of her mind, always there, always only a scratch away from the surface.

She'd tried to do her best, live a good life, be a good person, but every year was getting harder. Every year, she felt closer to the cliff, stepping closer to the edge. Every birthday felt like another lost opportunity. If she could just take a vacation, a month away from the grind, she could manage her feelings, but her job was too demanding, and sadly, she would have nobody to go with.

In the land of the free, she felt trapped by her career, her commitments, and her consumerism.

Defeated, she entered the small conference room, which was lined with dull Oakwood walls, filled with black furniture, and had no windows to open. The damp smell filled her nose, and she shivered as she thought about the germs that filled the room. She shuffled through her bag and found the hand sanitizer.

After cleansing her hands with a small spray of disinfectant, she opened her laptop and smiled when she saw an email from her mentor, Cindy Mendel, one of the few people that had stood by her side as the years crumbled away, one of the few people who had ever shown her love.

They'd met twelve years earlier; Cindy was seeking her out to help for a case in prosecuting fraud by one of her staffers. Since that case, Cindy had taken Law under her wing, always there for her, always available with advice, always backing her up when times were tough. Cindy felt more like family to her than her adopted parents ever did. There was affection and care in Cindy's voice, a warm and kind tone. She was perhaps the closest thing she'd ever had to a mother.

The email was nice, friendly, but it was the last line of the email that captured Law's attention:

*I hope the case conference goes the way you want today. Keep an eye on that defense lawyer. I've heard he's going to try and blame the wife, Kim Sulzberger.*

A knock at the door took her focus away from the email.

"Good of you to finally join me, Tex," Law quipped as Tex Hunter walked into the room. "I'm not wasting your time; I hope."

"How about we stop wasting everyone's time and drop these charges." He smiled, his dimples clearly visible. "You could save everyone a lot of time and effort."

"No can do, I'm afraid." She looked to the door, but nobody else walked through. "Your client didn't want to join us today?"

"You look disappointed he's not here?"

"I am. I expected him to come to this meeting about his future. I would've liked to put the deal to him myself, because I enjoy looking into criminals' eyes before I send them away."

"Then we have a problem because Robert Sulzberger is no criminal and you won't be sending him away. He was set up."

"Oh, this will be good." She rolled her eyes as Hunter placed his briefcase on the table, unbuttoned his jacket, and sat down. "I'll take a guess—you're going after the wife? She's going to be the person you pin this on? Say that she's the guilty party? If that's your plan, bad luck. The PD investigated her, the detectives investigated her, and this office has investigated her. We're satisfied that she wasn't involved. Her fingerprints aren't even in the basement."

"Don't you find that unusual—she had no fingerprints in her own basement?"

"You're suggesting her fingerprints were cleaned from the scene? I really hope you've got more than that to present."

"We have evidence, and we have a suspect."

"I don't believe you." Law shook her head. "I think you're trying to play us. You're trying to create a fake suspect so you can negotiate a reduced sentence. You're going to tell everyone that you're after Kim Sulzberger, that she's a real suspect. These tactics might work on a new prosecutor but I've seen every trick in the book, Tex. You'll have to do better than that. So, no. That tactic's not going to work this time. Not with this case. This man is too high profile for us to negotiate a reduced charge of second-degree murder. And it wouldn't look good for us if we gave out a reduced sentence without seeing the evidence first. I, for one, am not going to risk my job for a lying politician."

Hunter leaned back in his chair, waiting before he responded. "Finished your rant?"

"It wasn't a rant." She groaned. "Did he take the deal or not?"

"No."

"Will he consider another deal in the future?"

"He will."

"Good." She typed on her laptop. "I'll let my boss know, and we'll discuss the length of another deal, but you're not going to get second-degree murder unless we see new evidence." She stopped typing. "This meeting could've been done over the phone; you know? Or an email. We didn't have to have a meeting in the case conference room."

"I know." Hunter smiled. "But I wanted to do it in person."

"All you've actually done is waste my time. I'm a busy woman. I have a lot of other places to be and lots of other people to argue with."

"Are you any closer to identifying the victim?" He ignored her angst.

"Unfortunately not. We're checking across the country for missing persons or any files on her, but some states take longer than others to confirm their databases. So far, we've got nothing."

Hunter leaned back in his chair, crossing one leg over the other. "There's no evidence the woman came to the basement with Robert, and there's no evidence to say her presence was forced."

"What are you suggesting?"

"Perhaps she chose to be there, and perhaps she chose to be tied up."

"Kinky. Not my thing, but that's possible. And even if it were true, that still doesn't take murder off the table."

"Not for Robert…"

"You're suggesting Kim was the kinky one? She was in a relationship with a woman?"

Hunter didn't respond.

"What've you got?" she quizzed. "I really hope you're not withholding information from this trial."

"We're on the right path," he stated. "We've got a lead that'll prove he's been set up."

"You're good, Tex. You're very good. I was prepared for you to come in here with a new theory to throw me off course, and you've done well." She waved her finger at him. "But I still don't believe you. I still think you're just trying to position your team for a reduced sentence. Unless you have evidence, then we're not moving on twenty-five years. We can negotiate the privileges he'll receive in prison, but we need to stick to twenty-five years on this one."

"That's your choice," Hunter said. "And your loss."

"We're under a lot of pressure on this one. Mayor Quinn has even taken a keen interest in this case. She's even willing to testify about his behavior that day."

"That's not surprising, given who Robert is. She'll need to be prepared for any skeletons that come jumping out of his closet."

"It's more than that. She's very keen, if you understand what I'm saying. She's calling me every day for an update. We can't deal low, or there'll be people out of work." Law aggressively shut her laptop. "Next time, make sure you bring Robert along to the conference. I'll take great pleasure in seeing him before I put him behind bars." She stood. "And after that, I'm coming after you."

"For me? What for?" Hunter held his hands out wide with a smile.

"For wasting my time. I'm sure I'll find some legislation about that to pin on you."

# CHAPTER 20

"MAYOR QUINN. Thank you for taking the time to see me on such short notice."

"Mr. Hunter." Her handshake was firm. That was expected. With forearms that looked like they were chiseled out of stone, Mayor Nancy Quinn was an intimidating figure. Dressed elegantly in a black skirt and white blouse, she stood tall, even without the added stature of high heels. "I understand why you're here, although I should say that most of your questions should be directed at the State's Attorney's Office. The prosecutor on this case is very competent, and she'll happily answer all your questions."

"Michelle Law. We went to law school together. We had a meeting yesterday, and your name was mentioned."

"And you think there are questions I could answer that would help your case?"

"I do."

"Then please, come in." Mayor Quinn opened the door to her office, allowing him to enter the protected realm of the fifth floor in Chicago City Hall. "I'll try to help you any way I can."

Hunter stepped into the Mayor's private office.

Although it was a large room with many personal touches—two couches, a wide desk, and a bookshelf long enough to be considered a small library—it felt like the space was rented, waiting for the next mayor to be voted in. Photos of Quinn's extended family sat behind her desk under the large window, pictures with two presidents hung on the wall to the left, and next to those, her many degrees were proudly framed. In the age of minimalism, her office seemed busy and almost chaotic.

"I want to let you know that I'm going to be fully cooperative with this case, and I'll be testifying about my interaction with him that day. My advisors have instructed that I need to distance myself from Robert personally, however, I'll continue to show support for his wife. That poor woman." With an open hand, she pointed towards the leather chair in front of her desk. "And as you know, I spent twenty-five years in the courtroom, so I understand where you're coming from."

Hunter sat down. Not elegantly, nor smoothly—more with the thud of a man who needed answers. "I need to know how you saw Robert's decisions in the council."

"What can I say? I—"

"You can start with the truth. I don't need the media spin. I've read that in the paper."

Before she sat down, she paused. She wasn't used to being challenged. In her office, in her city, she was at the top of the tree, and anyone who challenged her risked losing their grip on the branches. "If you've read the papers, then you know how I feel and what actions I've taken to help the situation. There's nothing more I can tell you."

"I know that you threatened Robert with removing your endorsement of him if he didn't support the development of your new stadium."

She shook her head, a frown on her face. "I hope you didn't come here to make accusations, Mr. Hunter. If you have, this is going to be a very short meeting."

"Who needed to set him up for murder?"

"Set up? Oh, wow." She laughed. When Hunter didn't join in, she frowned again. "I hope you're not serious. I know he's pleading not guilty, but I thought you were going to push for insanity on the basis of a PTSD episode. That would've been the smartest tactic."

"Who needed him out of the council?"

"Everyone," she replied flippantly. She crossed her arms and leaned them on her desk, tilting her head slightly. "Even though he made his decision on the development to suit the city—"

"To suit your decisions."

"Not my decisions. He chose to change his approach for the benefit of this city. That stadium development will benefit everyone, not only a select group of people. But…" She looked away, towards the Bible displayed on her bookshelf. "But his ability to change decisions like that showed he couldn't be trusted. How could you trust a man that was willing to change his vote only to stay in politics?"

Hunter laughed, but this time, Mayor Quinn didn't respond. "So you forced him into a corner, used him to get your vote, but all the while, you knew you were going to burn him?"

"That's politics."

"This is more than a game; it's people's lives."

"We can't do everything by popular vote. As elected officials, we have to be bold enough to make the hard decisions. That's our responsibility. That's what the public has entrusted us to do. Whether we're loved or hated for it, that's what we have to do."

"The city didn't need the stadium." Hunter squinted. "But you did. Before you put forward the design of the stadium, you started to lose the polls, and your rivals were gathering pace. This wasn't about benefiting the city; this was about you creating something so big that the popular vote would come back to you."

"Power is the greatest aphrodisiac. And they say that when a leader is pushed into a corner, they should start a war. Something they can win. You create a win that makes you look powerful."

"And the stadium was your war."

"I prefer to think of it as my legacy. My way of leaving my mark on the city." She tapped her finger on the edge of the wide desk. "But I didn't anticipate the amount of backlash. I thought there would be a few small groups who could be cast as the enemy, and we would easily overcome them. I didn't anticipate the snowball effect the veteran's groups had. They were so vocal. So violent. You know that some of them even picketed outside my home for one week straight? They camped there. Pitched tents on the park across the road."

"These people went to war. They're trained to fight."

"There was so much hate, but I couldn't turn back. People don't like a quitter, nor do they like someone who goes back on their word—just ask Robert."

Hunter shook his head at how easy she found political double-crossing. "Who hated Sulzberger the most? Who had the most to gain from his downfall?"

"So many people hated him. Half the room voted against the stadium, so take your pick. Any one of them would've wanted him to go down, get his seat recast, and then challenge the vote. This is the most hated development of our time; it's split the city in two. People feel very passionate about this; they either love it or hate it. Who knows what could've happened?"

Hunter's phone buzzed in his pocket. He ignored it. "Who hated him the most?"

"Cindy Mendel felt the most betrayed, as did Edmond White. They were both veterans, and they felt personally deceived by his decision. The planned demolition of the community center was such a sticking point, even after we gave them a new place twice the size."

His phone buzzed again. "I've been trying to grab Edmond White; he's quite elusive."

"I don't know what you're looking for, Mr. Hunter. In my opinion, Robert has looked on edge for over a year. He looked like he was about to snap. Have a breakdown. Maybe he believes he didn't do it or maybe he had an episode and doesn't remember what he did. My advice, as a former lawyer, would be to plea insanity as a defense. If you use that tactic, you might even be able to get the public opinion on your side. If you bring in a couple of experts, and some former veterans, the jury will eat the story up. Saying he suffered a PTSD episode is your best option. But that's just my personal opinion."

"And my personal opinion is the city didn't need a

new stadium."

"You do what you have to do to stay in power."

"A young woman died because you needed to stay in power."

"How dare you!" She slammed her fist onto the table. "A young woman died because Robert killed her! Nothing to do with me! Nothing."

For the third time, Hunter's phone buzzed. This time, he removed his phone to check the message. It was Esther.

'New evidence has come in. You need to see this as soon as possible.'

"Saved by the bell, it appears." He put the phone away and stood. "I'm sure we'll talk again."

Mayor Quinn stared at him, long and hard. Hunter nodded and turned to leave.

"Mr. Hunter, people who walk too close to the edge risk falling off." Mayor Quinn stood. "Or there's a chance they might be pushed."

Hunter turned to look back at her. "What are you saying?"

"I'm warning you to think long and hard before you choose to bring this office into that mess. There are dangerous people out there..." Her eyes narrowed. "And in here."

# CHAPTER 21

WITH FILES spread out on the meeting room table in front of them, Hunter and his assistant, Esther Wright, stared at the papers, hoping an answer would leap out at them. The entire glass table was covered with different pieces of evidence provided by the prosecution; photos of the crime scene, police reports, witness statements. The weight of evidence against Sulzberger was impressive.

Behind them, the blinds had been pulled closed, shutting them off from the city late at night. When he first rented the office space, Hunter was sure he would need a boardroom—which professional wouldn't? —and he filled the space with slick office furniture, including a table large enough to seat eight people, a whiteboard and a projector. But over the years, he found himself using the room less and less, and now, it was only a shell, empty, except for the modern furnishings.

"How could they have missed it?" Esther pulled her hair back into a ponytail, a sure sign she was getting serious.

"They didn't miss it. They just weren't looking for it." Hunter looked over the file that stated there were strands of hair found on Jane Doe's clothing that weren't hers. "Female hair. Brunette. Found on the sweater of Jane Doe. That's all they've given us in this file."

Although this was the break he needed, disappointment was etched on his face. After Hunter pressured Michelle Law with the idea that Kim Sulzberger may have been involved, a review of the DNA evidence was ordered.

"But now we can see if it matches Kim Sulzberger's hair," Esther said. "We have a lead."

"Kim doesn't have a criminal record, which means there's no match for us. We would have to take her hair and match it via a private DNA company, but even then, we can't use it in court. The prosecution has no reason to believe it's Kim's hair, so she would have to volunteer the sample, and I don't think she'll do that."

"But it has to confirm our suspicions. Kim was there. She knew this woman." Esther threw her hands out and began to walk around the table. "This is what we've been waiting for."

"It's not quite the silver bullet. We don't even know if it's Kim's hair yet."

"Don't be so negative. This is a step in the right direction." Esther was pleading with her boss to see the significance of the new evidence. "We're almost there."

Although most of her work involved filing papers, organizing meetings, and emailing invoices, Esther thrived in the depths of a case. It was this work, the thinking, the problem solving, that she loved. When Hunter asked for an "Irish Coffee", a Grande Starbucks latte with a shot of Johnnie Walker Black Label, she knew it was thinking time.

"Possession is what the legal case is built around, that's what they're pinning their hopes on. I understand why they arrested him, common sense says he did it, but when you look at it, there's not much more evidence other than the girl was in Robert's house at the time she was found. There's not even any evidence that she died there. There's no video footage, and there's none of his DNA on her clothes—there's nothing else other than it's his house and he was alone all night."

"So it makes sense it was Kim." Esther pointed to the photo on the desk. It was a printout of Kim Sulzberger's Facebook profile—smiling, earrings on, hair perfectly straightened. The picture was at least five years old, but it was how Kim wanted the world to see her.

"Kim claims she was out of town for two days on a solo hike." Hunter rested his hands on the table. "And she doesn't look like the hiking type."

"There's no evidence of her trip?"

"None."

"GPS on her phone?"

"She left the phone at home—when questioned, she told the police that she went on a digital detox, which means there's no tracking and no photos from the phone. The last person to see her was her mother when Kim left her daughter with her for two days of babysitting."

"If she did set him up, then she's very clever. I read about a case like this once—a guy was caught with a stolen car in his driveway. He claimed he was set-up by his wife, as they had started to divorce." Dressed in a stylish, knee-length, dark blue dress, with sleeves coming to her elbows, Esther had the presence of a CEO more than an assistant. "That case ended with a suspended sentence even though he pleaded his innocence to the very end. They had nothing more than the car in his driveway, but that was all they needed to convince the jury."

Hunter stared at the photos of the crime scene. He hoped to see something out of place, something unusual, but there was nothing. "Anything with the assistant, Teresa Hardcastle, yet?"

"Not yet. Jones is working on it, but it's like she disappeared off the planet." Esther continued to walk around the table, tilting her head to stare at the photos of the crime scene. "I'd assume the missing girl is homeless or an escort."

"What makes you say that?"

"Nobody has reported her missing yet. There's no record of her on file, and if she was an escort, she's young enough not to have had a run-in with the police yet."

"Perhaps. Where would you look?"

"I'd start with the area around Wrigleyville in the north, and then move onto Bronzeville in the south. I've heard a few Johns were set up in bars around those places, and they're areas known for soliciting. If I walk around a few different bars with her photo, toss a few dollars to the ladies, I'm sure some of the girls will start to talk."

"We'll try that. At this point, anything that moves the case forward is going to be beneficial."

"Not that identifying her will make much difference."

He turned to look at her, raising his eyebrows. "Meaning?"

"The evidence clearly demonstrates he was the

only one home when this happened. He said it himself when questioned by the police. His wife was away, and his mother-in-law was babysitting his daughter. Unless we match the hair sample, he looks responsible. And if I were on the jury, I would find him guilty. We have to be able to connect the girl to Kim."

"Or someone else." Hunter moved a file across the table, the photo of one of Robert's adversaries clearly in view. "This person has a motive, no alibi, and the skills to make this attack. If we can match the DNA to her hair, then we can really go for her."

Esther stared at the file. "Her? Are you sure? That's risky."

"She's an option."

The two stared at the file on the table, the room filled with the fluorescent glow of ceiling lights, and the smell of Hunter's Irish coffee. Esther shook her head. She stood with hands on hips, a frown on her face. "Is Sulzberger set on fighting this? Any hint that he might take a plea deal?"

"He wants to fight it all the way. Actually, he wants me to prove he's innocent. Defending guilt is one thing; proving innocence is another."

"But that's what people believe we do. They believe we fight for the innocence of the client, and that's what he needs. If only the general public understood what we really do. We need to educate people out there. But," Esther raised her finger in the air, feeling an opportunity to share her life observations. "Education is not the answer when ignorance is not the problem."

"If ignorance is not the problem, then what is?" Hunter smiled.

"Belief."

"Belief? Please, Esther, enlighten me."

"You're his only hope. You're all Robert's got right now. His wife has abandoned him, his people have kicked him out of their organization, and the public needs blood. He has to believe you can save him, or he's got nothing left. You're the only symbol of hope he has."

"So what do I do for him? Tell him I'm looking for the guilty party?"

"What you should actually do is find the guilty party on this one." Esther stared at Sulzberger's file. "Robert Sulzberger is a good man. He's taken bullets for this country; for your freedom and mine. He's done more good in this world than most people have."

"But then he threw it all away and voted against the people he needed to support. And he possibly killed an innocent girl because he lost control."

"Do you really think that?"

"It doesn't matter what I think."

"It doesn't matter to your job, but you're still a human. You still have personal opinions."

"Did you drink all my whiskey?" Hunter chuckled. "Or did that last vacation in the Florida sun affect how you think? No more vacations for you."

"Lately, I've been doing a lot of studying after work."

"Really?" Hunter squinted. "I didn't know that. What are you studying?"

"Hindsight." She smiled. "And I've just graduated with first-class honors. I wish I knew ten years ago what I know now, but I can't go back in time, so the best thing I can do is pass all of this amazing wisdom onto you." She grinned as she walked closer to her friend, her boss. "My advice is listen to your gut. What does your gut tell you? What is your intuition saying? Innocent or guilty?"

"Nobody is innocent. Great people do bad things, and bad people do great things. Nobody is innocent, and if they think they are, then they're mistaken. Not you, not me, and not the religious zealot."

"You're avoiding the question."

"Deliberately."

"Don't be so emotionally detached. This is not one of those cases that you can just sail through. This isn't an easy case. If you want to win this case, you have to be all-in. Emotions and all."

Hunter shook his head.

"Tex, it's personal opinion time." Esther raised her eyebrows, pre-empting the answer. "It's time to acknowledge your emotions."

He ran his fingers over his chin, avoiding eye contact with the woman ten years younger than him. Answering that question would throw down the emotional walls he'd fought so hard to build.

It had taken years to make those walls solid.

"Tex?"

Finally, he conceded. "Innocent."

# CHAPTER 22

PRIVATE INVESTIGATOR Ray Jones looked like he was more suited to a biker bar, where sweat and testosterone were in abundance, than a loud and flamboyant karaoke joint. But it was in the confines of the music bar, with loudspeakers and flashing television sets, that he could let out all his pent-up emotions in a single high-pitched squeal.

The décor looked like it had been ripped out of an old Irish pub, but the shelves behind the bar, filled with specialized Japanese whiskey, dispelled that assumption. There was a large screen on the main wall, with three couches around it, and to the left, the doors to five reserved karaoke booths for those who wanted to sing and party in private. Two other patrons sat at the bar—wannabe singers who had found their confidence later in life. Ray Jones held the microphone in his hand and wiggled his hips, his large frame highlighted by the glow of red party lights, and the swirling disco ball. The Japanese hosts giggled as Jones attempted to hit the extraordinary notes of Freddy Mercury, singing along to another Queen song, and Hunter couldn't help but laugh.

Once, it was rare for Hunter to smile.

For years, he thought it was inappropriate to

express any sort of joy. His father was a convicted serial killer, and eight families suffered the loss of their daughters. Out of respect for the deceased, he'd refused to allow joy to enter his life. In his young adult years, he avoided all places of fun, and even when he felt happy, he held his smile inside. Only recently, since the death of his mother, had he begun to realize the fragility of life.

Ray Jones hadn't cared about Hunter's past. His father was a convicted killer also; however, when a dealer was shot in a drug bust gone wrong in East LA, the case didn't demand national coverage.

Although their relationship was built around their employment in the legal system, their personal relationship had flourished over the past decade.

"Out of all the martial arts, karaoke inflicts the most pain." Hunter smiled as Jones came and sat on the stool next to him, his destruction of pop music completed.

"Really? I'm a black belt in three martial arts, so let's see how accurate that statement is." He slapped Hunter on the shoulder. "It's good to see you again, Tex. I thought I'd better brush up on my Queen songs while I waited for you."

"But I'm early. You said to meet you at seven o'clock, and I'm five minutes early."

The waitress placed a beer in front of Jones, a smile on her face. "And he's been 'waiting' here for the last hour."

"Maybe I got my time wrong. And you know how much I love karaoke." Jones cradled his hands around his IPA like it was pure gold. He looked around the bar for any prying ears. There were none. "I wanted to keep you updated on how I'm going with the

Sulzberger file."

"What have you got?"

"I've located Teresa Hardcastle." Jones slid a piece of paper across the table. "That's where she's staying. Her phone is off most of the time, and she won't talk to me. Maybe you'll have better luck talking to her face to face. She's staying in Bronzeville with her stepdad."

"Thanks. I'll talk to her." Hunter placed the piece of paper in his pocket. "And Kim Sulzberger?"

"Nothing on the wife's whereabouts at the time of death. No social media posts, no check-ins, no footage of her car near the start of the two-day hike that she claims she went on. Kim Sulzberger claims to have gone to the Forest Glen Preserve, about a three-hour drive from Downtown, hiking overnight on the River Ridge Trail. So far, I've found nothing that verifies her whereabouts. I've left a call with the ranger who patrols the area she hiked, and if she went in there, he would know about it, but he's on a hiking trek in South America, and won't get back to me for a couple of weeks. There's no evidence of her signing in for the walk, although that's not unusual."

"Do you think she deliberately left her phone behind? Or did she leave it behind at all? Maybe Kim was home the whole time?"

"I'm not sure." He sipped his drink. "I've heard of psychologists recommending a digital detox to people who are struggling with mental health issues. That's not unusual, so if it were the case, you wouldn't expect to see any posts on social media about her trip, or any check-ins. Surveillance footage is rare near the start of the trail where she went, so again, that's not unusual. Most hiking trails are supposed to be an escape from technology."

"I sense a 'but' coming?"

"But there's no history of mental illness recorded anywhere for Kim. Nothing on her medical file, no mention of anything on social media. I find that suspicious." Jones sipped his amber liquid, and a smile instantly swept across his face.

"Robert's a politician; he might've wanted her to keep any mental illnesses quiet for the sake of his job. That sounds reasonable. The voters wouldn't want somebody whose wife is going through a hard time mentally—they need someone whose life appears stable and competent, even if it's a lie."

"I heard once that politicians and diapers should be changed often, and for the same reason."

"I didn't take you for a Mark Twain fan."

"Mark Twain? Never heard of him. I read that quote on Facebook," Jones said, taking another long gulp from his glass. "That could've been the killer's plan—they wanted to roll the dirty politicians out of the game. Change the politician, and you could change the stadium vote. But everyone has a plan—until you're punched in the face."

"Quoting Mark Twain again?"

"Mike Tyson." Jones grinned. "But here's something I'm sure you'll find very interesting."

"Go on."

"I was watching some of the news coverage that was being broadcast from outside Sulzberger's family home this morning, and I saw the prosecutor in the media scrum outside the main entrance. Now I wouldn't usually think anything of it, but she was lurking at the back, almost willing the media to interview her. Look."

Jones removed his phone and showed Hunter the YouTube clip on one of the news channels with Michelle Law standing in the background.

"I suppose that's not overly unusual. Maybe she was waiting for an interview?" Hunter suggested.

"That's not the angle the media wants at the moment. They'll get to that part of the story, but right now, this is the story of a celebrity war vet who fell apart under too much pressure. Nobody wanted her interview, and she would've known that."

"Maybe Michelle wanted her face on television."

"Maybe." Jones shrugged. "Maybe she wanted attention."

"Or?"

"Or she needs to know how Robert is doing."

Hunter squinted. "What are you saying?"

"Before this case began, Michelle Law, the prosecutor, had made numerous defenses of Robert Sulzberger on Facebook groups. She defended his decision to rezone the area for the stadium on public posts, defended his past, and got into arguments with people about his celebrity status. I was looking through the posts to see if I could find anything nasty, but her name kept coming up in his defense."

"Maybe she really wanted the stadium built?"

"Or this runs deeper."

"A coincidence, nothing more." Hunter shook his head. "I've known Michelle for decades. She's going through a hard time personally. She's not involved."

"Hey, you pay me to investigate, and that's what I do. I report the facts; you can interpret them however you want. What I'm saying is that you might have an option here. I think you could push her buttons— force her to make a mistake. She's defended

Sulzberger publicly on social media before, so there must be some sort of personal attachment. Exploit it." Jones threw his hands in the air.

Both men turned around as an older professional male took the microphone and started singing a Beyoncé classic, but singing was a loosely applied term—the man screeched like a dying cat. Jones raised his eyebrows when the man started adding dance moves. His friend at the bar started clapping along, completely out of time, but thoroughly enjoying the performance.

"What do you need me to do next?" Jones turned back to Hunter.

"I need you to go and talk to women in the bars around the Bronzeville area, especially anyone who might be an escort. Take a photo of our Jane Doe with you and see if anyone has ever seen or heard from her."

"What am I looking for?"

"Find out if any of them are missing. Show them a photo of the deceased, and see if they recognize her. Could be a lead about who the woman is."

"That's not Robert's council ward though? Do you think he'd drive out there to meet these girls? There would be closer areas he could go."

"You're right; it's not his council ward," Hunter stated, finishing his drink. "But it's a lead."

# CHAPTER 23

HUNTER EXITED his sedan with caution.

The yard in front of him was overgrown, there were five beer cans in the grass, and it smelled like a landfill site on a hot day. The waist-high brick fence was broken, chunks had fallen out of it, but the yard didn't look out of place. Every yard in the street was similar. Further down the road, around a block away, a group of men were loitering, watching Hunter's every move. His BMW sedan stood out on the streets of Bronzeville. Hunter stepped onto the front porch and approached the door. As he went to knock, the door swung open.

"Teresa Hardcastle?" Hunter asked. "My name is—"

"I know who you are." She stopped him from saying anything more. She stood behind the screen, one hand on the door.

"You're a hard person to find, Teresa."

"Deliberately."

"Can I have a minute of your time to talk about Robert Sulzberger?" Hunter asked.

"No." Her response was blunt.

Teresa Hardcastle was five-foot-five with dark hair and thick forearms. She wore black jeans and a loose blue t-shirt with the word 'Army' written across it.

"You can talk to me now or we can do it in a deposition," Hunter said. "The choice is yours."

She stared at him with agitation. "I'm not coming to the court to testify."

"I can subpoena you to do so. You're listed as a witness for the prosecution and you'd be in contempt of court if you didn't show. You could go to jail for that."

She folded her arms across her chest. She looked back into the house and then back to Hunter. She sighed, and then stepped out the door, pushing at the screen, before she closed the thick wooden door behind her.

"What do you want?" She stepped past him and leaned against the railing of the porch.

"I need to know where you were on the night of October 5th."

"It's in my police statement."

"I've read your statement. You claim that Robert asked you to organize prostitutes for him earlier that day. He denies he ever asked you to do that, and he denies he's ever slept with a prostitute. He claims your lying about this to make him look bad."

"Why does it matter?" With her left hand, she drew a cigarette and a lighter from the back pocket of her jeans and lit it. She took a long drag and then looked at the end of the cigarette. "He's going to prison now."

"You're left handed." Hunter stated.

"So what?" She stared at him and then took another drag. "Why does any of this matter?"

"It matters because your boss is stating that he's innocent."

"Not much of a boss," she mumbled and looked away. "More like a traitor."

Hunter was silent as he waited for her to continue.

"That prick betrayed us, everything my family stood for. He pretended he represented us and then he betrayed us like we were nothing." She leaned her elbows against the railing and looked out to the messy yard. "I served in the army, so did my sister. My stepfather was a veteran as well. He's inside. He's not doing well these days, not that he'd know what's happening. He doesn't have much of a memory left."

"I'm sorry to hear that."

"Sorry? Yeah, you and everyone else. You all stand up there and thank us for our service, but when we need you, we're overlooked. When war gets ugly, we're the ones that are there, but when we return a mental mess, we're the ones that are forgotten. Veterans need support, we need mental health services, and we need the community to support us. That's why the community center was so important. It was a family hub, a place where we were all comfortable." There was anger in her voice as she looked out to the street. "I went to Afghanistan and it was a horrible experience, but I felt like it was my duty to serve. I had to defend our country. When I came back, I knew I couldn't return to Afghanistan. I couldn't do it again. I knew my mind couldn't take it. I had to leave the family I loved in the army, but I had nothing as a civilian. I had no skills and there wasn't much work around. And then I saw a job working for Robert, and I thought, this is perfect. He believed what I believed in. He gave my people a voice. He gave people like my stepfather a chance to have their pain heard on the City Council. And at the start, that's what Robert did. He stood up for us, but when push came to shove, he let us all down. Prick."

"If he betrayed you, why didn't you just quit?"

"I don't have a lot of skills. Robert gave me a chance to improve my office skills, but I'm not the smartest person going around. I knew I couldn't get another job that paid as well as Robert paid me. I had to stay."

"But staying made you very angry," Hunter stepped closer. "Was it angry enough to kill?"

Teresa turned and stared at him. Her stare was cutting.

"Where were you on the night of October 5th?" Hunter pressed.

"I was here."

"Can anyone verify that?"

"My stepdad," she said. "But you won't get a lot out of him. He's lost the plot."

A beaten-up pick-up truck rolled up the street. It slowed as it approached Hunter's new sedan.

Teresa watched the truck move past, and once it was at the end of the street, she turned back to Hunter. "You have to go now. That car won't last much longer around here."

Hunter nodded, stepped off the porch, and walked back to his car.

He sensed that she hadn't told him the whole truth this time, but he knew it wouldn't be the last time he spoke to Teresa Hardcastle.

# CHAPTER 24

THE WIND whistled through the cracks of the tall door as the woman stepped away from the dull northern sunshine into the subdued mood of the church. The candles flickered, the artificial lights were turned down to a dull tone, and the stained glass windows presented a soft yellow glow along the pews.

The Roman Catholic Church wasn't only grand in its stature, but also its presence in Chicago. Old St. Pat's Church had stood by as Chicago developed, standing proud as its citizens looked for peace amongst the chaos. The church had stood strong during times of depression, fire, religious freedom, and abuse scandals. It was a place of worship, but also a place to ask for forgiveness.

The woman avoided the main door of the church; instead opting for a back entrance that led her to the calm area surrounding the confessional booth. Whether it was the cold in contrast to the outside warmth, or the presence of something more, a shiver ran up her spine as she stepped inside.

As she walked through the dimly lit hall, confused and disorientated by all the religious ornaments, she noticed a priest waiting patiently on a chair, resting in quiet calm with his eyes open.

"Hello, my daughter," he said in a slow drawl. "Please, come in. You're welcome here."

There weren't many places she felt welcomed any more.

Uncomfortably, she stepped closer to the priest. The building felt humid, and she felt the dampness seeping into her skin, seeping a sense of religion into her as well.

"Hello, Father." She bowed her head in respect. "I don't know if I'm in the right place." She brushed her hair over her ear. "I've come to confess my sins."

"Please, sit down." He opened his hands to her, gesturing towards the end of one of the long pews. "Tell me what's troubling you, my child."

The woman rested gently on a wooden seat, treating her surrounds with delicacy. Leaning forward, looking at the ground to avoid the gaze of the bearded man in his seventies, she went to open her mouth, but nothing came out.

As a man with time, the priest waited.

"I've…" She sighed, staring at the red carpeted floor. "I've come to confess my past sins, and ask for forgiveness of my future sins."

The priest continued to wait, acknowledging what was clearly a large amount of effort for the woman to be there. "Would you prefer to go somewhere quieter?"

"I think so." She nodded, eyes still focused on the floor, and followed the priest until she reached the dark confessional booth; a skinny wooden cubicle with two doors, no windows, and no lighting.

After she stepped inside one of the cubicles, her eyes took a few moments to adjust. A trickle of light came through a small gap in the door, and a wire mesh separated her from the next booth, reserved for the priest.

"Do I kneel?" She noticed the kneeling pad in front of her. In contrast to the grand main chapel, this booth was small and calm, a place of refuge.

"Only if you want to."

The priest ambled into his booth on the other side of the wire mesh, almost floating under his gown, providing the woman with the peace and solitude she desired. Hitching up her business skirt, she leaned her body forward, first coming down on her right knee, and then moving her left knee onto the pad with the assistance of her hands. She couldn't see the priest through the wire mesh, creating a sense that she was alone.

The thoughts of her childhood, the prayers every evening before dinner, flooded her mind. The moments when she refused to pray—when people shouted that she was a sick child—made her fists clench. Her family was so obsessed with the church and its traditions, but except for Sunday mornings, they weren't people of faith.

She couldn't remember the last time she went to church. She couldn't remember the last time she had faith in something bigger than her. She couldn't even remember the words to the Lord's Prayer.

When her depression snuck up on her, when she found herself alone in the world, she had time to question her mortality over and over again. With all that time alone, she questioned more than she had ever questioned before. Life, or maybe death, caused her to think deeply, and she didn't like the answers she gave herself.

"I have sinned more than most, Father. I have

sinned more than I can remember." She drew a long breath, filling her lungs with cool air.

"Go on."

"I've killed," she began. "I didn't mean to kill, but it happened that way. It was a young woman. She was just in the wrong place at the wrong time. That's all it was. It was an accident. No, not an accident. Fate. That's it. Fate. I've admitted that to myself now."

The priest didn't respond.

"I didn't want her to die. I didn't expect it. She was only supposed to pass out. I hit her, but I thought I only hit her hard enough to knock her out." She paused and looked at her hands, the ones that killed an innocent girl. "There are times when you have to accept your past, and I've done that. I've forgiven myself. She was supposed to survive. She was supposed to tell her side of the story, and nobody would've believed her. She was too drugged up to remember much anyway. It was all so perfectly planned. She was supposed to survive, and his life was supposed to fall apart. The girl was alive when I left that night."

It took a long time before the priest responded, "My child, have you told anyone else about this?"

"Nobody else would understand, Father. They would all try to persecute me. But can you understand that I didn't want to do it? Can you understand that I tried to tie her up, not kill her? She was supposed to wake up in the basement, struggle out of her ties, and yell for help. The neighbors were supposed to find her. Then his world would come tumbling down. My revenge was on him, not her. Do you understand that?"

"I'm afraid I don't," the priest replied in a low

tone. "But if you've come to ask for forgiveness, you've come to the right place."

"I'm not asking for forgiveness for that act. No. That was an accident. I don't need forgiveness because the blood is not on my hands. I'm free of that guilt," she stated. "I'm here, in this church, to ask forgiveness for what I'm about to do."

"For what you're about to do?"

"I've dug myself such a hole that the only way out is to turn the hole into a tunnel. I need to keep digging until I come out the other side. People are starting to ask questions. They're getting closer to me. They're asking the questions of the right people. And the more questions they ask, the closer they come to me. I don't want them to come any closer."

"Forgiveness doesn't work for future acts. You cannot build up a bank of forgiveness for what's about to transpire. The Good Lord doesn't work in that way," the priest replied. "We all make our own choices, and we must pay and repent for our decisions. If you know your actions are wrong, and you willfully chose that path, then you cannot expect forgiveness. You mustn't walk down the path of evil. You must choose the right path."

"You don't understand, Father. If I don't do this, then I lose everything. Everything. They'll find out who I am, and what I did. The lawyer and his investigator—they're already snooping too close to my business. They'll find out what I did." She sighed. "And the only way I can stop them is to get rid of the man at the center of all this. With him gone, nobody will continue to hunt for me. They'll forget about what happened, resign it to history. I'll make it clean. Make it so they don't find me."

"Are you saying you're going to murder someone in the future? I can't be an accessory to murder. I cannot watch idly by while someone loses their life at the hands of another."

Abruptly, she stood. "Thank you for your time, Father."

After she exited the cubicle, she hurried out into the main area of the church, dwarfed under the large chapel ceiling. Before she reached the main doors, she stopped and looked back to the chapel, back at the altar in all its glory.

"Forgive me, Lord, for I must sin once more."

# CHAPTER 25

HUNTER PULLED his black BMW sedan into the parking lot below his office building. Although it was Sunday morning, his thoughts were still rumbling through the Sulzberger case. He couldn't switch off. The older he became, the harder it was to let go. The desire for justice consumed most of his life. He had the gym, the bar, and the occasional game of golf, but the legal system filled most of his days.

He parked and then noticed the figure lurking in the shadows. He knew the figure, but he hadn't seen him for over a year. Hunter stepped out of the car, staring at the man coming towards him, walking into the underground lot before the automatic metal door closed. "Max? Is that you?"

"Uncle T." The boy spoke quietly, his face subdued in the dim light. "I need some work."

"Are you okay? Where have you been?" Hunter stepped closer to him.

"I need some work, man. I can't do all this other stuff. I can't deal with the emotion. I just..." Max looked around the half-empty lot. "I need money, and I want to work for it."

"I have to tell your father." Hunter reached for his phone. "Your father is worried about you. He needs to know you're doing okay."

"Not yet." Max held out his hand, hushing his uncle. "Please, don't call him yet."

Slowly, Hunter put the phone back into his pocket.

"Uncle T, I checked into the police department earlier this month. Patrick would've known that. I asked them to call him."

"You're calling him Patrick now? You're not even going to call him Dad?"

"I thought out of everyone, you'd understand." Max shook his head. "It's our family; you know how it is. Nothing is ever easy with our family."

Hunter stood silent as Max scratched the inside of his arm.

In the shadows of the parking lot, it was hard to see Max's face, shrouded under his hood, which covered a baseball cap. The lot was half-full, but the foot traffic was at a minimum. The street above them echoed noise through the space, creating a sense of activity, but around them, there was little movement. For a parking lot, it was clean, almost too clean, barely even a tire mark on the ground. The lines had been recently repainted, the numbers on the parking bays squeaking if someone drove over one.

"What are you doing here, Max?" Hunter stepped forward.

"Remember how you always said we were family, and no matter what happened you would always have my back?"

"Always."

"I need your help. I need some work. That's all I need." Max rubbed the indent of his elbow under his sleeve again, his eyes staring towards the ground. "I want to work for money. I don't want you to just give it to me. I need to earn it."

Hunter nodded to Max's arm. "Still using?"

"No, Uncle T. I've been clean for a month." Max rubbed his arm again. "I met a faith healer named Amos Anderson. He got me clean."

"A faith healer?"

"Amos Anderson told me to have faith in him, and he ran his energy right through me. It was such a powerful experience. I was crying afterwards. I haven't used any drugs since. I haven't even wanted to."

Hunter waited for him to continue, and possibly explain he was high on LSD when he met the man, but Max only waited in the uncomfortable silence. His loose clothes covered his skinny frame, but they couldn't cover his sunken cheekbones. This wasn't the promising young man that Hunter remembered.

"Why come to me for work, Max?"

"It's hard to find employment when you've had problems with…" Max drew in a deep breath. "When you've got our family history."

"I understand." Hunter nodded and placed a hand on Max's shoulder. "Come upstairs into the office. I'll find something for you."

Max shook his head. "Not an office. I can't go in there. I'm not good in enclosed spaces."

Hunter stared at his nephew, finally seeing his eyes, the sadness evident. Some people are born into a life of turmoil, some achieve it all by themselves, and others have it thrown upon them. For Maxwell Hunter, it was all three.

When he was fourteen, Max was the best-looking kid in school—the perfect jaw, the square shoulders, the flowing black hair. He had the infamy of being the grandson of a serial killer, and his fellow students were in equal parts attracted to him and petrified of his presence.

With his family's past came intense pressure, and the weight of anxiety built until he couldn't take it anymore.

When he was offered a hit of heroin after school from some of the older kids, Max found his escape; his retreat. He thought it was so cool, something to be proud of, a badge of honor to wear, but rarely does a person escape the white powder without addiction. When he was high, when he was buzzing, he felt free of the pressure to perform, and free from the pressure to meet his father's high expectations. His need for an extra hit grew every week, then every day, then every hour, until it was the only thing he could think about.

Before his father, Patrick Hunter, knew what was happening, his only son was deep in enslavement to the artificial high.

As a single father, Patrick tried everything to save his son, but nothing stopped the spiral. Nothing stopped Max's need for another hit, another moment of escapism. Their lives fell into a cycle of addiction—the more pressure his father put on him to quit, the more he needed to escape the pressure, the more he needed another high. Patrick tried his best for the boy he loved, but little did he know that he was only pushing him further away.

When he hit his lowest point, Max disappeared. Ran away. Walked the streets. Did whatever it took to get the next hit.

That was over twelve months ago.

"I can wash your car." Max nodded towards the

almost spotless black BMW. "That's got to be worth a twenty. I'll do a good job, Uncle T. I'll make it sparkle."

"We can do better than that." Hunter nodded, pulling out his wallet. "Remember how you were always good at sneaking behind people when you were young? You were the ultimate hide-and-seek champion. I need you to do that again. I need you to track someone on the streets."

"I'm good at that. The streets are my world now." Max smiled, rubbing his dry hands together. "Who am I following?"

Hunter checked over his left shoulder, and then the other. No other cars. "His name is Robert Sulzberger." He took a pen and small notepad out of his left pocket and scribbled a note on a piece of paper. "This is the address of his rented apartment, and his website, so you can find a picture of him."

"What am I looking for?"

"Anything, or anyone else that's following him, or lurking around. Any hint that someone is playing him. It's for a case I'm working on, and if someone is setting him up, then they're going to be keeping close tabs on him." Hunter stared at his nephew. "And look out for anyone that might be a killer."

# CHAPTER 26

TEX HUNTER took two shots of whiskey before he exited his car. He grimaced as the whiskey burned his throat, but he knew he couldn't make this meeting sober. He took five deep breaths, and then began his walk through the Cook County Jail as routine ordered. He greeted the administration workers at the entrance, nodded to the same guards as he had done for decades, and walked the same halls he always did.

He'd intended to come earlier, but the weeks had flown by with the Sulzberger case. Even then, he had only arrived fifty minutes before visiting hours were closed, squeezing the visit in at the last minute. He hated this journey. The yells of the mentally ill, of those pushed past their limits, filled the prison halls with distress. It was a feverish sound, a terrifying echo that bounced around the corridors. There was a scent of terror in the air, an angst that death was never far away.

Hunter was lead to a meeting room, and waited in the room longer than he planned. It was a game the guards liked to play. They liked to see how long the visitor would last before they complained. Hunter had learned the hard way to keep his mouth shut. Every complaint was only met with more waiting time.

160

The tight meeting room was cold, and the lack of windows didn't help. The paint was fading on the concrete walls, littered with scratches of the names that had come and gone, and the sense of hope had left the room a long time ago.

The metal door opened and Hunter stood. Alfred Hunter stepped into the room and smiled. "Tex."

Alfred Hunter was dressed in a white T-shirt and brownish-gray pants, hands cuffed together. He was becoming skinnier every visit. His clothes were baggier. His collar was looser. His Adam's apple was more pronounced. The man Hunter used to know, the man he looked up to for so long, was fading before his eyes. Hunter stood and hugged his father gently, afraid that he could crush him.

"I've seen you on the television; the trial starts in a few days, doesn't it?" Alfred lowered his body into the chair. "They're talking about the case back here. There's not a lot of evidence that he did it. What do you think? Did the politician do it?"

Hunter didn't answer.

"Thanks for taking the time to make an old man happy. I realize how much you love these cases and how hard it is for you to pull away from them." Alfred scratched his arm, then his chest, and then his face.

"You don't look well," Hunter whispered. "Have you seen a doctor?"

Alfred drew a long breath. He was a tall man, in his mid-seventies, with sunken cheeks, a thin neck, and wispy gray hairs on his head.

"Doctors? Not in here. I can't just call up and book an appointment." Alfred smiled. "My time is coming to an end, Tex. I can sense it. When I look in the mirror, I don't see myself anymore. I don't see that youthful man. I don't even remember what that man looked like. All I see now is an old person on his last legs. But it means that, finally, I'm going to escape these walls. After thirty years, I'm going to get out of here. It may be in a wooden box, but at least my time here will be done."

"It's not over yet. We can still get you out."

"No, no." Alfred waved his hand at Hunter. "I've lived my life. I've lived it with love. That's the purpose of life—to love. That's what I've learned behind these walls. Life is about love. I loved your mother. I loved my family. I loved my children." Alfred's tone was reflective. He'd had a lot of time for contemplation over the past three decades. "I've been lucky. Some guys in here have never had the chance to love. Some guys here have never had the chance to experience the joys of life. Some guys don't even know what love feels like."

Hunter didn't respond. He stared at his father, mouth open, the words escaping him.

Alfred Hunter was once a hard-working family man; a community centerpiece, always ready with a smile and a wave to his neighbors. Although he worked hard, he always had time for family. He coached the junior basketball teams, attended every school performance, and always volunteered when needed. When he was arrested for the murders of eight teenage girls, the community was devastated. How could they have not seen it? How could they have invited a serial killer to dinner? How did they miss all the signs? Hunter never asked any of those questions. He was convinced his father was innocent, and his opinion hadn't wavered in thirty years.

"How are you?" Alfred asked. "You haven't been here for a while."

"I'm okay."

"Girlfriend? Settled down yet? Maybe I've got more grandchildren out there?"

Hunter shook his head.

"Have you found love?"

Hunter shook his head again.

"How's work?"

"It's good."

"Keeping fit?"

"Sure."

"The weather good in the city?"

"It's getting cold."

For the next five minutes, the conversation continued in the same awkward fashion, only to be interrupted by a loud tapping on the door, followed by the deep voice of the guard. "Visiting time is finished."

Alfred stood. "Thank you for coming, Tex. I wanted to see you before..."

"Before what?"

"Well," Alfred shrugged. "Before I get a diagnosis. I want you to remember me as a happy, healthy man."

"It's not over yet." Hunter said. "I haven't stopped trying to prove your innocence."

"Thank you, Tex." Alfred nodded. "Hopefully, I'll see you again."

# CHAPTER 27

TONIGHT WAS her night. Her chance.

Her moment to finally end the stress. To see what was beyond her anxiety. To feel what it was like to live without the fear that she might be uncovered for who she was.

It was her escape.

Sulzberger's face was splashed all over the papers, another story, another angle, another headline. She was surprised the defense lawyer was still letting him go out in public, and even more surprised he hadn't tried to hide his identity. She couldn't believe that even as he faced the first-degree murder charges, he was still smiling. And smugly.

She waited outside his temporary apartment, nestled in the café across the road. When he left the building, she followed him down the street for five blocks. Even as she'd walked behind him, he hadn't recognized her under her baseball cap, sunglasses, and a baggy sweater.

She was always good at disguises. She'd loved to play dress up when she was young, and she still thrived on it. Some days, when she didn't like what she saw in the mirror, she disguised herself as someone else and spent the day pretending to be a foreign traveler at tourist hotspots. Her Russian accent was getting better by the week.

She'd watched from half a block back as he walked into the bar. She was surprised the bar was already open considering it was only 9 a.m. on a Sunday.

She understood why he went in there though.

She needed her first drink at seven every morning, just before her Soul Cycle Class. The taste of vodka was the only thing that got her out of bed. It was the highlight of her morning. The sting of hard alcohol filled her mind with dopamine and cracked a smile on her face when she desperately needed it.

She tried to hide it in many ways.

It was in her water bottle, a few drops of vodka after her workout. It was in her handbags—she'd sewn a small pocket inside her favorites. All she needed to do was go into the bathroom at anytime, take a small swig, and then her day could continue.

It was hard when every day seemed the same; when every day blended into the next. She needed a little push, a little bit of excitement. Without it, the days seemed useless.

She had thought about that night so much—how much she would be giving up if she pulled the trigger. Would she even be giving up anything? Life on the inside couldn't be much harder than it was for her now. Things couldn't get much worse.

Perhaps if they caught her, life would be better?

She had always liked discipline and routine, and prison would bring that to her. Or she could enjoy a life on the run. Fly to South America, perhaps Peru or Chile, and live her days drenched in tequila, sunning herself on the beach.

But she deeply feared that this was the best life

had to give, that this was heaven on earth. Here, she had luxuries, gifts, everything she'd ever dreamed of, but it meant nothing. Not the new couch, not the nice car, not the expensive watch. None of it made her happy.

But she needed the goods that she so desperately wanted to trash. They were her identity. Without her purchases, without her material goods, without the ability to spend, she was left with nothing but herself.

And she didn't like that one bit.

Robert had to go. That was her only choice now. If he were found not guilty by the court, then the Chicago PD would be forced to review the case, and more than likely find evidence that she was the perpetrator. She was sure she left something for them to find. She was sloppy, but then, she hadn't expected the girl to die.

She'd be cleaner this time. Leave no trace. No evidence.

Sulzberger's temporary apartment building was bland, a deliberate choice by the defense lawyer. If the media stalked Sulzberger, the pictures would be taken outside somewhere average, somewhere that could inspire a level of empathy from the public.

Sulzberger had reentered the apartment building at 5 p.m. He had two six packs under his arms, and he'd been in there ever since. For the last hour, after the café closed, she'd staked out the apartment from the back seat of her rental car, parked across the street, studying every person that entered and left the building. She was going to wait until later, perhaps midnight, but if he were drinking those beers quickly, then he'd be passed out soon. She didn't want that. She wanted him to be awake. To see her face before she killed him.

She had to move.

The building had a small foyer, just big enough for a small, unattended desk, an indoor plant, and the access to two elevators. To the side of the elevators was the door she wanted, the one marked 'Fire Escape.' After she left the car, with her head down, covered underneath a new black wig, she looked at her phone while she waited for a resident to exit the front doors. Once they did, she slipped in the open doors behind them.

She walked to the fire escape, opened the door, and was immediately hit by the musky smell. She had three options from there—an alarmed door to the street, stairs to the basement parking lot, or stairs up to the apartments above her. The cracked walls and broken lighting only added to the beats of her already pumping heart rate.

Bathed in dull light, she crept into the stairwell that led to his apartment door, her steps barely making a sound. She planned to call him on the phone and tell him to come to the stairwell. It was exposed, but it was empty. That was where she'd make her move. That was where she'd try to choke him. Just in case, she had her new weapon in her purse.

She'd studied the plans for the building the day before, calling the security company that managed it, reporting that the cameras in the fire escape were broken. They promptly told her there was no monitoring in the stairwell and she must've had the wrong address. She'd agreed before ending the call.

She scanned upwards through the gap in the stairwell, ensuring there were no movements above her.

Nothing.

She was safe to keep moving. The first flight of stairs was empty. The light was flickering in and out of use, on its way to the end of its life. There were stains on the stairs. Lots of them. Maybe water stains. Maybe liquid. Maybe something more sinister. She couldn't be sure.

She rested her gloved hand on the railing that led upstairs. She was still fit, but her heart rate was pounding.

Second flight of stairs.

Closer.

Closer to her destination, her target, her fate. She had to do this. She had to make him pay. She felt that deep inside of her. Stronger than anything she had felt in years.

Third flight of stairs.

She was there. His temporary home. At the heavy door that kept her shut out of the apartment floor where her target was waiting. With movements slow enough to deaden any noise, she pushed forward.

Her heart skipped a beat as she pried the door open.

With the door half open, her breathing became faster and faster.

"I can do this," she whispered and turned back to gaze at her escape, tapping on her chest to instill belief. "Tonight, everything changes. Tonight, Robert pays for what he did."

With a pounding heart, she took her phone out of her bag to make the call.

*Crack.*

A noise. Above. In the stairwell. A potential witness.

No.

Her heart rate shot up. Muscles clenched. She turned. Ran. Away from the open door. Back down the steps.

Without concern for the sound, she slammed the fire escape door shut, sprinted through the foyer to her car, and roared the engine to life. Back to the safety of what she knew.

She fled, gripping the steering wheel tight, hoping for the best.

When she was under the safety of darkness, she stopped the car and stared at the rearview mirror.

Waiting.

The noise hadn't followed her. Here, in her car, she was safe from the outside world. Robert had been lucky. He'd survived.

But she'd make sure his luck didn't last.

# CHAPTER 28

"A PACKAGE arrived for you."

As Hunter walked into the office, Esther smiled at her boss, pointing to the box sitting on the edge of her reception desk. The parcel was tattered and faded, in contrast to the clean and sleek office. In the two months since they took on the Sulzberger case, they'd received numerous threatening letters, all with varying degrees of danger.

With the trial due to begin the next morning, the case pushed through the system by the prosecution, the letters and phone calls had been coming in thick and fast. The media had loved the build-up. Every angle had been covered, and every social commentator had been interviewed. Television and radio show hosts expressed their opinions with high frequency. People on the street were quizzed, and letters to the papers printed almost daily. Few people avoided the opportunity to talk about Sulzberger's case.

Whenever Hunter's office took on a big case, he could almost schedule the delivery of letters. First, it started with media requests, then came the letters of outrage, and then, packages with no return addresses.

Arriving like clockwork.

"I thought we might've made it through this trial without a threat," Esther stated as she stood up behind her long desk. She peered over the two computer screens, looking at the package that rested on the coffee table. In the reception area of the lawyer's office was a comfortable three-seat couch, an almost fluorescent green indoor plant, and a wooden coffee table made from the carved slab of a Californian Redwood—a gift from a grateful client. "We were so close to making it through this one. If only this threat were delayed by a few days; it would've been a record for us on a big case."

"Are you sure it's a threat?"

"There's no return address, and it's the day before the trial. I'd bet your house it's not a love letter." She walked around her desk, coming closer to the package.

"That's nice of you to bet my house." Hunter smiled. "What's in the package?"

"I'm not sure yet, but I thought I should wait for you to arrive first. The delivery person wasn't one of the usual guys. He looked kind of rough, too, like he'd spent the night sleeping on the street. He was missing a few teeth and had the sort of skin that made him look twenty-five years older than he probably is. I had to watch him walk out to make sure he didn't steal anything as he left."

"Good luck to him if he decided to steal anything from you."

Esther Wright had a history of fighting. She'd spent most of her teen years as an awkward, gangly girl, outcast from the popular groups at school. She was picked on for her clothing style, height, and voice, but when one girl cut Esther's hair as a prank, her father dragged her to self-defense classes.

There, she found acceptance. Her love for fighting grew and grew, and she was once crowned female underage boxing champion of Illinois, but she tried to keep that a secret as she became older. Most potential boyfriends didn't appreciate the fact she could beat them up with the snap of her fingers.

Hunter moved cautiously towards the box. With the trial due to start the next day, he didn't have the time to pull open letters, and he was wary.

"Is there a problem?"

"I can't remember ordering anything, and there's no information on the outside of the box." Muscles tight with anxiety, he picked up the small box and put it to his ear. "At least it's not ticking."

"I'm pretty sure most bombs don't tick these days. This isn't the eighties; you know?"

"I've always thought of myself as MacGyver. If this were a bomb, I'm sure I could use your hairclip to defuse it."

"You think of yourself as MacGyver? No way. MacGyver was sexy, smart, brave, tall, funny, charismatic, and intuitive. You've only got one of those things."

"I'll take sexy."

"I was going with tall."

He grinned. "But if this is a bomb, I need you to start calling me MacGyver."

"I'll tell you what. If there is a bomb in there, I'll call you MacGyver, because if it's a bomb, and you try to defuse it, I'd say we have about fifteen seconds to live."

Hunter placed the small box on the wooden cabinet next to the entrance, away from Esther, and slowly pulled back the tape to open it.

He had never received a bomb threat before, but the thought was always in the back of his mind. He formulated a plan—grab Esther, run for the door to the office, then to the fire escape. Not much of a plan, but it was his way to calm the nerves.

It's not heavy enough for a bomb, he reasoned.

He moved the top flap, looking inside.

"There's nothing here." He searched the box. "Who sends an empty box?"

"There's a note," Esther pointed out, coming closer to look over his shoulder.

Reaching in, Hunter pulled out the small note handwritten on a white piece of paper. He slowly unfolded it.

'Robert is a criminal. He betrayed his own. If he doesn't pay in court, then I will make him pay. If you continue to defend that scum, then I will make you pay. Drop the case now, or pay the price.'

"Looks like it's from one of the people that hated him in politics."

"Or from the person that set him up." Hunter's statement was flippant. He looked inside the box again. Nothing else. "It's not too bad. We've had far worse threats here."

"Are you going to call the police?"

"There's no need." He shook his head. "I don't think it's a serious threat. Besides, there's no actual risk here. How's the person going to make him pay? Via credit card? Perhaps PayPal?"

"I think it's designed to be a physical threat." Esther smiled. "But at least it's not as bad as the five-page letter those hippies sent us when we took on the Dampier murder case."

Hunter laughed. "It was only once I'd read through to page five that I realized they were the ones that broke into the office the night before." He took a deep breath, looking underneath the box for any clues. "There's nothing to worry about here. It's only an idle threat. If they wanted to really threaten us, then they would've done something real—perhaps sent us a photo of the office."

"If you say so." She shrugged happily, returning to her desk.

"Esther." He turned to her. "You've worked hard enough over the past few weeks—why don't you take some early time and go home? Treat yourself to a massage or a glass of wine. We've got a big few weeks coming our way, and I need you fresh and ready."

"A bottle of wine might be better than a glass." She joked. "And thanks, I will take you up on the offer of an early afternoon. There's a series on Netflix I've been wanting to watch."

"Just keep an eye out for any disgruntled political advocates on your way home."

"Will do. Just after I run away from the hippies."

# CHAPTER 29

AFTER HE locked his office door, Hunter looked down the corridor that led to the elevators. Out the farthest window, the night sky was aglow with the buzz of city lights, and he tried to remember the last time he'd left in daylight. Not that he complained about the long hours. This was what he'd signed up for. He knew that the day he entered law school.

After he rode the elevator to the underground parking lot, he walked towards his car, briefcase in hand, his mind thinking about the first sip of whiskey. Then he spotted Esther's car still in her parking space.

Unusual, he thought, but concluded she must've gone to dinner before returning to her car. Perhaps even a date. A woman like Esther never found getting a date any real challenge. She could walk into any bar and instantly be the center of attention. Second dates, however, were a lot harder for her.

Hunter needed his whiskey tonight. It was his reward for getting through another threat, another note to add to the pile of idle extortions. He was building quite a collection. There were the regular letters from people who were still outraged by his parents' actions as if he had something to do with it, but mostly the threats came from the families of victims, the ones who wanted revenge on a criminal, and found he was the easiest target. Out of the hundreds of letters, there had only ever been one instance of violence. Good odds, if he were a betting man.

As he stepped closer to his car in the lot, something in the air didn't feel right.

He listened to the rain falling outside, and stepped over a puddle that was beginning to pool near the ramp that led to the street. The downpour was heavy enough to slow traffic, meaning his drive home was going to be longer than usual. With his keys pointed towards his car, he went to unlock it.

But in a moment of distraction, he stepped towards Esther's Volvo. The safest car. That was what she'd always wanted. She needed to feel safe as she drove around the streets of Downtown Chicago, the thoughts of gang violence never far from her mind.

The yellow sedan kept her safe from the terrors of the world.

As Hunter stepped around the car, he looked at the driver's side door.

Nothing.

No one in the vehicle.

He looked over his shoulder, back towards the elevators, then back towards the entrance to the lot. The heavy metal gates kept the cars in, but the gaps were wide enough for a nimble person to slip through. They never had any problems with the parking lot, which surprised Hunter. He kept expecting someone to slip through the gates, break into the cars to steal anything of worth, and then slip back out.

He heard a movement; a scrape along the edge of the car. He waited. Listened. No other sound. No other movement. His head turned, and he slowly stepped forward to the other side of the car.

"Esther!"

Lying on the concrete, head down, blood next to her, was his assistant.

"Esther!"

He fell to his knees, cradling her head, holding her tight, as he tried to wake her.

"Esther! Talk to me. Esther! I'm here." He held her, her face bloodied. "I've got you. I'm here."

"Tex?" She began to open her eyes, blood dripping from her mouth onto his jacket.

"I'm here, Esther."

"W-what happened?" she asked.

He looked over his shoulder, around the parking lot. No other noises. No other people.

"It's all right. You're safe now. That's all that matters. I've got you."

His voice sounded confident, firm, reassuring Esther, but in truth, he was filled with doubt. He knew this attack wasn't random.

And now, he had a new reality—neither of them was safe.

# CHAPTER 30

"HANG ON. Hang on! Wait."

Robert Sulzberger rubbed his eyes, kicked off the thick blankets, and then tapped the clock next to his bed.

5 a.m.

Too early for a casual visitor. Too early for a delivery.

He rolled out of bed and moved to the door of his apartment, the banging heavy against it. As he switched on a light in the narrow entrance, his first thought was about a fire. His second thought was there must be danger on the other side of the door.

The banging against his door became louder. Loud enough for other people on his floor to hear it. If he was in danger, then there would be witnesses, at least.

Leaning against the side of the wall next to the door, he called out, "Who is it?"

"It's your lawyer. Open the door!"

After rubbing his eyes again, he pried the door open far enough to peek into the hallway. As soon as the door was open enough, Hunter forced his way in, grabbing Sulzberger by the throat.

"Tell me who X is, or you're going to start paying a very heavy price." Hunter slammed his client against the wall. His grip was tight, fueled by anger.

"What?" Sulzberger murmured. "What's happening?"

"Tell me who X is!"

"I don't know!" he replied. "I don't know!"

"My assistant was attacked last night." Hunter's voice was more of a growl, his grip around Sulzberger's throat tightening. "She was attacked after someone made a threat about your case."

"I..." He shook his head. "I'm sorry. I have no idea who she is. I told you this. I don't know!"

Hunter grunted, wanting nothing more than to take his sleep-deprived anger out on his client. But he refrained, slowly removing his grasp from around Sulzberger's throat.

"Is Esther okay?" Sulzberger buckled forward, rubbing his throat as Hunter paced the room in the rented apartment.

"She's fine now. Still in the ER, and they're monitoring her, but she has her sister there." Hunter drew a long breath. "Late yesterday afternoon, someone sent a threat to our office—nothing major, only a note. We get them all the time. It was nothing to worry about so I didn't think anything of it. But then Esther was attacked from behind as she walked out of the office to her car in the underground parking lot."

"Did she see anything?"

"Nothing. She was sucker punched from behind, and the surveillance footage in the parking lot only monitors the entrance. No witnesses either."

"Coincidence?" Sulzberger raised his eyebrows. "Maybe a mugging?"

"Not a chance. She still had her handbag and all

her belongings. They wanted to send a message to us."

"To say what?"

"They want to derail us before the trial."

"Well, it's worked." Sulzberger threw his hands up. "Here we are at 5 a.m. in a rented apartment, and your assistant is in hospital. Whatever they were trying to do has worked."

Sulzberger moved to the coffee dripper in the kitchen, switched it on, and then paused to think for a moment. The kitchen was just big enough for one person; five cupboards, a sink, a bench long enough for a microwave, a coffee machine, and one hot plate.

"Beer?" he asked as he reached across the bench, shook an open beer can, and finished off what was left.

"No."

"Come on, it's…" He looked to the clock on the wall. "It's still nighttime. It's not really morning yet."

"I don't think time has stopped you recently." Hunter nodded to the empty cans next to the bin.

"Don't let me drink alone like a loser again." Sulzberger reached into the fridge, removed two cans, and tossed one across the room to Hunter.

Hunter nodded, popping open the lid.

"I'm sorry. I didn't think it would come to this. I didn't think she was violent. I knew she was passionate…" Sulzberger slumped onto the leather couch, next to the double bed, beer in hand, rubbing his eyes. "X and I would get hot and heavy in my car after every steal. It was a mix of passion, emotions, and pure lust. I'd never felt like that before, and I'm not sure I ever will again. I never knew her name. I never knew anything about her. We just stole things and were electric when we got naked."

Hunter gulped his beer and instantly wished he hadn't. It tasted like it was bottled straight from the Chicago River. Times had gotten tough for Sulzberger, and when he walked into a shop, he now looked for the lowest priced beer, and it tasted like it.

After placing the beer can on the table, Hunter removed his phone from his coat pocket and opened a picture of the note that arrived earlier. "Do you recognize this handwriting?"

Sulzberger looked at the note, perplexed. "Is this the threat?"

"It arrived at my office yesterday."

"From who?"

"That's what I'm trying to figure out."

Sulzberger stared at the picture of the note. "I don't recognize it. It could be anyone's, but it looks like they've written with their left hand."

"Why do you say that?"

"The direction of the smudge. Right-handed people don't smudge pens as a left-hander does. I'm left-handed. That's how I know that."

Hunter looked at the piece of paper again. The smudge of the pen moved from left to right, indicating the person wrote over the top of their sentence.

"It's not very threatening though." Sulzberger continued. "You would've thought if you were going to write a note like that, you would at least make it threatening. Write it in blood, maybe.".

"They're willing to back up what they've stated. Whoever wrote this is not messing around. They need you to pay for something."

"They need me to pay for what I did." Sulzberger

finished his beer in three large gulps. There had barely been a moment in the last five weeks where he was sober.

"Who would be this vindictive?"

"Where to start." He shook the empty can. "The whole city hates me now. Have you seen those comments on the news articles? On social media? Some of them are really nasty. Vile. People shout at me in the street if I go outside. This whole state hates me."

"Let's start at the beginning," Hunter grunted, still standing. "Who wants to hurt you the worst?"

"Probably X, but I know nothing about her. I've looked for her, Tex. Over and over. I've stalked the places we went. I've walked the streets. I've searched tens of thousands of online profiles. All the social media sites. I think I've seen just about every female face in Chicago except hers."

"You must know something about her. Tell me something, anything, that can give me a lead."

"I've tried so hard to find her. I've watched the security footage you sent me from those stores so many times, trying to find something. Anything." His head dropped. "But I know nothing more than what I've already told you. I thought she was a professional because she always had perfect makeup on. She looked like she had come from a mundane but well-paid job, just like me. I think that's why we bonded. We both needed the same thing—an escape from our lives."

"Professional, well dressed, loves to steal. That's not a lot to go on. Anything else? Come on, Robert. We need this."

"Nothing. I've thought about this so, so much,

and that's all I've got. Trust me, I've tried. I've searched so much online. I've sent messages to people, harassed others, and pressured everyone I know." Sulzberger crushed the empty beer can in his hand and threw it in the trash. "Even I'm starting to doubt she existed."

Hunter looked down. He hadn't received the information he needed.

"Are you sure it was X who did this to Esther?"

Hunter looked away. "Who else could it be?"

"Pick a number, and I'll give you the list of candidates."

"Then start at number two. Who hates you the most after X?"

"Right now, I'd say Cindy Mendel. She keeps sending me text messages of hatred. I've even stopped responding to them, but she sends them almost daily."

"You're accusing a politician of beating someone up in a parking lot in the dark?"

"She punched me; she's not scared of violence." Sulzberger stood and returned to the coffee dripper. He removed a coffee bag from the cupboard. "She'd be my number two candidate."

"And number three would be your wife."

"Kim? No, no." He shook his head. "She would never do that."

"She's a war vet."

"She also hates war now. She hates guns, hates violence—she hates anything that brings back those memories. It wasn't her."

"Did you say she hates guns?"

Sulzberger nodded. "Ever since... Ever since she saw a child shot at war, she's hated the idea of guns.

When she came back from her last mission, she cleared the house of any weapons. She didn't even like me going to the range to let off some steam. She used to go there a lot, but she refused to go anymore. It wouldn't have been Kim."

"Would you say your wife was struggling mentally before all this happened?"

"Of course," he whispered. "We both were. The separation was putting pressure on her as much as it did me."

"And what would you say if I told you that she bought a registered Glock just before Jane Doe was killed?"

"No." Sulzberger turned to Hunter, shock plastered over his face. "She wouldn't do that."

Hunter nodded his reply.

"Not Kim. She wouldn't, would she? She couldn't do that to Esther?"

"I don't know the answer to that question." Hunter began to move towards the door. "Watch where you step over the coming days, Robert. Someone is out to get revenge on you, and I don't think a court conviction is going to give them that."

"What will give them that?"

Hunter stopped at the door, paused and looked back at his client. "Only your death will."

# CHAPTER 31

WITH FIVE coffees to substitute for his lack of sleep, Tex Hunter felt fresh enough to begin the high-profile court case. He'd spent five minutes with green tea bags on his eyes, used half a bottle of 'Clear Eyes', and splashed enough cold water on his face to freeze a polar bear. He did his best to appear enthusiastic. For the next few days, his face was going to be stamped on every newspaper, his statements would be part of every television bulletin, and his words would lead every radio news announcement.

Before he stepped out of the black Chevy Suburban, he checked the news on his phone—no school shootings, no big weather events, and no other political disasters. Nothing else to distract the public. Nothing else but a celebrity murder case.

Hunter stepped out of the car and looked up to the somber, seven-story tower of limestone. The massive civic building was a homage to law and justice, a powerhouse hovering over the nearby prison. Robert Sulzberger stepped out of the car behind him, and Hunter handed him a mint. Sulzberger nodded, but no matter how strong the mint was, it wasn't going to wash away the weeks of alcohol abuse seeping from his pores.

When spotted, the media scrum snaked towards them in the early winter cold. The public had a fascination with power and corruption, and the case was popular enough to be a telemovie within a year. Every one of the reporters wanted a role in that movie.

"Head down and don't say a word," Hunter stated as the pack approached. "Don't even look at the cameras."

The media huddled around them, sticking phones and cameras in their faces, yelling at them, but the men continued to walk forward. The first time Hunter experienced the hustle of a loud media pack was when his father was first charged. He'd watched the footage on YouTube numerous times since—his younger self angry at the harassment as he'd tried to walk into the courthouse. He'd screamed at them with tears in his eyes, yelling that his father was innocent.

When he usually walked into the court, Esther would be by his side, keeping him organized, keeping him straight, keeping him focused, but she was at her sister's house, under her watchful eye until the trial was over. Hunter couldn't risk her being in court. She was the one person he felt obligated to keep safe.

As they were greeted by security at the front door, he spotted Kim Sulzberger stepping into the building, talking on her phone, staring at her estranged husband as he walked towards his fate.

Hunter did his best not to confront her over his suspicions of the previous night's events. His restraint was impressive.

His focus had to remain on the case at hand, the future of his client. In the hours since the attack on Esther, he had formulated a plan, a way to get what he needed from the courthouse.

They passed through the security checkpoints, leaving the desperate media behind them, and into the almost empty courtroom. The curtains on the windows were drawn closed, and the lighting was dull, making the dark brown décor appear almost black, not much brighter than the mood of the room. The prosecution team, five of the city's best legal minds, chatted around their table at the front of the room, busily readying themselves for what would take place over the coming days. Two of the younger assistants stood behind the lead prosecutors, eager to learn everything they were doing.

As Sulzberger walked into the room, he looked up to the judge's chair, its power impressive in its height, and then to the jury box, desolate in its emptiness. He knew this court would soon be full, and his fate would be cast in this room over the coming days. He hadn't felt nervous until now.

During the process, he'd felt a range of emotions. Fear, anger, confusion, and helplessness were his daily cocktail of emotions, but now, in the courtroom, he felt the full weight of his coming fate. This room would be where his future was decided.

It was out of his hands now.

Out of his control.

"Good morning, Tex." Michelle Law, the lead prosecutor, dressed immaculately in a black pantsuit, looked up from her computer. "It's good to see you again. And you must be Mr. Robert Sulzberger. It's a pleasure to meet you in person. I'm a fan of your reality television work, and also your time as a politician. My name is Michelle Law."

Sulzberger didn't respond, staring at the

prosecutor. She offered her hand, but he didn't react. Even as Hunter sat down, Sulzberger was still staring at the woman who had gone back to her computer, typing and readying herself for the case.

"Robert," Hunter said, "you're supposed to sit next to me over here."

In a daze, Sulzberger walked to his seat. He sat down, mouth still wide enough to catch a fly.

"Are you okay?" Hunter asked. "I understand there's a lot of pressure here, but we need you to appear together when the jury walks in. Would you like some water? Coffee? I could even sneak you a stiff drink. You've gone quite pale."

"Tex." Sulzberger turned to his lawyer.

"What is it?"

"Her. Michelle Law." He stared at the woman opposite them. "That's her."

"What are you talking about?"

"Her. That's her."

"I don't follow."

"That's her." Sulzberger's eyes were focused. "That's X."

# CHAPTER 32

"THIS HAD better be good." Judge Dirk Harrison looked at his watch as the prosecutor and defense lawyer entered his chambers. "We have an absolutely packed courtroom, the media are hungry, and we're due to start this trial in a matter of minutes. You'd better have a mighty fine reason for this conference, Mr. Hunter."

Judge Harrison sat behind his desk in the narrow chambers, his heavy arms spread wide, staring at the defense attorney, waiting for the excuses to come. His morning wasn't going how he planned, and he was a man who didn't like surprises.

He liked defense lawyers even less.

As they walked towards the desk in the dimly lit room, Tex Hunter stared at Michelle Law, looking for any crack in her armor, any hint that she knew what was coming. But there was nothing. Not a smile, not a twitch, not even a sideways glance.

"Your Honor, I state that the lead prosecutor in this case has a significant and intimate personal relationship with the defendant and should be excused on the grounds of a conflict of interest."

"Pardon?" Law pretended to be surprised, her head tilting to the side. She stood in front of the judge's desk, prepared to go toe to toe with her opponent. "That's an outrageous accusation. Your Honor, this is merely an attempt by the defense to stall this case. Nothing more. We've pushed for a speedy trial because it benefits the community for this person to be convicted of this crime. It benefits everyone. Stalling it on the back of outrageous accusations isn't going to help the community."

"Do you know the defendant on a personal or professional level?" Judge Harrison turned to the prosecutor, the soft light coming through the window behind him.

"No, Your Honor. I've never met the defendant before in my life. Of course, I know who he is, half the city does, but today is the first time we've met in person. I have no relationship with him—personal or physical."

Judge Harrison turned to the other man in the room, raising his eyebrows at the defense attorney. "Are you sure there's no mistake here? Could your client be mistaken?"

"My client is willing to sign an affidavit declaring how he knows the lead prosecutor on a personal level."

"And I will sign one that states I've never met this man before in my life!" Law turned her attention back to the judge, clearly prepared for the attack. "This is an attempt by the defense to stall this case, to throw it out. He's looking for anything that can slow this case down. That's all. The process of law should be above these petty games. The waiting public won't accept the attempts at stalling from the defense."

The judge stared at her. "If it's found you do know this man, then I'm sure you're aware of the penalties and the risk to your career."

"I'm very well aware it would be perjury to declare such a false statement in this court. But I will say it again: I have never met that man before in my life."

"And you will declare this in court, that you don't know this man?"

"Yes, Your Honor. I don't know the defendant."

"Mr. Hunter, if your claim is true, and they have had a significant personal relationship, then I'm sure you have evidence of this?" Judge Harrison sighed, agitated. "I'm sure if they knew each other on a level that could be deemed a conflict of interest, then there must be photographs of them together? Communications between them, at least. Perhaps you could show me the text messages, emails, or phone contact between them?"

"It's complicated, Your Honor."

"How so?"

"They've had a secret relationship where code names were used, and no information was exchanged. They know each other intimately, but have never taken a photo together or swapped details."

"Oh my." Judge Harrison threw his hands up. "This is worse than I expected."

"He must've mistaken me for someone else," Law rebutted. "I haven't had a secret relationship with that man. In fact, I've never had a secret relationship with any man. These accusations are completely false."

"I assume you have evidence to the contrary, Mr. Hunter? And I really, really hope you have something to back these accusations up with."

"She's made comments in his defense on Facebook."

Judge Harrison waited for him to continue.

He didn't.

"That's all we have at the moment." Hunter was confident and firm.

"That's it? You can't be serious. That won't do. Do you have anything concrete, Mr. Hunter? Anything that proves your claim there has been an intimate relationship between the prosecutor and the defendant?"

"At this point, no, Your Honor."

Judge Harrison shook his head again, groaning. "Then it's his word against Law's. If you're willing to declare there's no conflict of interest in this case, Ms. Law, then I must rule in your favor. Unless you have something more to add, Mr. Hunter?"

Hunter stood silent, staring at the woman next to him.

He had nothing. Not a phone call, not a note, not a text message. His client didn't even know the woman's real name until a few minutes earlier.

There was nothing he could prove in court.

Judge Harrison indicated to the door. "Then get out of my chambers and stop wasting my time. This case must proceed."

# CHAPTER 33

AS THE attorneys walked back into the courtroom, Sulzberger stared at his former lover, mystery woman, and fellow thief. She didn't give him the pleasure of a smile, not a wink, not even a glance.

"What happened?" Sulzberger whispered as Hunter sat down.

"Nothing happened." Hunter kept his eyes focused forward. "The case will go ahead."

"What do you mean nothing happened?" Sulzberger leaned closer, feeling the eyes of the packed crowd on him.

"Just that. Michelle denied ever having met you, and Judge Harrison needed evidence of you and her in a relationship. But we have nothing. We have no evidence at all. All we did was make Judge Harrison angry, and he's not going to be on our side in this case."

"What do we do now?"

"We have to win the case, Robert." Hunter whispered to his client. "This courtroom is our best chance to expose her. We can force her to make a mistake, and then we'll have an opportunity to pounce."

"And if she doesn't make a mistake?"

"She will." Hunter responded, although he wasn't sure how he could force her to expose her identity and involvement with the case.

Sulzberger's mouth hung open for a moment, and then he looked across to X.

Despite feeling his eyes on her, she didn't turn around. She couldn't. She didn't want to give Sulzberger the satisfaction. At that moment, she was ahead in the case, and she didn't want to give the defense even a sliver of hope, not even a grain of optimism.

As the court listened to the bailiff's instructions, Hunter was still shaking his head, rubbing his fingers over his brow, his posture slumped, defeated in his chair. As he backtracked over the timeline, it all began to fall into place—Law's specific request to be on the case, her desire to meet Sulzberger, her need to know how Sulzberger was emotionally handling the process.

But theories were one thing; proving it in court, under the pressure of a media-hungry trial, was something else altogether. Over the coming weeks, his every move would be watched, his every word overheard, and he'd barely be able to move sideways without the social media universe being informed.

With the case scheduled to run for five weeks, Hunter was already consigned to the fact that his movements would be between his office, the court, his home, and if he could, a sneaky trip to his favorite bar.

Although Hunter had one week scheduled for evidence, he planned for most of the work to be done during the prosecution's case. His intention was to plant an element of doubt in every testimony, discredit the witnesses' credentials, and demolish any evidence they presented. The prosecution's case relied heavily on Sulzberger being the only person present at the scene of the crime. There would be witnesses who would testify that Sulzberger was a loose cannon, building a picture of a broken man on his last legs. The case would be as predictable as it was plain. There would be no bells or whistles in the prosecution's attack.

Hunter had a plan. He intended to expose the holes in the wife's testimony, expose the lack of direct evidence, and question every step of the quick police investigation.

But everyone has a plan until they're punched in the face, and Tex Hunter had just been given a solid right hook to the jaw.

"One minute," the bailiff called out, warning that the judge would enter the courtroom in a few moments, and the event would begin.

Judge Dirk Harrison walked into the room as a dominant figure. This was his courtroom, and anyone who dared get in his way would be crushed. He wouldn't stand for theatrics and had even less patience for distractions. His hair was all but gone, and his skin looked like it had spent too many vacations in the Miami sun, but his mind was as razor-sharp as his voice was fierce.

After Judge Harrison had introduced himself and taken the court through the details of the trial, he asked for the bailiff to bring in the twelve regular, unqualified people that were about to assess the workings of the law.

The jury selection had been arduous—trying to find people who weren't influenced by the blanket media coverage was difficult. In a city with a history of political corruption, the news outlets had created a monster in this case.

Despite the defense's objections during selection, the jury was exactly who Law needed in the box. Nobody too political. Nobody with a past in the armed forces. And nobody who might fall for Tex Hunter's charms.

Judge Harrison spoke to the twelve chosen individuals, telling them that they needed to listen to the evidence, or lack thereof, to determine their judgment for this case. They needed to make no assumptions, provide the defendant the presumption of innocence, and assess the guilt of the defendant on the evidence alone.

The jurors all nodded in agreement, but they were only human. They'd already made their first impressions of the defendant, perhaps even weeks ago.

Hunter had spent hours teaching Sulzberger how to sit, stand, and react to the statements in the court. To prevent him appearing defensive, he advised Sulzberger that he couldn't fold his arms, slump in his chair, or look away from a testimony. He couldn't lean backward, sigh, yawn, or appear disinterested. His shoulders had to be relaxed, his facial muscles calm, and his demeanor attentive. He needed to take long, slow, deep breaths when the testimonies about his guilt were spoken.

But that strategy was also gone.

The shock and unease written on the faces of the men at the defense table spoke more than any witness testimony.

Looking across to Law's desk while she prepared to deliver her opening statement, Hunter saw a woman prepared. Everything on her desk was perfectly organized and set out. Her laptop was ready, her pencils were sharp, and her notepad was open. She knew Hunter was going to object to her presence, and if there were evidence she was X, he would've presented it already.

She'd played him, played him well, and he didn't like it one bit.

*****

"May it please the Court. On the morning of October 6th, Ms. Martina Lopez was due to clean the residence of Mr. Robert Andrew Sulzberger, starting her routine at 9 a.m. She was late, starting at 9:15 a.m., and she walked into the house using the key that the owner had given her. She noticed nobody was home, and she cleaned the house as usual—starting with the kitchen, the bathrooms, and then the bedrooms. On this day, the first clean of every month, she would go to the basement. The door to the basement was unlocked.

When she walked into the basement, what she found was disgusting. Utterly horrifying. She found the dead body of a young woman tied to a chair.

She screamed.

Ms. Lopez raced outside and called 911 on her mobile phone.

She waited outside, in her car, with the engine running, until she saw the first police car arrive. She was on the phone with the 911 dispatcher, and the operator confirmed it was the car indeed dispatched to the property.

Ms. Martina Lopez will tell you she did not directly call Robert Sulzberger, the owner and resident of the home, out of fear for what he could do. She will tell you she did not hang up the phone from the 911 dispatcher out of fear for what Robert could do. She did not wait inside the house out of fear for what Robert could do to her.

She will tell you she was terrified of the man.

What the police found when they entered the property was an unidentified woman, her arms and legs tied to a wooden dining room chair. When the paramedics arrived, they pronounced her deceased at the scene.

We still don't know who the young woman was. We have no record of her. There is no record of her missing, no file on her fingerprints or DNA. What we know is the young woman was around 21 to 24 years old, of Latino descent, and she died in the basement of Robert Sulzberger's home.

For the purpose of this court case, we will call the deceased Jane Doe.

The medical examiner will testify that Jane Doe was killed by a blunt force to the skull, one strike, and she was deceased between two to six hours before Ms. Martina Lopez found her body.

Jane Doe died as a direct result of a blow to the face. When she was hit, the bone in her nose severed the ophthalmic artery in her brain, causing a massive internal hemorrhage, and this caused her death.

She was alone, cold, and helpless.

Robert Sulzberger told the police he was the only person staying at his address that night. When taken in for questioning, Robert Sulzberger stated he was there all night. He stated to the police that no one else was staying at the property.

Robert Sulzberger killed Jane Doe, and as such, he should be convicted of murder in the first degree.

My name is Michelle Law and, with my team, I will present the reasons why you must find Robert Sulzberger guilty of such a cold-hearted crime. A cold-blooded murder.

My team and I will present expert witnesses to illustrate how Jane Doe died, and who killed her.

Witnesses such as Detective Thomas Rodman will detail why he was able to deduce that Robert Sulzberger was the killer and make the arrest after questioning the defendant. He will show the evidence that proves Robert Sulzberger was not only there, but also caused the death of Jane Doe.

We will present expert witnesses who will talk about the blood found only yards away from the body. That DNA sample matches the DNA of Robert Sulzberger.

Expert witness, Medical Examiner Dr. David Bardon, will explain exactly how Jane Doe died.

Witnesses will testify they saw Robert Sulzberger at the scene of the crime only hours before Jane Doe's body was found.

You will hear from colleagues of Mr. Sulzberger, including the Mayor of Chicago, Mrs. Nancy Quinn, who will testify about his behavior on the day before the murder. You will hear from Mr. Sulzberger's assistant, Teresa Hardcastle, who will testify that Mr. Sulzberger had asked her to organize prostitutes in the past. Cindy Mendel, a City Council member, will testify about her friendship with Robert Sulzberger. She will explain that Robert didn't seem himself in the weeks leading up to the murder. She will testify that something felt 'off.'

You will hear from witnesses who will testify about the drug problems that have plagued the accused's life, and how he could not control his behavior when drunk on alcohol. We will hear that when he was arrested that day, he admitted he was drinking the night before.

You will hear from the neighbors of Robert Sulzberger who will testify that things did not appear right in the Sulzberger household leading up to the murder. They'll testify that Robert seemed angry and annoyed in the days prior.

You will hear from expert witnesses who will detail the crime scene, and explain exactly how the evidence shows Jane Doe was murdered.

As a member of this jury, you have a valuable role to play.

You have to listen to the facts. You have to listen to the evidence. And you have to decide whether Robert Andrew Sulzberger murdered Jane Doe in his basement on the night of October 5th.

But I'm not here to convince you of the guilt of Robert Andrew Sulzberger. I won't have to do that.

The evidence you hear will speak for itself. The evidence in this case will make the guilt of Robert Sulzberger abundantly clear to you.

There will be no dispute. There will be no doubt.

After you have heard the facts, there will be no choice but to find Robert Andrew Sulzberger guilty of the crime of first-degree murder.

At the end of this case, I will talk to you again and ask you to think about the evidence and the facts that have been presented to you. It's at this point you will be asked to conclude, beyond a reasonable doubt, that Robert Andrew Sulzberger is guilty of the callous, planned, and horrible first-degree murder of Jane Doe.

Thank you for your service to the court."

\*\*\*\*\*

Law delivered her opening statement with passion, intensity, and fire. When she sat down, her team quietly congratulated her on a job well done.

Rattled by the revelation that his opponent was Sulzberger's mystery woman, Hunter barely took in a word of the statement. He spent his time staring at the computer in front of him, thinking of a way to expose the woman. Social media was out, surveillance footage was out, phone location data was out—without a slip up from her, without a mistake, he had nothing. The key to his case was sitting next to him, tempting him, laughing at him, and he had no way to expose her.

"Mr. Hunter," Judge Harrison interrupted his silent reflections. "The court is waiting for you to begin."

Hunter looked up from the computer, all the eyes of the court on him, waiting for him to rebut the opposition, but he was lost in his train of thought, lost in his sense of attack.

\*\*\*\*\*

"May it please the Court. In this case, how Jane Doe died will not be in dispute." Hunter began reading off the page in front of him. His voice was monotone, and his mind was elsewhere.

"We know Jane Doe died of a forceful blow to the skull on October 5th. The Cook County Medical Examiner's Office has come to this conclusion and has stated as much in their statement of death. We know where she was found by the cleaner, Ms. Martina Lopez, on the morning of October 6th.

That's what we know. Those are facts. Indisputable.

But that's not what this case is about."

Hunter began to find his rhythm, his tempo. His voice.

"This case is about what we don't know. This case is about what's missing. This case is about where reasonable doubt exists in the assumptions made by the prosecution.

When the prosecution has finished with their case, you'll feel that all the questions have not been answered. You'll feel like there are missing pieces of the puzzle—and that's because parts of the puzzle are missing. The important parts. The parts that actually show you what this picture is.

We do not know what caused the blow to Jane Doe's face.

We do not know where Jane Doe died.

We do not know who killed Jane Doe.

There is no evidence, no evidence, that proves any of those important questions. And without answering those questions, reasonable doubt will continue to exist. It must.

There are no witnesses to Jane Doe's death. There is no evidence which states Robert Sulzberger caused her death. There is no evidence to state Robert Sulzberger had any hand in Jane Doe's death.

My name is Tex Hunter, Criminal Defense Attorney for Mr. Robert Andrew Sulzberger, and with my team, I'm here to serve the court. The way I will do this is by ensuring the process of justice is administered fairly and justly. Putting an innocent man away for a crime he did not commit is not justice. That's not fair and ethical.

As jury members, I need you to remember that, right here, right now, Robert Sulzberger is an innocent man. Right now, Robert Sulzberger has a clean slate.

Despite what you've heard, he doesn't start this case as guilty. You cannot assume that because the prosecution claims he's guilty means that he is. No. The onus of proof is on the prosecution. The onus to present evidence is on the prosecution.

And the proof must be compelling enough to alleviate all reasonable doubt.

All reasonable doubt.

The prosecution will try to explain their case to you using science, testimonies, and fanciful stories. But no matter what they tell you, no matter what they present to you, remember that no evidence answers three important questions. Remember that they've missed the important factors of the case.

Where did she die?

Who killed her?

And why did she die?

The prosecution will present evidence they think will prove the assumptions, but you must remember that none of their evidence proves anything. The evidence they'll present does not prove their theories about how Jane Doe died.

And they're just that—theories.

Nothing more.

At the end of this case, you will ask yourself questions about the charges against Robert Sulzberger.

Is there enough evidence to prove he conducted this act?

Is there enough evidence to prove he murdered this person?

At the end of this case, you will have reasonable doubt in your mind. And you will have that doubt because there's not enough evidence to prove these charges beyond a reasonable doubt.

No witness saw Robert Sulzberger and Jane Doe together. No DNA evidence proves the prosecution's theory. And there are no fingerprints that prove their assumptions.

That's because Robert Sulzberger did not have a hand in her death.

There is nothing, I repeat, nothing, which proves Robert Sulzberger caused the death of Jane Doe.

Nothing.

You may feel sad for the loss of a young woman's life, but don't let that feeling cloud the fact that there's not enough evidence to convict this man.

At the end of this case, I will stand before you again and highlight all the missing pieces in the prosecution's story. You will have a feeling about this case. You will feel it deep inside. That feeling will be reasonable doubt.

At the end of this case, you cannot find Robert

Sulzberger guilty because there's simply no evidence to say he committed the act.

And that means you must find Robert Sulzberger not guilty.

Thank you for your service to this court."

# CHAPTER 34

THE JURY took to the prosecution's first witness, Detective Thomas Rodman, immediately. He appeared as every mother's dream and every father's wish, but his broad shoulders, perfect grooming, and wide smile were a cover for the pain, tragedy, and agony he'd witnessed in his twenty-five years on the job. Walking into the basement to find a beaten Jane Doe tied to a chair didn't even rank in his five worst moments as a detective with the Chicago PD.

Michelle Law's questioning was textbook perfect—establish the witness's credentials as a wonderful servant to the community, outline his world as one of family, church, and decency, and reiterate his ability to do a service to his community with honor. After the groundwork was solid, she began the character attack on Sulzberger.

"When you arrived at the house of Mr. Sulzberger, what did you find?"

Rodman cleared his throat. "First, we had to find the cleaner, Ms. Martina Lopez. Dispatch informed us that she wasn't waiting inside the house, and she was, in fact, waiting across the street in her car with the engine running."

"Did she explain why she was waiting there and

not in the house?"

"She said she was scared of Mr. Sulzberger and his power. She needed to make sure we weren't corrupt police officers, and that the police department knew we were there. She had to confirm this with the dispatcher before she would exit her car."

"How was Ms. Lopez behaving when you first talked to her?"

"Understandably, she was very shaken and scared. She barely said a word to us. Her arms were folded across her chest, she was very pale, and she was sobbing. She cried the whole time we talked to her."

"Did she show you the scene of the crime?"

"She led us to the location of the body, but she wouldn't reenter the basement. By the time Ms. Lopez had shown us to the basement door, the paramedics had also arrived. Ms. Lopez waited at the top of the steps to the basement while we went down to investigate the scene. Once we determined the room was secure, and there was no further threat, we entered the room."

"What exactly did you find when you stepped into the basement?"

"We found Jane Doe tied to a chair. The paramedics entered after us and checked her pulse and her vital signs, but there were none; however, that was clear to everyone in the room. Her face was bloodied, her head was tilted to the side, and there were no signs of any movement from her."

Law tapped a few keys on her computer and the images taken by the police photographer appeared on the court monitor. "Was this the scene you were confronted with?"

There was an audible gasp from the jury. That was

understandable. Most people didn't see the dirty underground of city life in their daily grind. They went to their coffee shops, sat in their air-conditioned offices, and spent their evenings at the gym or in a restaurant, all the while ignoring the horrors of human behavior that existed only a a few feet away from them.

Heads in the gallery turned away as Law continued to scroll through the pictures.

"That's the scene we entered into. You can see the body is tied to a dining room chair and placed in the middle of the room."

"Was Ms. Lopez a suspect in the crime?"

"At that point, yes. Everybody was a suspect before we started the investigation, but we quickly ruled Ms. Lopez out as a suspect as she had an alibi for the night before—she'd been working since midnight at her other cleaning job at a Downtown office building, and surveillance footage and other workers later confirmed that. She worked from midnight until 8 a.m. when she then left to go to her job at the Sulzberger house."

"And is that when you made the call to take Mr. Sulzberger in for questioning?"

"It is. I made the call to dispatch, and Detective Jemma Knowles was close by his office. She went to talk to him. After a quick discussion, she brought him down to the station and into a room for questioning. At that point, he was very open about talking with us. After I talked to him for an hour at the station, it was clear I should place him under arrest. He stated, very clearly, he was the only one home that night."

The next twenty-five minutes were spent detailing the detective's impression of the crime scene. If a picture painted a thousand words, then the prosecution made sure they used every single one of those words to emphasize the brutality of the attack. When she was done with questions about the scene, Law moved her focus to Sulzberger's first interview with the police, where they pulled apart the transcript, seemingly line by line. For more than two hours, the jury hung onto every word from the detective, convinced by his deep voice, piercing eyes, and show of authority. First impressions counted, and the prosecution had started well.

It was now the defense's turn to change that.

Hunter began his cross-examination seated behind his desk. When instructed by the judge to begin questioning, he turned and stared at Michelle Law for a number of long moments. He needed her to know he was coming for her. He wasn't going to let her walk away from this.

"Detective Rodman," Hunter began. "Was Mr. Sulzberger present when you entered the house?"

"No. He advised us he had left the residence at five o'clock that morning to go to the gym and then to his office."

"Was this the usual routine for Mr. Sulzberger?"

"He claimed it was."

"Were you the one who called him at his office?"

"No. As I stated earlier, we sent another detective to talk to him at his office, Detective Jemma Knowles. Detective Knowles asked Mr. Sulzberger a number of questions and then asked him to come to the station to talk further. Mr. Sulzberger voluntarily came to the station for questioning. At that point, he wasn't in custody, and we advised him he was free to leave at any time. And—"

"But he didn't leave?"

"No. He chose to stay and answer the questions."

"At that point, you'd advised him that a woman was found deceased in the basement of his home and he still chose to answer all of your questions. Is that correct?" Hunter flicked a page over in front of him, reading over the lines on the paper file.

"Yes. And when it became clear he should be charged with the crime, and we made the decision to arrest him, we read the Miranda warnings to him. It was then he exercised his right to remain silent."

"But he'd chosen to talk freely before that?"

"That's correct."

"Did he have to talk to you when questioned? Before you read him the Miranda warnings?"

"No, he didn't have to talk to us."

Hunter paused, allowing the information to sink into the minds of the jurors. He tapped his index finger on his top lip, demonstrating to the jury that he was thinking about the importance of that information and they should too. When he saw a number of heads nod in the jury box, he continued.

"Detective Rodman, were there any blood splatters on the floor around the placement of the body in the basement?"

"No, you can see in the pictures that there weren't any."

"In an attack like this, would you expect to see blood splatters around the body if this was where the attack took place?"

"Not always. You can see the impact of the strike is directly on the nose, not across the cheekbone. Any blood present may have dripped directly onto the victim's body—if that was the case. Or the perpetrator may have cleaned the blood from the scene."

Hunter looked over his shoulder. Kim Sulzberger's eyes felt like they were burning into his back. He was describing the scene at her home, her place of sanctuary, her escape from the pressures of the world.

"In your testimony with the prosecution, you stated you had enough evidence to charge Mr. Sulzberger with murder. Do you have any direct evidence that Robert Sulzberger touched Jane Doe?"

"It's hard to say. There's certainly—"

"Please answer the question directly, Detective Rodman."

"If we are to look at—"

"Yes or no, detective."

"What was the question again?" Rodman stalled.

"Did you then, or now, have any direct evidence that Mr. Sulzberger laid a hand on Jane Doe?"

"It's complex. He—"

"It's not complex. It's a yes or no answer to the question. Did you then, or now, have any direct evidence that Mr. Sulzberger touched Jane Doe?"

"Objection," Law interrupted. "The question put to the defendant is complicated and requires further explanation."

"I argue that it doesn't," Hunter responded. "It's a simple and direct question. There can only be a yes or no answer. He either has the evidence that this happened, or he doesn't."

Judge Harrison grunted. "The objection is overruled. It's a direct question that can be answered with a direct answer. Please answer the question, Detective Rodman."

"No," the detective mumbled.

"And do you have any evidence that directly places Mr. Sulzberger in the basement that night?"

"He said he was the only one home that night. He said—"

"Again, this is a yes or no question, detective. Is there any direct evidence that places Mr. Sulzberger in the basement that night? Did he make any statements about being in the basement that night?"

"It's not that—"

"Yes or no, detective. Is there any evidence that Mr. Sulzberger was in the basement that night?"

"No." Detective Rodman moved around in the chair.

"Is there any evidence that Mr. Sulzberger handled Jane Doe?"

Rodman sighed.

"Please answer the question, detective. Is there any evidence that indicated Mr. Sulzberger handled Jane Doe?"

"No."

"Did you find any evidence on Jane Doe that indicated Mr. Sulzberger had touched her?"

He shook his head.

"Please answer the question verbally, detective. Did you find any evidence on Jane Doe that indicated Mr. Sulzberger had touched her at all?"

"No."

"Did you find any evidence, anything at all, that stated Mr. Sulzberger gave drugs to Jane Doe?"

Rodman looked to the prosecution lawyers. They avoided eye contact. "No, we did not."

"Did you find any fingerprints from Mr. Sulzberger on Jane Doe or her clothing?"

"No."

"Did you find any DNA from Mr. Sulzberger on Jane Doe or her clothing?"

"No."

"Did you find any evidence there was blood from Mr. Sulzberger on Jane Doe?"

"No."

"Did you find any evidence there was blood from Jane Doe on Mr. Sulzberger?"

"No."

"Did you find any evidence that Mr. Sulzberger had tied Jane Doe to the chair?"

"No."

"Detective Rodman." Hunter chuckled and shook his head, leaning forward on the table, eyebrows raised to relay his fake surprise to the jury. "During your police investigation, did you find any direct evidence that stated Mr. Sulzberger knew the deceased person?"

"It's not that simple. It's—"

"It is that simple, Detective Rodman. In fact, it's so simple that you may answer the question with a simple and direct yes or no. During your police investigation, did you find any direct evidence that stated Mr. Sulzberger knew Jane Doe?"

"What we found—"

"Yes or no, detective."

"Listen, what it was—"

"Detective Rodman!" Hunter slammed his fist on the table. "It appears you're avoiding the question. This is a simple question. Yes or no?"

The detective looked around the room, and then at the judge who nodded that he should proceed. He sighed. "No."

"And, Detective Rodman, do you have any direct

evidence, anything at all, that indicates Mr. Sulzberger struck Jane Doe?"

The crowd started to murmur. Hunter raised his eyebrows further.

Detective Rodman looked away. "No. We don't."

# CHAPTER 35

ALTHOUGH HE hadn't had a cigarette for many years, the craving still hit him sometimes. That moment of relief, that rush of nicotine, that momentary distraction from the day's events to ease him into relaxation like a two-hour massage in one single hit.

As he waited in the courthouse foyer, Hunter wondered if someone around him had a spare Malboro. A strong Cuban cigar would've been even better. Followed by a glass of whiskey. And then perhaps the bottle.

A person pushed past him in the foyer of the courthouse, their own worries to concern them, and the smell of cigarette smoke lingered. Suddenly, Hunter didn't need a puff anymore. He couldn't stand the dirty smell of secondhand smoke.

He moved to the side of the busy foyer, its low roof creating an echo of rushing shoes. He leaned against the concrete wall, gazing out the small window to the front steps. He'd spent much of his life in the dimly lit building, and he often wondered if he would miss the intensity of the place when he retired. But after much thought, he always came to the same conclusion—he could never retire. He would work until his last days, pushing a pen with his frail hands. He couldn't imagine a life without this building, without this passion.

Sulzberger came up next to him, rubbing his hands together after leaving the bathroom. He smelled like a mixture of vomit, sweat, and vodka.

"I still don't understand," Sulzberger said as he stood next to his lawyer. "Why can't you arrest her? It's clear she's the killer."

"There's no evidence, Robert. All we have is your word, and that looks like a defendant trying to save his own skin. Your statement wouldn't be worth the paper it's written on."

Sulzberger ran his hand through his hair. "Why would she do this to me? Who would do this to anyone?"

"I can't answer that question for you."

Hunter looked over his shoulder, through the window, at the gathering media crowd, eager behind the police barrier, waiting for them to walk out of the building and down the stairs.

"Are they waiting for us?" Sulzberger asked.

"They're waiting for Michelle. I've already said we won't be making any statements about this case, but Michelle is loving the limelight. She's been volunteering to give interviews, and now I can see why. This is all a game to her. Your life, your history; it's a game."

Sulzberger's eyebrows squinted together. "I didn't know anything about her. Not her job, not where she lived, not even her real name. I'm sorry, Tex. If I knew, then I would've told you. I would've said something earlier."

"She declared before Judge Harrison that she'd

never met you. Do you have any evidence, anything at all, that could link her to you? A text message, or a photo together? If we can do that, we can get her off this case on a conflict of interest, possibly stall for more time, and give us the chance to build a case against her for murder. At the very least, the state would be willing to strike a better deal."

"I've got nothing." Sulzberger shook his head. "We had no contact outside of our designated meeting spaces. Not even our names were exchanged. No photos, no messages, nothing. And she was always wearing a disguise in the surveillance footage."

"I find that hard to believe."

"I find it hard to believe myself." He tapped his fist against the wall. "I can't believe I'm here because of my own stupidity."

Hunter noticed the media crowd had started moving together like a sea of snakes. They were preparing for their attack. He turned in the other direction. Out of the elevator, still inside the building, stepped the junior prosecutor, perfectly dressed in a pinstripe suit, pocket square neatly arranged, followed by another equally well-dressed member of his team.

Walking tall behind them, shoulders back, full of beaming confidence, was Michelle Law. She pulled a loose strand of hair back, smiled, and walked out the elevator door towards Hunter and Sulzberger.

Looking up at them, she grinned. "What a rush this case is."

Sulzberger stared at her, unable to say anything.

"Is that what it's all about for you, Michelle? The rush?" Hunter stepped closer, closing in on her personal space.

"It's strange what gets people excited. Some of us

get a rush by having affairs in parking lots, others by prosecuting criminals, and others by killing prostitutes."

"And you've done all three." Hunter was firm.

"I wouldn't sink that low. That's for the lowest scum of society. The ones that can't find their rush elsewhere. The cheap ones. The nasty ones. But the world is lucky that people like me are determined to get revenge for the innocent."

She lingered for a moment, then turned and walked away. Sulzberger stared at her, his face expressionless.

"She set me up," he finally stated as he watched through the window as the media began mobbing her. "I have no doubt about that."

"If we can find something…" Hunter began to move, "then we still have a chance to win this."

# <u>CHAPTER 36</u>

ON THE second day of the trial, the testimony of the cleaner, Ms. Martina Lopez, went as expected.

Yes, she was there. No, she didn't see Sulzberger that morning. Yes, she was distressed by what she saw. All very factual, all very convincing; however, none of the facts stated that Sulzberger was the killer. Tex Hunter made sure of that.

The third witness, next-door neighbor Marcy White, was much the same. Yes, she saw Sulzberger there that night. No, she didn't hear any commotion. Yes, she heard the cleaner scream the next morning.

Solid witnesses, but nothing game changing. Nothing that could swing a jury.

When the fourth witness, Medical Examiner Dr. David Bardon, walked to the stand, Law continued her process of asking very factual questions. She was attempting to build a mountain of small facts, a massive pile of little truths until it became beyond possible that something so big could be anything other than a certainty.

She questioned the doctor, and Hunter objected at every possible opportunity, disrupting the rhythm of the prosecution. When Law finished her examination of the autopsy report, she turned the witness over to the defense, winking at Hunter, a small grin on her face; the type of grin that comes from knowing you were slowly knocking your opponent into submission.

"Dr. Bardon," Hunter began, seated behind his desk, laptop open in front of him. "In your report, you've stated that the deceased died between 3 a.m. and 7 a.m. The cleaner found her at 9 a.m., and there is surveillance footage of Robert entering the gym at 5:30 a.m. like he did every second weekday morning for the past five months. It took Mr. Sulzberger between 25 and 30 minutes to travel to the gym, meaning he left the house at around 5 a.m. Does that leave any possibility the death occurred when Mr. Sulzberger was not home?"

"A simple deduction would tell you there's a timeframe during the time of death estimate when Mr. Sulzberger wasn't home."

"It certainly does. According to your report, there's the possibility the death occurred when Mr. Sulzberger wasn't home. How long after the strike to her face do you believe Jane Doe died?"

"Within a very short timeframe after the strike. If not ten minutes, then 20 minutes at the most. The impact caused the bone in her nose to be pushed backward, and this severed the ophthalmic artery, causing a massive internal hemorrhage, which caused her fatal brain injuries. The body's response in a situation such as this is to shut down and cease breathing."

"That means, according to your report, there's a two-hour window, under darkness between 5 a.m. and 7 a.m., when Mr. Sulzberger wasn't home, where the deceased could've died. Is this correct?"

"I'm here to testify on the medical report I've

finalized. I'm not here to comment on whether Mr. Sulzberger was home at the time. What I can tell you is the death occurred approximately between 3 a.m. and 7 a.m."

"Thank you, Dr. Bardon." Hunter turned to a file on his desk, opened it and removed a piece of paper. "Did you conduct a toxicology report on the deceased?"

"I did."

"And what was found in the toxicology report?"

"The deceased's blood alcohol reading was 0.15, which is associated with being very drunk and having significant effects on coordination and comprehension, especially for a petite, young woman like our Jane Doe. We found an acceptable level of codeine, meaning it wasn't higher than a prescribed dosage, but it was also found the deceased had very high levels of diazepam, which is more commonly sold as Valium. These levels could be deemed fatal."

"How does alcohol interact with diazepam?"

"Not well. The body processes alcohol and diazepam in similar ways, meaning the effect of alcohol may be increased. Common side effects of this interaction may be extreme drowsiness, and the victim's breathing may have slowed significantly."

"And what are the significant signs of a diazepam overdose?"

"When a person consumes too much of the substance, the body may react with certain signs. Each person is different, but the signature indicators of a diazepam overdose include a deep sleep and slowed breathing rate. Other signs may include fatigue, confusion, lack of awareness, and uncoordinated movements. Jane Doe may not have been responsive at all before her death."

"Is it possible that even without the impact of the strike, Jane Doe may have died from an overdose of diazepam, due to the interaction with alcohol?"

"With the levels of drugs we found in her blood, yes, that's possible, but death by overdose is very distinctive, and that's not what happened to this young lady. It's clear in the autopsy she died because of a strike to the face and subsequent hemorrhage."

"But do you believe, in your medical opinion, she would've died if she wasn't struck in the face?"

"I believe that without medical assistance she would've died within a few hours."

Hunter turned and stared at Michelle Law. She avoided eye contact. "Dr. Bardon, do you believe she took the drugs herself?"

"I don't know how to answer that question."

"Let me rephrase it for you." Hunter paused and looked at the report in front of him. In truth, he didn't need more time, but he was coaxing the jury to pay attention. Silence can be a sharper weapon than any amount of words. When the jury's eyes were locked onto him, Hunter continued, "Was there any evidence she was forced to take drugs? Perhaps a mark on her throat, or around her neck?"

"Not that I found in the examination." The medical examiner shook his head. "There's no evidence she was forced to consume the drugs that night. We found track marks on her arms, indicating she had previously injected drugs; however, these marks were healed, and from an earlier time."

"With those levels of drugs in her system, would she have been aware of her surroundings?"

"Drugs affect everyone differently, but with the

levels we found in her blood, I don't believe so, no."

"Do you think she would've been able to scream for help?"

"It's my professional opinion that she wouldn't have been coherent, and depending on what stage she was at during the overdose, she may not have been able to talk at all. Certainly, before her death, she wouldn't have been able to communicate clearly."

"Do you believe that, with the levels of drugs and alcohol in her system, she may have fallen and hit her head, causing her death?"

"What we know is that she was tied to the chair at some point shortly before her death, and her wrists and ankles show signs of struggle against a rope. If she were tied to the chair after her death, then there would be no signs of a struggle."

"Could she have been tied up, struggled against the ropes, untied herself, fallen and hit her head, then been tied up again?"

The medical examiner's head tilted to the side before he shrugged. "I suppose that's possible, given the evidence that's available. Unlikely, but yes, I suppose it's possible. However, I would say, given the nature of the impact on the nose, the strike is most likely to have come from a left-handed punch, or a right-handed backhand, rather than a fall."

Hunter flicked over his paper file on the desk. "That wasn't stated in your report."

"The report focuses on the facts. The fact is the strike that caused the death of Jane Doe was from the direction of the left of the attacker. That's stated in the report. However, I'm here for my professional opinion, and in my professional opinion, I would state the strike was from the fist of a left-handed person or from a right-handed backhand."

Hunter looked across to the table next to him, the pen resting in Michelle Law's left hand. He stared at her, his mouth hanging open.

"Defense?" Judge Harrison asked when the questioning didn't continue.

"No further questions," Hunter whispered, thoughts racing through his head.

After the witness was excused, Judge Harrison called a recess for the day's proceedings, and the large crowd murmured their way out of the courtroom.

"Tex?" It was Sulzberger, next to Hunter, desperate to know what was happening. "What's wrong?"

"Nothing's wrong." Hunter began to close the files on the table. "Everything is just falling into place."

# CHAPTER 37

HUNTER FELT the pressure continue to build each night.

The mystery woman, 'X,' was right next to him, teasing him with her presence, but he couldn't find a way to expose her in court. He had nothing. While Ray Jones investigated the link, Hunter's focus had to remain on winning the trial. His focus had to be on securing a not guilty verdict.

By the third morning, when Law called her next witness, the trial tactic had become clear—she would use people in respectable positions to question the mental stability of Robert Sulzberger. She knew the jury would respond better to emotions than cold hard facts. And once the jury was emotionally invested in the outcome, Law would call expert witnesses to the stand, adding to the puzzle piece by piece until there was an overwhelming feeling that Sulzberger had to be guilty.

The first witness to talk about Sulzberger's mental instability was the Mayor of Chicago, Nancy Quinn, a strong voice and a respectable presence. Quinn was always going to lay it on thick. She was going to use the public platform to inform people that she'd asked him to get help for his mental health issues in the weeks before the murder. For her, walking to the stand wasn't about convicting a killer; it was about protecting her public image.

"Thank you for taking the time to talk with us today, Mayor Quinn." Law began, seated behind her desk, one leg crossed over the other. "Do you know Mr. Sulzberger, the defendant in this case?"

"I do. I'm the Mayor of Chicago, and Mr. Sulzberger is a member of the Chicago City Council. He works as an alderman in the 44th Ward. I've known Mr. Sulzberger for several years."

"In your interactions with Mr. Sulzberger, was he violent?"

"Objection," Hunter stated. "This is prejudicial. The defendant has never been charged with a violent crime, and this information is not relevant. It's of no significance to this case and if included, could be seen as harmful to the fairness of this trial."

"I argue it's relevant, Your Honor," Law retorted. "We're asking the witness to describe her personal experiences, and the things she has personally witnessed. We're not asking her to relay anything she hasn't seen."

"I'll allow it," Judge Harrison responded. "However, Mayor Quinn, you must only talk about your personal experiences and the things that you've personally seen."

"Let me rephrase the question for the benefit of the court." Law looked across to Hunter, smiled, and then continued. "During the time you've known Mr. Sulzberger, have you ever witnessed him behave violently?"

"A few times." Quinn's voice was firm. "He had a fire inside him, and he was known to be aggressive. I saw him push another City Council member during a heated debate in my office, and that person fell to the floor."

"Were there any other incidents of violence that you witnessed?"

"Yes. I saw Mr. Sulzberger punch a man in a bar. I'm not sure what they were arguing about but I was sitting down in a booth, and Mr. Sulzberger and this other man started pushing each other, and then Mr. Sulzberger threw a punch, which knocked the man over. I think that—"

"Objection to the word 'think,'" Hunter interrupted. "It calls for characterization."

"Sustained."

"Your Honor," Law responded. "Mayor Quinn can testify about what she saw."

"She can testify about what she saw, but she's not allowed to add her personal opinion to them." Judge Harrison was firm and turned to the witness. "As a former lawyer, I expect you to know that, Mayor Quinn."

"Very well." Law turned a page in her file. "Mayor Quinn, did you speak to Mr. Sulzberger the day before the body was found in his basement?"

"I did." Quinn moved in her seat. "We had a discussion about the stadium approval. Mr. Sulzberger talked to me in my office, and he said that he was thinking about withdrawing his support for the project. I told him that this was a very bad idea, and that the community needed the project to go ahead. Of course, the approval had already been given for the stadium, so withdrawing his support would've had little effect, however, it would've damaged his public image."

"How do you think Mr. Sulzberger was feeling that day?"

"Objection to the word 'think,'" Hunter stated. "It's hearsay."

"Sustained," Judge Harrison replied. "Ms. Law, please stick to the facts when asking your questions."

Law nodded, irritated that Hunter had interrupted her rhythm. "How did Mr. Sulzberger behave that day when he was in your office?"

"He slapped his hand on the desk numerous times. He raised his voice and was quite aggressive towards me. He was so aggressive that my secretary called my phone to make sure I was alright. He even threw a file across my office."

"During this interaction on the day before the murder occurred, did you feel threatened by his presence?"

"Yes. Mr. Sulzberger is a large man, much bigger than I am, and he has a presence when he becomes angry. I felt threatened during that conversation. If I'd known what he was about to do—"

"Objection. Speculation."

"Sustained," Judge Harrison agreed. "Mayor Quinn, you know better than that. If you wish to make those sorts of accusations, then I will have to hold you in contempt."

Quinn nodded, and then Law continued. "On this day, just hours before the body was found, how did Mr. Sulzberger's voice sound?"

"Objection to the use of the word 'sound,'" Hunter interrupted again. "It calls for characterization."

"Sustained."

"Your Honor," Law responded, increasingly

frustrated. "Mayor Quinn can testify to what happened in her office."

"She can testify to the words she heard, but she's not allowed to characterize what happened." Judge Harrison was firm.

"Very well." Law turned another page on her desk. "Mayor Quinn, did you think Mr. Sulzberger was about to become physically violent?"

"Objection to 'think.' Again, it's speculation."

"Sustained."

"Right." Law looked at her notes, struggling to maintain her focus. "Did you advise Mr. Sulzberger to do anything that day?"

"I did. I advised him to seek help for his mental health. It was clear he was struggling, and I advised him that I knew a very good therapist who could assist him. I wanted to help him with any issues he had."

"Was this the only time you had advised him to seek help for his mental health?"

"No, it wasn't. I'd been advising him to seek help in the weeks before this. I was asking if he was ok, and checking on him, but it was clear to me that he needed professional help." She drew a breath. "I did all that I could to help, but in the end, he had to make the decision to seek assistance himself."

"After the events of that day, were you surprised to hear that Mr. Sulzberger had murdered someone?"

"Objection!" Hunter called out. "The question assumes facts not in evidence."

"Sustained." Judge Harrison's response was flat. "Ms. Law, I won't warn you again. Please stick to questions that are able to be answered by the witness."

Law smirked as she looked across to Hunter. She knew exactly what she was doing. She was planting a seed in the minds of the jurors, planting a tiny drop of information that would be given the chance to grow in the coming weeks.

"No further questions." Law finished.

Hunter waited a few moments before he began. He opened a file, read the first few lines, and then stood and walked to the lectern at the side of the room. He didn't have many questions to ask Mayor Quinn, however, he needed to highlight the lack of direct evidence in her statement.

"Mayor Quinn, did Mr. Sulzberger ever hit you?"

"No."

"Did he mention Jane Doe during that interaction with you on October 5th?"

"No, he didn't."

"Did you witness Mr. Sulzberger be violent towards Jane Doe?"

"No, of course not."

"Did you witness Mr. Sulzberger and Jane Doe together?"

"No."

"Did you witness someone entering Mr. Sulzberger's home that day?"

"No, I wasn't even at his home."

"Did you witness Mr. Sulzberger punch anyone that day?"

"No."

"It appears you didn't witness a lot, Mayor Quinn," Hunter said. "No further questions."

Before Quinn could be excused from the witness stand, a man from the back of the crowd rose to his feet and announced, "Sulzberger's a traitor and a killer! Don't let him go free!"

"Shut your mouth!" Judge Harrison roared. His face was red. "There will not be any shouting in my courtroom! Get out of this room. Bailiffs remove him!"

As the bailiffs removed the man from the courtroom, holding onto his arms, Judge Harrison asked Law for a redirect, which she declined, before he excused the witness from the stand. He then turned to the jury and instructed them to disregard the interruption from the yelling man.

The tension in the courtroom was building, and it wasn't finished yet.

# CHAPTER 38

AFTER ANOTHER day and a half of witnesses, Law called Sulzberger's assistant, Teresa Hardcastle, to the stand. As the time drifted into Friday afternoon, Teresa Hardcastle was the last witness for the week. It was a transparent tactic from the prosecution—they needed the jurors to leave for the weekend thinking about the mental stability of Robert Sulzberger.

Hunter had spent his time torn between finding evidence to link Michelle Law to Sulzberger, and focusing on winning the trial. After the first week of the case, he wasn't succeeding at either.

Teresa Hardcastle walked to the stand with her shoulders back. She wore a black suit, complete with trousers and a jacket. Her black hair was pulled back tightly into position, not a strand out of place, and her make-up was poorly done. She hated being paraded in front of the judging eyes in the courthouse.

"Miss Hardcastle," Law began as the witness struggled to find a comfortable position to sit. "Can you please tell the court how you know Mr. Sulzberger?"

"I've worked as his assistant for the past five months. I work out of his office in the 44th Council

Ward."

"Would you describe yourself as close to Mr. Sulzberger?"

"No." She shook her head. "He wasn't a very nice man to work for."

"And why is that?"

"He was angry a lot of the time, and he used to throw things around the office when he lost control."

"Lies," Sulzberger mumbled under his breath, shaking his head.

"As his assistant, did you have a lot to do with his personal life?"

"I did."

"Did he ask you to organize anything in his personal life?"

"He did. He'd sometimes ask me to organize inappropriate things."

"Can you please give the court an example of an inappropriate request?"

"He asked me to organize a prostitute for him."

"I did not!" Sulzberger slapped his hand on the table and leaped to his feet. "That's a lie!"

"Mr. Sulzberger!" Judge Harrison was loud in his response. "There will be no outbursts like that in this courtroom. Let this be your one and only warning to keep your mouth shut!"

Sulzberger drew a deep breath, nodded, straightened himself out, and sat back down. "Sorry, Your Honor. It won't happen again."

Law waited a few moments before she continued. "And when he asked you to organize a prostitute for him, did you?"

"No. I told him I wasn't comfortable doing that. I didn't want anything to do with that sort of behavior."

"And how did he react when you told him no?"

"Angrily. He shouted at me, and then told me to go home."

"How many times did he ask you to organize a prostitute for him?"

"Twice."

"And what was the last time he asked you to do this?"

"October 5th."

One jury member gasped, and then covered her hand over her mouth. Once Law heard this, she nodded to the witness and then turned to Judge Harrison. "No further questions."

Hunter waited a few moments before he began questioning Teresa Hardcastle. Hardcastle squirmed in her chair, anxious to finish her public appearance.

"Miss Hardcastle, do you ever drink at work?" Hunter asked, staying seated behind the defense table.

"Uh," Teresa stumbled over the answer. "I don't usually."

"You don't usually?" Hunter sighed. "How many times did your employer officially warn you about drinking at work?"

"I don't know," she whispered.

"Ten." Hunter's response was blunt. "Your employer, Mr. Sulzberger, wrote you up for drinking at work ten times within five months."

"I drink because sometimes the scenes I saw at war get too much." She kept her voice low, embarrassed by her behavior. "The drinking helps numb the nerves and the thoughts of war."

Hunter nodded and lowered his voice as well. He didn't like attacking Teresa Hardcastle on the stand, but he had to do his job. "Were you drinking on October 5th?"

Teresa took a few moments, looking around the room. "That day was a hard one. I'd woken up with some issues, and I needed a drink that morning."

"And did Mr. Sulzberger send you home at lunchtime?" Hunter's tone was soft.

She nodded.

"Please respond verbally for the court."

"He did," she said. "He could see I was struggling so he sent me home."

"And what time did he ask you to organize a prostitute for him?"

She looked away from Hunter, the tears building in her eyes.

"Miss Hardcastle?" Hunter questioned.

"He must've asked me in the morning."

"And where was he that morning?"

She shrugged.

"He wasn't in the office. In fact, that day, he only interacted with you for fifteen minutes, and that was when the publicist for Mr. Sulzberger, Ms. Mary-Lou Jones, was also in the office. It was in that fifteen minutes that he could see you were struggling and sent you home. Ms. Mary-Lou Jones has also provided a statement to the court. So, I'll ask you again, Miss Hardcastle, what point during the day did Mr. Sulzberger ask you to organize a prostitute for him?"

"I..." She paused and dropped her head. "I must've gotten my days mixed up."

"Are you saying now that Mr. Sulzberger didn't ask you this on October 5th?"

"That's right," she said. "I must've gotten my days

mixed up. He didn't ask me on that day."

The entire courtroom went silent. Teresa sat on the stand, frozen.

"Your Honor, we have no further questions for this witness, however, we reserve the right to recall her as a defense witness."

Hunter closed the file in front of him, shaking his head. He saw one of the jury members do the same. Judge Johnson instructed the jury on how to respond to the testimony of Teresa Hardcastle and then called an end to the week's proceedings.

"They're all lying. How can they do that?" Sulzberger leaned close to Hunter and asked as the crowd moved out. "How is that allowed?"

"It isn't." Hunter's response was blunt. "But it gives us a chance to throw this whole mess out on appeal."

# CHAPTER 39

AFTER THE close of the fifth day of the trial, Hunter couldn't get out of the courthouse quick enough. He pushed through the yelling media pack waiting outside the doors of the building, ushering Sulzberger behind him, the yells close enough to feel the spray of spit on his face. There was desperation in the media push; desperation to get a sound bite from Sulzberger, something to play on the evening news. And if they could get that sound bite, they would play it over and over and over again on the twenty-four-hour news channels.

The uniformed police tried to hold the reporters back, arms spread wide, but one of the young journalists pushed too hard, too eager, and his microphone hit Hunter in the face. It was a rookie error.

Hunter stopped.

The crowd ceased pushing. They saw the look in his eyes. Everyone took a step back, their voices hushed by his intense stare.

"Sorry, sir." The young reporter sounded like he was begging for his life.

Hunter didn't respond. Instead, he guided Sulzberger to the curb, and the remaining reporters parted ways, allowing safe passage to the waiting SUV. The noise of the pack became muted, all of them aware they had overstepped the mark.

Hunter opened the back door to the waiting black Chevy Suburban, allowing Sulzberger to enter first before he turned back to the crowd.

As he looked over the crowd, he spotted his nephew on the steps of the courthouse. Max looked nervous.

Once he entered the rumbling car, Hunter took out his phone and called Max. "Max. Walk to your left. We'll circle the block and then pick you up."

After the car with tinted windows had done a lap around the city block, most of the media pack had already dispersed, the remaining ones conducting live crosses to their networks, with Michelle Law waiting for interviews with numerous crews.

"Max. Are you okay?" Hunter asked, after he opened the door for his nephew to climb inside.

Sulzberger moved across the back seat, creating enough room for the skinny eighteen-year-old to sit.

"I'm good, Uncle T. It's all these cops; they make me nervous." His eyes scanned the man next to him. "I've been following you."

"Pardon?" Sulzberger turned his head to stare at Hunter. "He's been following me?"

"At my request," Hunter stated. "I needed somebody who would blend into the background, somebody who wouldn't be noticed. I had a suspicion that someone would need to keep tabs on you, and I needed to know who was interested. He—"

"I've got something," Max said, his actions jerking. "Go on."

Max looked at the driver, then out the window,

then back at Sulzberger. Being trapped behind the tinted windows made him uneasy. The car was slowly edging forward, muffled in the workday traffic. The new car smell was still strong inside, the leather seats still squeaky new. It wasn't the type of place Max had been used to in the past year.

"Someone is following Robert," Max continued.

"Who?"

"A woman."

Hunter sighed and leaned back in the seat, his shoulders dropping from their height of tension. It was a revelation he wished had come a day earlier. "I know, Max. There she is over there, talking to the media."

Hunter pressed the button to wind down the window, and he pointed to the television cameras as Law began to answer questions, the mobile spotlight beaming on her.

"Where is she?"

"The woman there." Hunter pointed to the media again. "The woman talking to the reporters with the dark hair."

"Where?"

"The woman with the spotlight on her, where the television camera is pointing."

Max squinted. Michelle Law was only twenty-five yards away. He blinked and stared intently.

"Uncle T, that's not her."

"Take another look, Max." Hunter shook his head.

Max stared again, almost leaning out the window.

"Uncle T, that isn't the woman that's been following Robert everywhere."

"Are you sure, Max?" Hunter leaned forward again.

"Absolutely. There was a different woman following him." Max scratched his chest. "And the woman looked like a killer."

# CHAPTER 40

DESPITE THE long, tiring week she'd had, this was the moment she had been looking forward to.

Listening to all those people tell their stories, trying to frame Sulzberger for what she did, she occasionally smiled—not a smile wide enough to let anyone know what she was thinking though. She tried to hide those moments under her long hair.

But even with the court case, even with the charges leveled against Sulzberger, she wasn't sure it was enough to take revenge.

She wasn't sure whether it was enough to stop him. That lawyer, the son of a serial killer, was clever. She knew that. He might even get him off the charges. Set him free.

She had to finish the job. Get her revenge.

When she accidentally killed the prostitute, although it wasn't planned, she thought it was quite serendipitous. Prison could've been the right answer for Sulzberger. She thought it would've been sufficient. But now that he was facing a future behind bars, she knew it wasn't enough. There wasn't a sense of satisfaction for her. There wasn't a sense of achievement.

She had to do more than that.

She had to make him pay for what he did—the way he rejected her.

And if Sulzberger beat the charges, then she wouldn't be able to stop him. He'd keep doing what he always did—using people, using the system. His lawyer looked confident, and it filled her with a sense of dread.

Her life relied upon her being seen as a respectable citizen. A person who had it all together. Her reputation had to come first. She needed to be seen as someone with all the answers.

That was why she had to finish off Sulzberger. He was the crack in her armor. He was the reason she could no longer sleep at night.

She had to finish him.

She looked at the gun, cleaned and ready, sitting on the kitchen bench. The room was dark, lit only by the city lights pouring through the open curtains. She preferred it that way. Despite all the furnishings, despite all the goods in her home, it felt cold and empty. Lonely. Love hadn't been in that room for years.

She'd polished the gun, and she took great joy in making sure it was perfect. Not a spot on it.

Having the gun in her hand brought back so many feelings. So many thoughts. Her messed-up childhood. Her mistakes. All of her bad decisions. That childhood, laced with pain and fear, had haunted her for so long—always in the back of her mind. Always there, always present. She had never been able to shake it.

Someone had to pay. Someone had to be taken out. It had to be him.

He was so much like the men from her childhood.

So much like the men that caused her pain. Killing him would be the answer she had looked for. Better than any therapy, better than any drugs.

He probably knew it was her. She almost expected the door to swing open and the police to charge in. There was a chance he could point the finger.

She couldn't let him do that. This was her only opportunity.

This time, she wouldn't back away. She wouldn't run in fear.

This time, she would finish the job.

# CHAPTER 41

THE APARTMENT stunk of testosterone. Hunter sat on the edge of the bed, Sulzberger on the couch next to it, both men tapping their feet with nervous energy. The place looked like it belonged to college students—clothes hanging over the furniture, beer cans piled up next to the trash, empty takeaway boxes next to the sink. The room was narrow and dark, creating a sense that the walls were going to close in on them at any second. Both men stared at the floor, bonding in a moment of quiet reflection.

When the knock on the door echoed through the room, Hunter leaped to his feet and opened the door. Ray Jones walked in without a word.

"It didn't go well in court today?" Jones shut the door behind him.

"It could've gone better," Hunter said. "A lot better."

"I'll give you the good news first then," Jones stated. "We can rule the wife out."

"Kim? You've ruled her out?" Sulzberger was surprised. "That's great news."

"Her story that she was out of town on a hike checks out. I managed to talk to the ranger of the preserve. He'd been on a three-month vacation in

244

Peru, and I couldn't get hold of him until recently. He said he clearly remembered Kim because she seemed so underprepared for an overnight walk. He took down all her details, including the car registration, and said she had to be back within two days or he would send a search party out for her. He described her perfectly, so she now has an alibi."

"Could be a setup?" Hunter turned to Sulzberger. "We could be dealing with two killers here."

"So why wouldn't she have mentioned the alibi before?" Jones sat down on the black couch, leaning back with a relaxation that escaped the other men. "It's a stretch to suggest she set this up and then forgot about it when you pressed her for an alibi. If it were a setup, it would've been the first thing she said. She would've been prepared to answer the questions."

"It's a stretch, but it's not impossible," Hunter said. "What about Michelle Law? Did you find anything that ties her to Robert?"

"Unfortunately, I've got nothing. I've checked video surveillance footage, I've asked people that know her, and I've spent hours upon hours searching online. All of that work has amounted to nothing." Jones shook his head. "If you could get her on the stand, we'd clean this thing up within an hour. The case would be over."

"Unfortunately, it's not that easy."

"Why not? You know she's the killer, and you have the skills to nail her. I've never seen a better interrogator than you. I'm surprised the CIA haven't come knocking, asking you to question their targets."

"We can't put her on the stand without proof," Hunter stated. "And right now, we haven't got anything."

"What's your play then?"

"She claimed she didn't know Robert and stated that directly to the judge. If we can find one piece of evidence, one piece at all, that links them together, then we can get her off the case and onto the stand in a different trial. That's our opportunity."

"You'd destroy her career," Jones stated.

"She's a cold-blooded killer." Sulzberger went to the fridge to look for more beer. "There's a chance my daughter is going to grow up without a father because of her. Her career is the last thing you should be worried about."

"We don't know she's a killer yet. So many people—" Hunter turned to look at Robert. "Sorry, Robert, but so many people hated you. Just because you were having an affair doesn't mean she's a killer. I look at her, and I don't see a killer. I see a woman that's falling apart, maybe an alcoholic, but I don't see a murderer. I thought X was our best hope, but I don't think Michelle Law is our answer." Hunter stepped closer to Sulzberger and pushed the fridge door shut before the man could reach for a beer. "If we can delay the case because of her conflict of interest, then we're a step closer to winning."

Sulzberger nodded and turned away from the fridge.

"That's going to be hard." Jones stood up. "So, Tex, what do you need me to do?"

"Ray, I need you to find out everything about Michelle Law's past."

# CHAPTER 42

HE WOULD pay.

She was sure of that.

She had never felt more betrayed, more hurt after what he did to her. He had her heart in his hands, her future, and he unremorsefully squashed it. She'd lose everything because of what he did to her. Everything she fought so hard to build. Everything she'd pushed for.

She had been scoping out the apartment from the street for an hour, waiting patiently in a café with a baseball cap on. The café was quiet, the five round tables only sparsely filled, and the staff behind the long counter were more interested in checking their phones than watching their customers.

In her handbag, under her arm, was her balaclava, and underneath that, her gun. The one that would solve all her problems.

Revenge had always been her greatest weakness. She wouldn't let this chance slip by her. She would have her revenge.

As two tall men exited the apartment building, she put her head down, the cap covering her face. She pretended to read an article on her phone as they walked past the café window without saying a word to each other. The solemn look on their faces was what she expected.

They were men of action, not big talkers. She was surprised one of them was a lawyer, but that's what happens when you grow up with serial killer parents.

After they had left the building, she crossed the road, and followed another resident to the secure entrance, slipping in behind them. She walked straight to the stairs and began her walk up to her fate.

This was her chance. Her time for revenge.

If she could do it with a knife, she would. It'd be quieter that way. Perhaps even more enjoyable.

If it had to be the gun, then that was what she'd do. She was confident she could outmuscle him, take him down. She knew she could do it. Quickly in and quickly out. That'd been her plan for the past two days now.

He had to pay.

She would have her revenge.

# CHAPTER 43

HUNTER AND Jones walked out of the apartment building in silence, past the residents returning home, past the travelers mingling on the sidewalk, and past the youths congregating near an alley. There wasn't much left to say between them. They'd come together, investigated a case, and faced a trial, but they were staring at defeat when the answers were so close.

"What did you find in Bronzeville?" Hunter asked as they crossed the road.

"A lead, but nothing certain. I've got my best girl on it; she's asking around the area. We'll know in the next twenty-four hours."

"I really need that magic, Ray. I really need something."

Jones nodded.

When they reached the car, Jones stopped and looked back at the apartment building, almost shrouded under darkness. "They have to be connected somehow. Robert and Michelle Law—there must be something that links them. Something, somewhere."

"There has to be," Hunter stated. "I've thought about it so much, and I've come up with nothing.

Even if we could match the location data on Michelle's mobile phone with Robert's, it still doesn't prove anything. It only proves she was in the same place at the same time, perhaps coincidentally. She could even argue that Robert was stalking her, and she knew nothing of it. We've got nothing on her."

"It would prove there's at least some doubt to her story that she doesn't know him."

"But it doesn't prove she was involved in the murder of Jane Doe either. It wouldn't prove anything, and any judge in Chicago will laugh at that evidence. All we have are a few social media posts about how she likes his work as a celebrity and politician."

"Maybe you could request the judge to release her mobile phone data? Track her movements via her data on the night of Jane Doe's death?"

Hunter laughed. "Good luck with that. Could you imagine trying to get a prosecutor's location data on the back of a hunch? She's good friends with every judge in town. We wouldn't even make it in the door before they'd kick us back out."

"True." Jones smiled. "There are two kinds of lawyers—those who know the law, and those who know the judge."

"Just as well I know the law then. I need DNA evidence. It wouldn't be admissible in court, but it could give us leverage. Do you think you could get a DNA sample from Michelle?"

"Easy enough." Jones shrugged. "I should have it by the morning—perhaps a drink bottle or a strand of hair. Should be very easy to get some DNA from Michelle."

"We'll work on it. Let's get her DNA. I need you

to focus on that." Hunter checked his coat for his car keys. He patted down his pockets, then his trousers, and then he opened his briefcase, searching for them. "Ah."

"What's up?"

"I've left my keys on the bench in Robert's apartment."

"Just call him. Get him to bring them back down."

"No, I'll head back up. I don't need Robert walking around out here, gathering attention. It wouldn't be a good look at this time of night, and I'm sure there'll be some media vans around here waiting for a late night snap."

Jones nodded, leaning against the car. "Don't leave me too long out here. You never know what could happen with those media types."

"That's right." Hunter turned and began to walk back towards the apartment building. "In a case like this, you never know who is hiding what."

# CHAPTER 44

SHE WAS at the door of the apartment.

It was close to the fire exit. In a quick sprint down the hall, it was four seconds away, maybe five. Perfect. Once she was in the room, there would be no talking, no explanations. She would do what she needed to do and then make a quick exit. If there were no fuss, she'd walk quietly with her head down. It'd be at least twelve hours before anyone found his body. She'd have her story straight then. One, maybe two, alibis.

She was good at propping doors open, not that the apartment door was hard. Her years of training had never left her. With a simple twist, a turn of her credit card in the gap next to the doorknob, and a light shove, it was pried open.

She was in.

Stepping into the dimly lit apartment, she heard the shower running in the room at the end of the suite. That'd make it easier. Cleaner. He'd be naked and defenseless.

She liked that.

Taking his life when he was naked. Leaving him there to die slowly in all his vulnerability, stripped bare before her. The way he started life would be the way he ended it. She wasn't nervous—only filled with the sense of satisfaction that came with knowing her revenge was moments away. All her troubles were in the shower.

Leaving the door slightly ajar for a quick exit, she walked towards the back of the room, hand gripping the knife tightly. She'd reclaim her life now.

This would be the second phase of her life, the time to start again. She could come back, try to rebuild her career. No one would ever know what she had done. They couldn't.

There was a knock on the apartment door.

It was loud. Heavy.

She froze.

Room service, maybe. She waited to hear if the water in the shower stopped. It kept running.

She reached for her gun. Placed the knife back in her bag.

Another knock. Louder this time.

The door was open.

She was exposed.

Vulnerable.

And there was nowhere to hide.

# CHAPTER 45

TEX HUNTER knocked on the door again. No answer.

"What could he possibly be doing?" he moaned to himself. "Robert?" he called. "I need my car keys. I left them on the bench."

He stepped back, checking the number on the apartment door, ensuring he'd gotten the right one, but then he noticed it was slightly ajar.

"Robert?" He leaned forward, pushing on the door. "Robert? Can you hear me? I need my keys."

He leaned into the apartment. Hearing the water running in the shower, he sighed and pushed the door open further. He walked inside, looking for the light switch.

The shadow hit him. From behind, right at the base of the skull. Shock pulsed through his body. He fell to the floor.

In the dark, he saw the shadow reaching for the door. Dazed, he lunged at the person.

Grabbed it.

The shadow swung again. A gun was suddenly in his face.

Hunter let go, and on instinct, flung his left hand towards the weapon, knocking it away.

It fell.

The shadow, dressed in black, face covered in a balaclava, kicked him between the legs. He buckled, but then lunged again. The shadow's hand caught on the doorframe, ripping what sounded like a shirt sleeve.

Hunter stretched, pushed at the hand, but the shadow was nimble.

The shadow let out a yelp, clearly feminine.

She kicked again. Connected between his legs again. He was stunned.

The shadow was quick. Before he knew it, she'd collected the weapon and was heading towards the fire escape.

Hearing the commotion, Sulzberger stepped out of the bathroom with a towel wrapped around him. "Tex?"

Without a word, Hunter stood and looked down the corridor.

Gone.

"There was someone here." He looked back to Sulzberger. "They had a gun."

"What?"

Hunter took out his phone. "Ray, get to the fire exit. Stop whoever comes out of it."

"On it," Jones said.

Hunter hung up. "I don't know who it was." He looked back at Sulzberger, then at the doorframe. "But that's going to help."

He pointed to the doorframe that had caught the edge of the woman's arm. The fabric from her sleeve was left on the edge of the frame.

And so was her blood.

# CHAPTER 46

AFTER HE spent the weekend talking to the police, Hunter walked back into the George N. Leighton Criminal Courthouse. He hadn't had more than a few hours' sleep in days. The hours he slept in his office that morning weren't even deep. Not that he needed sleep. Adrenaline was coursing through his veins.

On the previous Friday night, Jones was too late to get to the fire escape door, but he saw the shadow race across the street. He tried to chase her, but his heavy frame wasn't designed for sprinting more than a few hundred yards. The shadow was as nimble as it was determined.

Hunter took a swab from the doorframe, bagging some of it up before the police arrived to do the same. They viewed the security footage and asked for witnesses, but they got nothing.

Tex Hunter entered the courtroom, Sulzberger behind him, and Esther trailing them. Esther insisted she was able to help with Sulzberger's case, even with a headache that had lasted days.

Michelle Law sat at the front of the room, ready for the day ahead, busily typing on her laptop.

"Late night on Friday night, Michelle?" Hunter

stepped close to her.

She turned, looking perfectly awake. "I've had enough beauty sleep if that's what you're asking."

He stared at her for a few long moments before leaning closer. "We have you, X."

She squinted before leaning back to look at Sulzberger. "X is a figment of Robert's imagination. A way to explain what's happened in his past—it's quite common in people with PTSD. If X were a real person, you'd have evidence she existed, right?"

"You won't get away with what you did Friday night." Hunter was blunt.

"Friday night?" Her eyebrows scrunched together. "What are you claiming X did on Friday night?"

Hunter stared at her again for a long moment. "You can only hide for so long. We've got you. This game is over."

"I was at home Friday night, rereading this file." She waved the paper in the air. "The work never stops."

Hunter stood back, his heart banging within the walls of his chest. He needed patience. His time would come. He was sure it was a woman who attacked him. He told the police as such.

They questioned him for hours and took the DNA evidence away from the scene, but it would be weeks before the results came back. He pressed the police for a quicker turnaround, but they wouldn't hear it. They had enough work to do before they started to worry about a politician and a defense lawyer—not their favorite people in the world. At least a month, he was told.

He didn't have that long.

Hunter considered asking for a court recess, a

break in the case to deal with the attack, but this was his chance, his opportunity to turn the screws on Michelle Law. He sat at the defense table, staring at nothing, trying to think of a way to expose the prosecutor.

As Judge Harrison walked in, and the jury was ushered inside, Hunter watched Law closely, looking for any hint of fatigue.

She showed nothing—no bags under her eyes, not a yawn, not even a cup of coffee on her desk. As she questioned the first witness of the day, another medical expert, her voice sounded fresh and awake. There wasn't one missed step; not one missed beat.

He had no doubt she was X.

But he was starting to doubt whether he could prove it in time.

# CHAPTER 47

AS LAW called the next witness of the day, Hunter had his head down, studying the holes in his case. He didn't doubt Sulzberger's innocence now. The life of the innocent man next to him rested in his hands, but he wasn't sure he could save him. The chance to save a guiltless man was a horrible, unbearable weight to carry. One small mistake would mean Sulzberger's death.

Hunter looked around the courtroom. Kim Sulzberger was sitting in the front row of the public gallery; her hair was a mess and her makeup barely done. He stared at her for a few long moments before Law's voice caught his attention again.

"Thank you for joining us today, Mrs. Cindy Mendel. Can you please begin by telling us about your relationship with the defendant?" Law began her questioning, sitting behind her desk, laptop glowing in front of her.

"The relationship between Robert and I used to be quite tight. We ran for office off the same platform, and we shared a lot of the same values in politics. Obviously, we were both members of the Democrats, but it was more than that. We bonded because we both wanted to help the veterans of our country, state, and city."

"Are you a veteran of the army?" Law questioned her mentor.

"That's correct. I served in Iraq, but was medically discharged after one year." Cindy rubbed her left shoulder. "I didn't serve with Robert, but we had a common understanding of each other's outlook on life."

"And your husband, Liam Mendel, may he rest in peace, did he serve his country as well?"

"He did. He suffered a lot after we returned from war, and eventually, it all became too much. He committed suicide. I walked into my kitchen one afternoon and found him hanging from the roof. He couldn't deal with what he saw in Iraq." She paused for a moment and looked at the ground. "That's why I went into politics—to help returning veterans like my husband. I wanted to make a difference. Robert Sulzberger and I began politics together, and I almost felt like we were a team, helping our people."

"And did Mr. Sulzberger maintain this value? Did he keep representing veterans?"

"No. No, he didn't."

Hunter read the notes in front of him, trying to steer his attention away from Law and back to what he could do for the case. After Friday night's events, he was hopelessly underprepared for the week ahead.

He reread the witness' file, spotting things he hadn't seen before.

"What did Mr. Sulzberger do that made you question his ethics?"

"Robert Sulzberger was voted into politics on the back of his ability to defend this country and what he could do for the brothers and sisters that have done the same. But did he? No, he didn't. He abandoned them. He voted to close down an essential community support center for returned veterans to build a new stadium. He abandoned his people for the sake of a stadium."

Hunter continued to read the file.

"Could you make a difference without Mr. Sulzberger?"

"Without Robert's support in the Council, I'll be out at the next election. That's why we were so good together."

"Did you feel Mr. Sulzberger was unstable?"

"Very. He changed ideas faster than anyone I know. He stood for nothing. He'd lost his spine."

Cindy Mendel was a veteran. Familiar with death.

"Did you think he was unhinged?"

"He pushed me once when I got too close."

She had a violent past. Lost control and attacked when approached by a group of teens. Got off on self-defense.

"Did you feel threatened by him?"

"Of course. He's a sizable man. He's tall and broad. He's very threatening."

She hated Robert and the decisions he made for his political career.

"Do you think he's capable of killing?"

"He killed people at war. We know that."

Hated him enough to make him pay for his decisions.

"And when he had the deciding vote for the policy you were pushing for, what was his reaction?"

"Betrayal." She coughed. "He betrayed his people."

Hunter looked up from the file.

Michelle Law handed a glass of water to her mentor.

Cindy reached out her left arm, the sleeve of her shirt rising up.

And that was when Hunter noticed the large, fresh cut on her wrist.

# CHAPTER 48

TEX HUNTER looked across to Cindy Mendel, then to Michelle Law, then back to Cindy.

The shock and confusion on his face was clear, and when Law turned to see what was taking him so long to begin the cross-examination, she squinted. This should've been a simple witness. Nothing wild. No accusations. No surprises. Cindy Mendel was a respected citizen, a politician, a person who worked to better the community.

As Hunter began to turn his attention to the witness, an email notification appeared on his laptop screen. It was from Jones. Quickly, he opened it, read it, and it had everything he needed to see.

"Mr. Hunter?" Judge Harrison was impatient. "Would you please pay attention to this court and begin questioning the witness?"

Hunter paused, then turned his attention to the woman on the stand.

"Thank you for taking the time to talk with us today, Mrs. Mendel."

"My pleasure," she replied, chin up.

"Are you tired this morning? Perhaps you would like a cup of coffee?"

She stared at him. Intently. "I'm fine."

"As a politician in the 4th Ward in the Chicago City Council, do you do a lot of work in the community?"

"I represent the community and I do a lot of work with the disadvantaged. I give them a chance. I work hard to help the people that need an opportunity in life. It's draining work. It takes its toll."

"What toll has it taken on you?"

She squirmed in the chair. "It's no secret I've suffered through depression. I've stated that many times before in interviews. That's the toll it's taken out on me, but it's worth it. It's worth it when you're able to help someone that needs it."

"But who's helping you?"

She shrugged, looking away from the eyes on her. "I help myself."

Hunter turned to Law. Law's head was down, unable to watch her mentor's testimony.

"Your medical file states you were discharged from the army after a psychotic episode. Have you had any episodes since?"

"Objection. That's not relevant to this case," Law called out.

"I'm establishing the witness' credentials, Your Honor."

"At this point, I'll allow it, but get to your point quickly, Mr. Hunter," Judge Harrison stated.

"Please answer the question, Mrs. Mendel. After you were medically discharged from the army, did you have any further psychotic episodes?"

"I did." Cindy leaned forward, closer to the microphone. "But not for many years now."

"Did your husband handle these episodes well?"

"Objection." Law's hand slammed down onto the

table, defending her mentor. "Relevance."

"Withdrawn," Hunter replied, before standing to approach the witness. "Mrs. Mendel, have you been prescribed any medicine to deal with your depression?"

"Xanax, Valium, and codeine for my back pain."

Hunter took his time, allowing the answer to sink into the minds of everyone in the courtroom. "Are there a lot of veterans living in your council ward?"

"There are."

"And so, you would've been upset, perhaps even angry, when Mr. Sulzberger rezoned the area for the community center to make way for the stadium development?"

"Of course I was angry. That's no secret. This was my community, this was my place, and we supported people from all over the city, including residents from Robert's council ward, and these bigwigs came in and decided it would be better used for a new sporting complex. No way. This community center made a real difference to people's lives; it didn't just entertain those on television."

"Without Robert's support, you'll be out at the next election, is that correct?"

"That's possible."

"And did the fact you may lose your job make you even angrier?"

"I love my job, and I would hate to lose it."

"Were you angry enough to kill?"

"Objection!" Law threw her hands out, confusion written on her face. "Accusation!"

"Sustained." Judge Harrison was just as confused. "Strike that from the record. Jurors, you'll ignore that question. Defense, I won't have that type of unfounded accusation in my court."

"Withdrawn." Hunter kept his stare on the witness. "Do you support the local women of the area as well as the veterans?"

"Of course I do. I represent everyone in my area."

"Even the women employed as prostitutes?"

She shook her head. "As you know, prostitution is illegal in this state."

"You didn't answer my question."

"I don't know what you're referring to."

"The women that you tried to change."

"I don't know what you're talking about." She shook her head.

Hunter walked closer to her. The seed had been planted in the witness' mind.

"Mrs. Mendel," he began. "Can you please advise where you got the cut on your left arm from?"

Shock washed over Cindy's face as she covered up the cut with her sleeve. "Just…" She faltered. "I cut myself at home over the weekend."

"Really?" Hunter feigned surprise. "Interesting. I'm sure you're aware of how DNA works."

He stared at her. She squirmed.

"If you cut your arm on a door, and left your blood on its frame, then a DNA swab from the door would match a sample taken from you."

She looked away.

"Are you left-handed, Mrs. Mendel?"

"I am."

"And when you help girls from the street, do you usually give them your Valium?"

"No." Her voice was soft. Scared. Just the reaction Hunter needed.

"Did it make you happy to give drugs to these

girls?"

"Objection. Accusation."

"Did you enjoy drugging girls from the street?"

"Objection! Your Honor!"

"Sustained!"

"Did you love taking advantage of them?"

"Enough!" Judge Harrison shouted. "The objection is sustained! Defense, you're on your very last warning. Don't let me discipline you again!"

Hunter paused, walked back to his desk, and tapped his finger on the top of a paper file. "Mrs. Mendel." His voice was calmer. "In your 4th Council Ward, does the area include Bronzeville?"

"That's correct."

"A council ward that's known to be a base for many escorts. Is that right?"

"When I returned from Iraq..." She squirmed again. "I worked with women who were exposed to sex work and tried to rehabilitate them. I didn't persecute them; I helped them."

"Did they get under your skin—these women that wanted to sell their bodies for money?" Hunter closed the gap between them again.

"It's horrible what some women have to go through." She looked away. "They needed to be saved."

"Saved? Did Jane Doe need to be saved? Did any of the girls need to be saved?"

"They all need to be saved!" Cindy shouted. "They all do! Nobody deserves to go through what I went through! I wanted to help them!"

"And when you found Jane Doe that night, did you intend to kill her?"

"Objection!" Law called out. "Your Honor!

Accusation!"

"Sustained!" Judge Harrison shouted. "Defense, you will not make that sort of accusation in the courtroom!"

"Did you mean to kill her, Cindy?"

"I didn't kill anyone!"

"Cindy! Was she meant to die?"

"Objection!"

"Sustained! You're out of order, Mr. Hunter!"

"Cindy, you drugged her! You drugged her with your Valium!"

"No!"

"Mr. Hunter! Control yourself!"

"You killed Jane Doe for a vote!"

"No!"

"You killed her!"

"She wasn't meant to die!"

The courtroom went quiet. Stunned. All eyes were fixated on Cindy Mendel.

Hunter waited.

Cindy looked to the door. Too far away.

He walked closer.

"You didn't mean to kill her, did you?"

"It wasn't meant to happen that way." Cindy buried her face in her hands. "She wasn't meant to die," she repeated, softer this time. The fight in her voice was gone. "She was meant to survive. I didn't mean to kill her. She wasn't supposed to die."

The court hustled, the reporters desperate to get the news out first.

"But Jane Doe did die." Hunter's voice matched the softness of Cindy Mendel's. "And you killed her for revenge."

Hunter stared at Cindy Mendel as she started to

cry. He had exposed a criminal. He had exposed a murderer.

But he wasn't finished. Not yet.

# CHAPTER 49

"IS IT true you're going to fund a new center, near the old one?" Esther asked from the back seat of the BMW.

Tex Hunter drove through the traffic, racing through the orange lights, speeding through the backstreets, trying to keep ahead of any trailing media vans.

"While waiting for the trial, I adjusted my will to leave them one million dollars, so they could set up a new center." Robert Sulzberger sat nervously in the front seat, sweat starting to build across his brow. "And I've sold all my shareholdings. I have the cash to help them, so I will. I'll buy a new place for them. It's the least I can do."

"I even heard that some people are happy you were innocent. It's going to be a good write-up in the Tribune tomorrow," Ray Jones called from the back seat, next to Esther, his hand holding onto the bar above the window.

"Some people are quick to forgive." Hunter looked up and down the street before screeching his tires forward again. "And some people aren't. Some of the men and women won't talk to Robert ever again, but that's not why he's donating the money to them. He's doing it because helping those veterans is the right thing to do."

"The right thing to do?" Esther teased him. "Now I've heard it all—Tex Hunter telling the world he has some sort of moral compass."

"I didn't say I had a moral compass. I'm only interested in the truth." Hunter smiled. "I'll leave the morality for other people to grapple with."

"But you're correct." Sulzberger bounced in his seat as Hunter raced over another bump in the road. He was clearly breaking the speed limit. "It was the right thing to do. I got into politics to help people, and I'm no longer in politics now. I'm done with that. I want to try and help people outside of the paperwork in City Hall. I'll buy a place nearby, and the veteran support groups can use that for their new base. My assistant, Teresa Hardcastle, even contacted me and apologized for trying to kick me while I was down. She was angry with me and I get it—I betrayed her and her family. Hopefully I can help them and do the right thing."

They were closer now.

"I read about Cindy Mendel." Jones checked over his shoulder for any trailing media vans. "She had a large write-up in the paper only a few weeks back. She lived a pretty tough life."

Only three blocks to go.

Straight from the courthouse, once the piles of administrative papers had been signed off, Sulzberger made the call he'd been waiting months to make.

"I was sorry to hear it was her." The nerves started to grow in Sulzberger's stomach. "But it all made sense to me. Everything she did, everything that happened; I should've known it was her."

"She was a cold-blooded murderer, Robert. Don't be too sorry." Hunter pushed the BMW faster.

"I know." Sulzberger shrugged. "But still, she always tried to do good in the world, didn't she? That was always her motivation."

"She killed an innocent woman, punched Esther in the back of the head, and tried to kill you in your apartment. That's not doing good in the world," Hunter stated. "She'd seen a lot of hatred in her life, and a lot of pain. That's got to come out somehow."

"What about the thief?" Esther asked. "The prosecutor, Michelle Law. What happens to her? Does she just get away with what she did?"

"Robert got away with stealing; why shouldn't she?" Hunter turned another corner.

Two blocks now.

"I didn't get away with it." Sulzberger's voice was shaky. "I lost my job. My reputation. My entire life has been turned upside down, and I can never return to the City Council after that. But not Michelle Law. She defied every ethical standpoint for a lawyer, laughed in our faces, and you're just going to let her go back to the same everyday life she led before?"

"That's probably painful enough." Jones laughed, holding on tight as the car raced faster. "For me, her life would be worse than prison."

One block to go.

"Tex, just because she's your old-school alumni doesn't mean she should get away with it," Esther argued. "She played you the whole time. She betrayed the entire justice system just so she could see Robert on the stand. He dumped her, and she took us all for a ride. There's got to be a part of you that needs to take her down?"

"I don't need to take her down, even with her distinct lack of ethics, but I will hit her with some truths. She won't get away from this without a reaction from us," Hunter responded. He looked in the rearview mirror at Jones. "Did you get those DNA samples I asked for?"

"I did. I still have them." He looked at Hunter quizzically. "But the case is over."

"This isn't over yet. Who do you know in the DNA field?"

"I have a few good friends everywhere. But what do you need it for?"

"A hunch."

\*\*\*\*\*

The nerves of a young child are like nothing else.

Waiting on the front steps of her home, Lucy Sulzberger couldn't stand still. She hopped from foot to foot, staring at every car that drove past, her eyes filled with tears. Her body was completely consumed by nerves, starting from her belly, reaching out to drench every limb in anxiety.

She hadn't seen her father in months, and she didn't want to wait another second. She didn't know if she could. All she wanted was to hug the man she worshipped.

At five years old, she saw none of her father's faults or mistakes. Even after her mother explained where her father had been, all she knew was that she wanted to feel his hug again.

The black sedan screeched to a stop at the side of

the street.

Lucy stopped bouncing.

The door to the sedan opened.

"Daddy!" She spotted him in the distance. "Daddy!"

A child doesn't care about her father's issues. They don't care about his problems. They don't care about the arguments he has with their mother. All Lucy cared about was if her father was there for her. There to hug her, to read to her.

Dazed by the Chicago sun, Robert Sulzberger stepped out of the front seat and looked up at his house. His eyes lingered for a second before his focus moved to his daughter running towards him, crying, arms wide open.

He knelt, the force of her hug almost knocking him backward. The connection was an explosion of emotion, tears, and love. She cried. He cried more. He held her tight for the first time in months. This was his moment. His second chance at life. He'd faced death, looked it in the eye, and his only thought was about his family. His daughter. The people he loved. Holding his daughter, holding her so tight, he never wanted the moment to end.

This was everything to him.

When Lucy finally pulled out of the hug, the shoulder of his shirt was soaked in tears. He wiped his eyes with the back of his wrist, not wanting his daughter to see him as such a blubbering mess.

He didn't know what to say.

"Where have you been, Daddy?" Lucy held onto his arm, desperate not to let him go again.

"I'm sorry, sweetie. I'm so sorry I haven't been here. I'll be here more. I promise."

"You'd better make that promise to me too." Kim Sulzberger stood near them, arms folded across her chest, not sure how to feel.

Sulzberger nodded. "I will. I'll be here. I want to be here. I want to try again. With us, as a family. That is if you'll let me stay?"

He looked up at her with wet eyes. She looked away. Sniffed back a tear.

"Please?"

"I would like that." Her response was quiet, but it was her truth. "I would like that a lot."

Tex Hunter walked around the front of the car, provided Kim a nod, and Lucy a smile.

"Thank you, Tex." Sulzberger stood with Lucy attached to his left hip as he held out his right hand. "You saved my life."

"Helping you felt like I was helping my father. After he was arrested, nobody assisted him, nobody helped him search for the truth." Hunter shook Sulzberger's hand firmly, and nodded. "I have to go."

He stepped back into the driver's seat, started the engine and drove away, desperate to avoid the picture of a happy family.

# CHAPTER 50

"WHAT HAVE you come to do?" Michelle Law took a sip from her water bottle, placed it back in the bottom drawer so nobody else would see that it was filled with vodka, and then stared at Tex Hunter. "Whatever it is, make it quick. I've got too much work to get through. I'll be here until midnight even without this meeting."

"I'll be quick." Hunter shut the door behind him.

The feeling in Law's office was frantic, instantly tightening his shoulders. Law sat behind her large desk, everything perfectly organized but almost overflowing with files. She had three computer monitors on one side of the desk, all open with different documents, and large paper folders rested underneath. There were no family pictures in her office, no personal touches—not even a nice cup to drink coffee from.

"But, Michelle, you should clear your calendar for a few days, maybe even a few weeks. This may take a little longer for you to work through."

"You're going to try to nab me for stealing with Robert? No chance. I don't have time to deal with that." She waved him away and then looked back at her computer screen. She attacked the keyboard frantically, the noise from the tapping keys filling the room. "I still have my own midlife crisis to deal with, thanks."

Hunter stood in front of her perfectly organized desk, waiting for her to stop typing. After a few moments, she stopped, unable to ignore his presence any longer.

"You broke the law, Michelle. You're a prosecutor, a symbol of justice, and you repeatedly broke the law."

"We were only stealing small things. And we didn't hurt anyone."

"But what's next? Bigger items? More stealing? Or perhaps you'll move on to a more serious crime."

"I'm not the son of a killer. Killing people is not in my DNA."

"Maybe it is." Hunter held a file in his hands, not quite sure what to do with it yet. "I was sad about Cindy Mendel."

"So was I." Law relaxed her shoulders, leaning back in her chair. "They identified the deceased girl. Anthea Grace. She was a runaway who found herself in the sex trade. Apparently, Cindy picked her up in Bronzeville."

"You were close with Cindy, weren't you?"

"She was the closest person I had in my life. We met more than twenty years ago, and she's been in my life ever since. Always there for me when I needed advice. She was like my family." She held her emotions back. "But I guess, in the end, she was a cold-blooded killer. A felon. There isn't anything more I can say about that. I can't justify what she did just because she was my mentor."

"Family is the world's greatest masterpiece, and I

truly believe that even after everything my family has been through." Hunter looked at her more intently. "Did you tell Cindy about your relationship with Robert?"

"I told her we were dating, but I didn't tell her about the things we did." Law shook her head, and the sadness in her eyes was clear. "I turned to her when he broke it off with me. I was truly heartbroken, and I had to talk to someone, but she was the only person I ever told. I cried about Robert, a lot, and she comforted me."

"Has she written to you since the charges were laid against her?"

"She's written letters, but I haven't read them." She blinked back a tear. "And I don't intend to. She's gone. Like everyone else in my life. They all go away."

Hunter let the silence sit in the room.

"What is it that you needed, Tex? Did you come to gloat that you won? Because the killer is behind bars—that's a win for me too. There'll be no gloating here. And if you're going to try and pin the stealing on me, you'd better be prepared for a fight."

"My investigator took your DNA from a water bottle that you used at the gym."

"What?" She laughed. "Are you trying to prove I stole with Robert? You must know that's inadmissible evidence."

"I know it is, but at the time, we needed a lead for the case. We thought that you, the mystery woman, X, would provide that, so we took your DNA."

"Why tell me that now?" She closed a paper file on her desk.

"Because the result of your DNA sample is about something bigger than this case. This is something that you should know."

"What are you talking about?"

"There's a match to your DNA. It was a hunch of mine, and it turned out to be true."

Her mouth hung open.

"There's more than just a resemblance between you." He tapped the file in his left hand. "Maybe everyone didn't abandon you."

"Tex."

"You must've known. You must've had an idea for all these years."

"Don't say it."

"Did you know? Somewhere, deep down, you must've known. Maybe subconsciously. It was obvious to everyone else."

"Don't do this, Tex. Don't do this."

"We ran a test on the DNA and matched it with another DNA sample we took from the night Robert was almost shot."

"Tex."

"Your mother has been by your side for all these years."

"No." She shook her head. "No."

"People do strange things for their families. She knew who you were and she needed retaliation for what Robert did to you. She needed revenge for you. That's why she went after Robert. It was all for you. It was your revenge."

"It can't be true."

"Michelle, the DNA proves it." Hunter placed the file gently on the edge of her desk. "Cindy Mendel is your birth mother."

The shock didn't last long. For some time, deep down, she'd known the truth. She'd recognized their resemblance. She'd felt their bond. Her tough exterior melted away. Her head fell into her hands and she burst into tears, flooding out like a river. The family she longed for was so close, so near, but so far away.

Hunter walked around the table and rested his hand on her shoulder. An imprisoned family member was something they both had in common, and now, they shared that pain.

# CHAPTER 51

THE WALK through the entrance of the cemetery filled his stomach with nerves. It always did.

The grass was perfectly manicured, the path well trodden, and fresh flowers lay at the foot of a few gravestones, but this wasn't where Tex Hunter was going to stop. He was headed to the back of the yard, where the grass was long, the path was cracked, and flowers were a rarity—where they buried a convicted serial killer.

After he had left Michelle Law with the DNA file, he made the drive to the Queen of Heaven Cemetery in the suburb of Hillside, a yard Hunter had thought was secure enough to protect his mother's gravestone. Although her gravestone had been spray-painted with words of hate twice, he was content with the choice of resting place.

Next to the trees, near the fence, well out of the way of any foot traffic, Patrick Hunter stood in his best suit, looking down at the grave, hands clasped in front of him, saying a few quiet words.

Hunter patted him on the back when he arrived.

"Nice flowers." Hunter laid a bunch of white lilies at the base of the small gray headstone, next to a bunch of purple chrysanthemums. He had to go to five different stonemasons before one would agree to engrave his mother's headstone, and they were out of state. "You don't usually bring flowers."

"They're not mine." Patrick's voice was cold.

Hunter stood, turned, and looked down at his older brother.

"Purple was Natalie's favorite color." Patrick was in no mood for niceties. "She must've ordered them."

"Natalie's back?" Hunter's voice rose. "Have you heard from her?"

"No, Tex. And I don't need to hear from her." Patrick kept his eyes on his mother's grave. There were no graves beside their mother's; no one wanted to be buried near a person with her criminal record.

"She's your sister, Patrick. If she's in town, if she's in the country, we have to find her."

"No, we don't." Patrick's voice calmed. "She left three decades ago, and I'm glad she did."

"You could forgive her for what she did."

"Never. I will never forgive her. If you see her, don't tell me about it." Patrick knelt, kissed the top of the gray stone, and then nodded to his brother.

"She's your family, Patrick."

"She's not my family."

"How can you say that?" Hunter stood tall.

"Family are the people you choose to love. It isn't always blood. Family are the people you choose to do anything for, the people you want to protect. Natalie, our father; they're not my family. They betrayed me. Betrayed us. They pretended we lived an average life. They were always smiling. Laughing. They waved to the neighbors. Dad even coached the junior basketball team. But behind closed doors, they were killing people. Cutting their throats."

"You don't know if Natalie had anything to do with it."

"I don't care if she did anymore. She's not my family. You, Maxwell, our mother..." Patrick paused. "You're my family. You're the people that I hold here." He tapped his chest.

"I saw Maxwell." Hunter was direct.

"What?" Patrick's voice softened. "Why didn't you tell me?"

"I'm telling you now." Hunter turned to look at his brother again. "He came to me for money and said he'd stopped using. I gave him some work, but right now, he doesn't want to talk about what happened. Not to me, and not to you."

Patrick's mouth hung open, unable to respond.

The cold breeze blew around them, the leaves rustling overhead. The sun struggled to find a gap in the clouds, but when it did, at intermittent times, the warmth of the day jumped. The weather was as confused as the look on Patrick's face.

"Family is the world's greatest masterpiece, Patrick. You have to accept that one day. You have to accept that all this is your family."

"Long ago, I accepted that our father is a convicted criminal. You should too." Patrick exhaled, shook his head, and began to walk away.

Hunter watched his brother amble down the path with his head dipped and his hands in his pockets, and then turned back to the gravestone. He bent down and rested his hand on the ground, feeling the damp earth. He drew a long breath and sighed.

"Mom, if Natalie's here, I'll look after her. She's family, and I fight for my family. I haven't stop trying to clear our name. I'm getting closer to the truth, and

I'm going to uncover what really happened to my father. I'm going to get him out of prison." He stood, dusted the grass off his knees, and blew a kiss to his mother. "And I won't stop until I find the truth."

# THE END

# AUTHOR'S NOTE

Thank you so much for reading Power and Justice. I hope you enjoyed the twists and turns in this story. This is the first novel about Tex Hunter and his family, and there are many twists to come about his father's past, which will be revealed throughout the series.

This story was written while I was in New York, working at various co-working spaces, including The Writers Room in Lower Manhattan, and Bat Haus in Brooklyn. Thank you to those places for the support, and a special thank you to Parliament Co-working. To all my amazing family and friends, thank you. To my editor Lara, many thanks for the tips and the ideas for the plot. And thank you to Bel, my cover designer, on her amazing work.

In my travels, whether it's at a co-working space, in a bar, or on a tour, I always come across fascinating people. I believe that everyone has a story, and I love to hear them all. To all the people I've met during my travels, thank you. You've inspired these characters.

And if you enjoyed this book, please leave a positive review. Reviews mean the world to authors.

You can find my website at: peteromahoney.com
And if you wish, you can contact me at: peter@peteromahoney.com

Thank you, Peter O'Mahoney

# ABOUT THE AUTHOR

Peter O'Mahoney is the author of the best-selling Tex Hunter, Bill Harvey, and Jack Valentine thrillers.

O'Mahoney is a criminologist, and uses his experience in this field to guide his stories. He has a keen interest in law and is an active member of the American Society of Criminology.

O'Mahoney was raised on a healthy dose of Perry Mason stories—the pace and style of these books inspired him to write as a teenager, and he hasn't stopped since. He loves exciting characters, breathtaking plots, but more than anything, he loves a great twist. He has worked with various authors on plot design; including J.J Miller, Patrick Graham, and William Thomas. His thrillers have entertained hundreds of thousands of readers around the world.

O'Mahoney splits his time between Chicago and the wide open beaches of Australia.

# ALSO BY PETER O'MAHONEY:

*****

In the Tex Hunter Legal Thriller Series:

**FAITH AND JUSTICE**
**CORRUPT JUSTICE**
**DEADLY JUSTICE**
**SAVING JUSTICE**
**NATURAL JUSTICE**
**FREEDOM AND JUSTICE**

*****

In the Jack Valentine Private Investigator Thriller
Series:

**GATES OF POWER**
**THE HOSTAGE**
**THE SHOOTER**
**THE THIEF**

\*\*\*\*\*

In the Bill Harvey Legal Thriller Series:

**REDEEMING JUSTICE**
**WILL OF JUSTICE**
**FIRE AND JUSTICE**
**A TIME FOR JUSTICE**
**TRUTH AND JUSTICE**

\*\*\*\*\*

# SAMPLE CHAPTERS:

## FAITH AND JUSTICE

## TEX HUNTER
## LEGAL THRILLER
## BOOK 2

# CHAPTER 1

THE CHURCH steps were filled with parishioners, smiling in the winter sunshine, their Sunday morning gossip filling the air.

Thirty potential victims, at least.

Criminal attorney Tex Hunter stood at the edge of the street, looking up at the church steeple, in awe of the structure built almost a century ago. When bells began to ring through the still air, he watched the Baptist church members line up to shake the hand of Reverend Noah Darcy. Reverend Darcy was young, fresh-faced and uncomfortable; still coming to terms with the fact that he was now the leader of the congregation at only twenty-nine years old.

Hunter walked up the concrete steps, hands in his coat pockets, his collar turned up to the damp air. Tall oak trees lined the street, their long shadows dulling the warmth of the sun, and the steeple of the brick church poked out above them. The stained glass windows looked impressive, almost as impressive as the building itself. There was a sense of history in front of Hunter, of a past fought long and hard. This church had seen many battles, and the latest battle against racism was challenging its people to the core.

"You shouldn't be here." An old lady, half his height, brushed past Hunter, ensuring her elbow connected with his arm. "Nobody wants you here."

"This is a place of worship." Darcy intervened, turning to Hunter when he heard the woman's aggressive tone. "Your murder investigation has no place here."

"You wouldn't return my calls, and I thought I'd find you here on a Sunday morning." Hunter stepped up the final concrete step and stood next to the pastor. "And I've heard you preach that the chance for true forgiveness can only come when we're tested."

"You're certainly testing me, Mr. Hunter." Darcy held his hands out wide as two males came up behind him, both as tall and as broad as Hunter. "I'm sure you can understand why I wouldn't want to interact with you—you're defending the man who murdered our Reverend Dural Green."

Hunter looked to his left, past the faces snarling at him, past the hatred that these people had for him, and spotted a white van on the road. It was moving forward at a crawling pace, despite the road being clear.

Hunter had seen the dented white van circle past the block once already. It wasn't unusual for a twenty-five-year-old van to be driving the streets of Grand Crossing in Chicago; rather, it was the new cars that stood out.

The vehicle slowed as it approached a group of children on the sidewalk, almost as if the passengers were staring at the children, focusing on them.

"That's why I was calling you, Reverend." Hunter kept watching the van out of the corner of his eye. "I wanted to hear your opinion on something."

Five children.

No older than ten.

The men behind the African American pastor stepped closer, but Hunter didn't flinch. He'd been in enough fights, and had enough training, to know that he could take them both. One quick left hook, followed by a straight right punch, and the problem would be taken care of.

The van turned around. Slowly edging up the road again.

Closer.

"Mr. Hunter, I don't feel that this is the time or the place for this conversation," Darcy continued. "This is a place of worship, not a place for a controversial law discussion. I've avoided you because, quite simply, I don't want to talk with you. I thought that would have been clear to a man with your intelligence. I don't want to be a newspaper headline."

Hunter didn't respond.

He watched the van, tires rolling forward, then turned his attention to the children, who were clapping their hands together in perfect rhythm.

Closer now.

Something was not right. These were dangerous times for the church. Controversies were as regular as the Sunday service.

There were three girls and two boys on the sidewalk; all dressed in their Sunday best.

Smiling. Innocent.

Carefree.

Hunter moved, ignoring the minister and his congregation. He dashed back down the steps.

The van stopped.

"Mr. Hunter?" Darcy called out. "Are you leaving

already?"

The tinted window of the van rolled down. It had stopped under the shade of a tree. Hunter couldn't see inside; there were too many shadows.

It was only a second before Hunter saw the rifle. It was pushed out of the window, resting on the door of the van.

Hunter looked at the children.

So happy. So free.

The grins on their faces, the laughter in their voices.

Their clothes were so pristine, so perfect. The two boys had neatly trimmed hair, the three girls each had their hair pulled back into a ponytail, not a strand out of place. They were in the third grade, starting to find their own voices, starting to discover their individuality. For them, life was still a perfect collection of days spent with friends; learning, laughing, growing. They knew danger was alive in their suburb, they'd practiced school shooting drills earlier that week, but it was always an arm's length away.

The gun pushed further out.

The children didn't sense the danger. They were completely unaware of the menace lurking beyond the street.

Hunter ran.

"Move!" He screamed for the children to take cover. "Get down!"

The first gunshot rang out.

It was unmistakable, echoing through the neighborhood.

Muscles clenched. Instincts kicked in.

Hunter raced to protect the children.

He shot past the shocked faces of the adults, past the people stunned with fear. He reached for the youngsters, moving faster than he had in years.

The second shot came quickly after the first.

His arms wrapped around the children, his back to the white van, huddling the children together.

He felt the third shot before he heard it.

It hit his shoulder.

And when the blood from a girl splattered against his face, his world became a blur.

# **CHAPTER 2**

PLEASURE IS nothing without comparison to pain.

Tex Hunter took great comfort in the idea that a person who had felt the deepest sorrow was best able to experience the greatest joy. It had been more than thirty years since he had felt free, more than three decades since he felt a flash of pure delight. Pain was a constant companion, an acquaintance that was always there for him, a reminder of who he was. Despite his past, despite the decades of pain, he had hope for the future, hope that one day he could experience joy again.

He often thought that if he were ever to get a tattoo, it would be the words of poet Ella Wheeler Wilcox: 'Weep, and you weep alone.' But he wasn't a fan of ink, nor did he trust anyone enough to write on his body.

Oak Street Beach, in the neighborhood of the Gold Coast, Chicago, had the potential to hold great delight, and in his past, it once did. Sitting on the park bench at the edge of the beach, under the branches of a young tree, he listened to the calm waves lap gently against the sand. Only joggers dared to venture to the beach in late February.

Reminiscing about the days when his family drove

from their home in Logan Square, he smiled. There was a purity to their life then. The way they threw the Frisbee around, the way they laughed, the way that their love for each other was unmistakable. He remembered his older brother talking to every girl that walked past, his mother reading fiction under an umbrella, and his father teaching him how to throw a baseball. Those days the sand was too rough, the sun too hot, and the beach too busy, but it didn't matter.

Those summer days were special; days that would never be forgotten, as they were the last days before his father was arrested for the murder of eight teenage girls. The events of that summer changed him; he lost his innocence, his youth. He was forced to grow up far beyond his years.

After that summer, he never let his guard down again.

Love, peace, and calm became foreign notions.

"There's nothing more you could've done." Esther Wright rested a hand on Hunter's right shoulder, the one not covered in bandages under his suit, and handed him a takeaway coffee. "You did everything right. You didn't pull that trigger."

His assistant sat next to him on the park bench, crossed one leg over the other, and looked over Lake Michigan.

"What if I'd moved quicker, Esther? More to the left?" Hunter grimaced as he reached for his drink. "I could've taken more of the bullet. I could've saved her."

"No, Tex." Esther shook her head. "You did everything right. She's still alive, and by all reports, she's a fighter. You gave her a chance. Without you, without the risk that you took, that girl would've been dead. There were no casualties because you stopped them. You did everything right. No one else was brave enough to dive in front of those children."

The paper reported Hunter as a hero, a man who risked his own life to save the innocent, but that was a concept he was uncomfortable with. He reacted on instinct, not heroism. The real heroes, he'd always argued, were the people who used their working hours to save others—the firefighters, cops, paramedics. Of course, the paper didn't print that quote; instead, they chose to print an old quote from his father: 'Don't persecute my boy. He'll be a hero one day.'

Hunter hated that quote.

His father had said it from a prison cell when Hunter first graduated from law school, and the media ran photos from his graduation. The law community already hated Tex Hunter, and that quote only further cemented their dislike of him. Many people were the same—although he had nothing to do with his father's actions, and was only ten when his father was arrested, they held him responsible in some way.

Esther Wright gazed out at the view, and a jogger running past winked at her. She smiled as if she was very used to male attention, and then slurped her coffee loudly.

Hunter recoiled, as did the jogger who also shook his head. Esther, Hunter's long-term assistant, was a woman who had been blessed with the gift of splendor—her eyes were a mesmerizing shade of cobalt, her smile melted the coldest of hearts, and her honest demeanor drew most people in. Her sandy-blonde hair rested just beneath her shoulders, even in winter her skin was lightly tanned, and her figure was a healthy feminine shape. She was almost perfect; except nobody had ever taken the time to teach her any manners.

She slurped her coffee again; this time, it was loud enough for a young child, who was twenty-five yards away, to lean forward in a stroller, and stare at her. She smiled and waved, oblivious to the disgust of the world around her.

"How did you even know I was here?" Hunter asked as she took the drink away from her lips.

"You weren't in the office at 9 a.m., and you're never late." She gulped a large mouthful of coffee. "And when you need time to process something in the morning, I usually find you here, looking out at the lake."

It was nice for someone to have his back, but Hunter wasn't used to it. He was used to standing on his own, swimming against the tide, without even a life raft in sight, but the longer he spent with Esther, the more he became comfortable with her caring nature.

"Do they have any leads for the church shooting?"

"They haven't got a thing, Esther. The van wasn't registered, there's no CCTV footage around the church, and the witnesses didn't see much other than a white van. Fifty people outside the church and they saw nothing of value." He shut his eyes as a gust blew into them, bringing a sprinkling of sand with it. "And all I saw was a rifle poking out of the passenger window. I didn't see any faces in the van."

"It must be tough for the police. They've already got so much racial tension around your case with Amos Anderson murdering the minister, Dural

Green, and then something like this happens. They know they have to tread softly here. There's so much hate in the city at the moment, and it's threatening to turn into a riot. I remember studying the LA riots in school, and nobody wants that here."

"That doesn't mean they should stop doing their job and avoid catching a shooter. If the shooter has done it once, then they're going to do it again." He watched as a young biracial couple, one African American and the other Caucasian, walked past hand in hand, snuggling into each other. "There are rumors the White Alliance Coalition is associated with the church shooting, but there's no evidence, and nobody's claiming it. This was more than a random attack. These people are filled with hate."

"I've heard about the White Alliance Coalition—a small group of deadbeats living on the outskirts of the city. I heard the leader on a documentary saying that people of color should be segregated. It's a pity; I thought those attitudes were left behind in the 1950s."

"People love nostalgia."

"If there was one thing I learned studying history at school, it was that history belongs in the past."

He smiled. "These people don't have the same morals that you and I do. They receive funding from an anonymous source, and they're actively recruiting. They're playing off people's fear and filling the world with hatred. The media is giving them a voice, even though they only represent a tiny portion of the population, because readers respond to them with loathing. That emotion, that drama, sells papers."

Esther forced a smile.

She looked out at the beach and remembered the

time, ten years earlier on her twenty-first birthday, when she went skinny-dipping there. It was past one in the morning on a cold spring night, and her friends dared her to do it. Never one to back away from a dare, she stripped down and leaped into the water. She only lasted a few seconds before the chill in the water almost froze her to the bone.

"Once, there was a man in a police interrogation room." She turned to Hunter. "And the man said to the cop, 'I'm not saying anything without my lawyer present.' And the cop said, 'But you're the lawyer.' 'Exactly,' he replied. 'So where's my present?'"

Hunter chuckled.

"What did the pirate say when he turned eighty?" She waited a few moments, a grin stretched across her face. "Aye matey."

"That's so bad it's funny." Hunter laughed out loud. "But I fail to see how that's relevant."

"It's not." Esther shrugged. "I'm just trying to get your mind off current events for a few moments."

"I only know one joke and it's a blonde joke. So, why are blonde jokes so short?"

"So, men can remember them." She retorted quickly before he could answer.

"Well, that joke took an unexpected turn."

"Not if you'd asked for directions."

He laughed loudly again. They sat for a minute, enjoying the buzz of laughter, taking in their moment of joy. It was a rare reprieve from their stressful lives, but it wasn't long before their thoughts turned back to the inevitable, back to the unavoidable depravity that they encountered every day.

"Come on, we should get to the office. We have a case to prepare for." Hunter stood and drew a deep breath of fresh air, ignoring the sharp stab of pain in his shoulder. "It's going to be a busy month."

Esther waited a moment longer, and then stood next to her boss, looking up to him.

"I guess the question is: are you going to pass on the current case with the faith healer Amos Anderson? You could step away. You've only had the case on your desk for a week. You haven't poured a lot of work into this yet. You don't have to defend the man charged with killing Reverend Green. You'd only be inviting more hate into your world."

"I won't pass on this case. Not now." Hunter buttoned up his coat. "This case was the only reason I was at the church. It's the only reason I was there to save those children. If I was a man of faith, I would say that it was a sign from above."

"You don't have to invite this danger into your world, Tex. You could step back, take it easy for a while. Maybe even take a vacation. Relax a little—go south and get some sunshine."

"Esther, I'm not a person that runs from danger."

"I know," she whispered as he walked towards the parking lot. "That's what I'm afraid of."

# CHAPTER 3

CAYLEE JOHNSON ran her finger over the Glock handgun. It felt so cold, so emotionless, but so inviting. She loved the weight of the gun. The way it rested in her hand.

Her shotgun leaned against the fence post behind her, looking strong in the country breeze. The weapon was a tenth birthday present from her father, her very own shotgun, the best present she had ever received. Her father painted the handle bright pink just for her, although the years had faded the paint. She was so happy that day. It wasn't the first gun she had fired, but as she entered her second decade on the planet, it was the first one she owned.

Falling in love with the handgun almost felt like she was cheating on the shotgun, but the heart wants what the heart wants. She reasoned that there were so many guns in the house, most stored in the garage, that she had the right to choose which one suited her best. The Glock had been her favorite since she'd turned twenty, almost a year ago. There was something real about the kickback, the authority. Something raw about the intensity of power.

It was always her father's aim to influence the policymakers. He wanted to be remembered as a game changer, someone who shifted the course of history. The family had enough guns in the shed to arm every member of the White Alliance Coalition and start a riot on the streets of Chicago. They could start a riot big enough to change policy, a riot that could change their city forever.

Her father, Chuck Johnson, talked about the moment when they would reach a turning point, a point when they would have an opportunity to be remembered in the pages of Chicago's history.

Her Uncle Burt believed every word of the speeches, although he was gullible enough to believe anything her father told him. He would do anything for the White Alliance Coalition. Their numbers had dwindled a lot over the years, down to ten people at the last meeting, but Uncle Burt had enough blind passion for twenty men.

"The White Alliance Coalition will rise," her father had said before the meeting. "We will conquer."

The guns gave them power, the feeling of supremacy. Her father often said that they would be nothing without the guns, nothing without the explosives. They didn't have much money, only enough to get by, but the weapons were their treasure trove; their fortune and wealth.

Their home backed onto the Spring Lake Nature Preserve, outside of Barrington, Illinois; a place of tranquil peace and quiet. She had long felt a kinship to the land.

Most of the homes on their road were regal, with the type of entrance that demanded tall swinging gates. The nearby properties had seven-bedroom monstrosities that sat back from the road and had horses, gardeners, and full-time housekeepers.

Not the Johnson's home.

The old metal gate across their driveway was overgrown with weeds, and held two signs: one warning people not to trespass because of the dogs, and the other warning them not to trespass unless they wanted to get shot.

The other residents complained about them often: the constant gunshots, the overgrown weeds, and that their dogs killed the wildlife that dared to venture onto their thirty-acre property.

The property had been in the family for five generations; passed from one racist Johnson son down to the next. The original residence, little more than a hut, still sat near the road and their current family home; a one level, four-bedroom brick house built in the sixties to replace the previous weatherboard dwelling, sat at the end of a long driveway.

Chuck Johnson had won a payout due to a work accident when he was only twenty and spent most of his life on the property puttering from one thing to the next.

The two-door garage that sat next to the house contained most of their gun collection. There were fifty guns at last count. Not to mention the C-4 explosives that Caylee's father had recently gotten his hands on. It amazed her what was available on the black market.

There were five old broken down cars behind the house; two of them being rescued and worked on by her uncle. Cars were the only thing he understood.

Behind the cars were the dogs' cages; four Dobermans, who were often barking loudly.

The police were regulars to their property, but they had visited more frequently over the last month. First, they came to question her father about his whereabouts on February 1st—the night that Reverend Dural Green was murdered—and then they were back to ask if he was involved in the shooting at the Baptist church last week.

They asked her Uncle Burt questions too, so many that his answers got mixed up. It wasn't hard to confuse Uncle Burt.

The police didn't ask Caylee a single question. Not one.

She had never been good at lying. If they'd asked her the right question, she might've collapsed under the pressure. She almost wanted that to happen; to relieve herself of the guilt that she was carrying on her shoulders, to take the choice away.

She was getting to an age where she had to make a decision between her family or her friends.

Her friends didn't know who her father was, who her family were, and they wouldn't like it at all, but family was family. It was all she had.

She held the handgun tightly, pointing it towards the tree.

The slow squeeze of the trigger was what she enjoyed the most; the anticipation of the power that was to come. She smiled, waiting for that moment.

She aimed at the beer can sitting on a log that backed onto the lake. She was never too sure who would be out on the lake, out there having fun. That only added to the intensity of it all.

When she had no margin for error, no chance to flinch, no chance for a misstep, the melody began. It was when her entire body was engulfed in adrenaline, stinging her senses, pulsating fear through her being. One wrong breath, one slight lean of the body, and she would miss her target, sending the bullet on its own path to destruction.

The sound of the six shots resonated around the woods that surrounded their house. It felt good—that rush, that power. She smiled again as she looked at her handgun.

She would end this.

All of it.

She wasn't going to let this war go on any longer.

This was her destiny.

# FAITH AND JUSTICE IS AVAILABLE TO BUY NOW

Made in the USA
Monee, IL
11 November 2023